THE DEVIL WORE

BLACK

MARK L. FOWLER

In Memory of Ito Maitin and Ron Cason

CHAPTER ONE

She was running flat out now, the icy air ripping into her lungs, feet pounding at the loose gravel as she came onto the stone bridge, crossing over the stream towards St Barnabas church. First light breaking on a grim Sunday morning in early November.

The road ahead appeared deserted as the young woman, clad in black Lycra with yellow flashes, like a wasp out of season, thundered past the long-abandoned stables, the iconic bell-tower of Trentham Hall looming into view a hundred feet above her. Ignoring the path that snaked past the church, she opted instead for the wider lane between the woods and the newly renovated terracotta villas.

Another fifty yards and she would reach the stiles, before taking her customary left turn into Trentham Park for the final stretch.

She was panting hard, taking no prisoners; already beyond the villas, the rectory set back over to her immediate right. Still maintaining a relentless pace, she was checking her stop-watch when something in the woods dimly registered in the corner of her eye. The first rays of morning slanting through the trees, illuminating an anomaly; something out of place.

Something that shouldn't be there.

Pulling up suddenly, she edged towards the wire fence that marked off the perimeter of the woods. The cold air was brutal, as sharp as a knife in the throat, and raw on the lungs; it held the promise of a long and bitter winter.

The path ahead stretched beyond the entrance to the park, and all the way up to the private golf course at the top. The park and the golf course were generally well-used, but this early on a Sunday morning there wasn't a soul around.

The intense loneliness of the hour began to dawn on her. There were no dog walkers, golfers, or even like-minded runners getting in the miles before the world caught up with the day; no-one to relieve the sudden sense of isolation.

In the eerie silence, the woman reached the wire fence, peering through into the gloom beyond.

She couldn't see anything but trees; the woods stretching all the way to the church, which stood out of sight on the far side. Taking a few steps backwards, she tried to glimpse again whatever it was that had snatched her attention, interrupting the climax of her run.

Wondering if she had imagined it, she was about to resume her run when, edging a couple of feet over to the right, she saw it. It was unmistakable now. She blinked, pressing her face into the wire; seeing it, and at the same time not quite believing what she was seeing.

The early morning light was playing tricks, it had to be.

Pulling her face away from the fence, shaking her head, she was mumbling to herself, looking quickly behind her, up and down the path. Still no-one was coming.

Panic was setting in, bringing the first prickle of tears, and the urge to run, and run fast; to put mile upon mile between her and this impossible, unspeakable thing that she was witnessing.

Forcing herself to look back through the wire fence, she half expected to find nothing but configurations of mist. Hoping against hope that what she had seen had been nothing more than phantoms generated by the dawn light.

None of that happened. The obscenity was still there.

She was beginning to shake, wanting to cry; her eyes blinking in disbelief. The light of the day appeared to intensify, making the grotesque scene that she was gazing on harder to deny.

There, in the densest part of the woods; a figure tied to a tree. No, not a tree; what, then?

A ... *cross*?

A man, his arms outstretched, not moving, not making a sound. *Naked.* An old man, tied - or else nailed - to a wooden cross. "Christ," said the woman, backing away from the fence. "Christ - help!"

She swung around to see the first of the early morning dog walkers approaching from the direction of the park entrance. A man, in his early thirties, perhaps, was looking at her; a puzzled, concerned look animating his face, as though he believed himself to be in the presence of madness.

Dimly she heard him say, "Are you alright?" But she couldn't answer, couldn't speak. She was pointing through the fence, back into the woods, her voice returning and the words coming out in an almost unintelligible squeal.

"In there ... an old man ... *crucified.*"

7

CHAPTER TWO

Detective Chief Inspector Jim Tyler sat in the unmarked car watching Detective Sergeant Danny Mills trudging up the lane towards him. He had never seen Mills looking so weary and forlorn. In all the years that DCI Tyler had worked down in London, and in the brief time that he had spent in this strange exile in the City of Stoke on Trent, he had witnessed nothing that had shaken him so deeply to the core. What he had seen in those woods marked for him a new chapter in the depravity of the species.

Tyler remained silent as Mills climbed into the front passenger seat, and almost a minute passed before he said, "Father William Peterson: Rector of St Barnabas church. Stripped and crucified. Found by a young woman out jogging. I am awake, Danny. I am not dreaming. I have not been drinking or sniffing the flowers."

Danny Mills sighed as though succumbing to the weight of a diabolical world pressing down on him. He looked pale, and the shining edge of his graveyard wit for once appeared dull and lifeless. "Berkins is waiting for us back at the station," he said, his tone as flat as the day.

"Well, then," said Tyler, starting up the engine. "We'd better not keep the Chief waiting."

As Tyler drove towards Hanley, his mind repeated on the scene that had become imprinted far beneath the level of conscious thought. An old man, a dead priest:

Father William Peterson, his arms outstretched, his hands nailed to each end of the horizontal beam, a single nail driven through both of his feet, securing them to the lower part of the vertical beam. His body cold, naked, frail, desecrated; black duct tape covering his mouth, keeping his screams locked inside him as his failing body had fought desperately, pointlessly, for God-knows how long, but hours, most likely, writhing in unimaginable agony and torment until it had finally given out, given up the ghost.

Tyler recalled the dozens of crucifixes depicting the broken body of Jesus Christ that had adorned each and every room of the orphanage back in Leicestershire. St Saviour's: another place of pain and suffering.

As Tyler pulled onto the car park at Cedar Lane Police Station in Hanley, in the centre of Stoke on Trent, he looked at Mills and thought: *Are you reading my mind*? Do you know enough about me to imagine that I have already solved the case? That some refugee from St Saviour's, or somewhere like it, has handed out retribution for the sins committed by this priest?

Switching off the engine, he said, "You've got it wrong, Danny, if that's what you're thinking."

"Sir?"

"I keep an open mind, always have done and always will."

"I would expect nothing less, sir. The facts, that's the name of this game. You've taught me well."

"The chief will be pleased to hear that," said Tyler. "He's going to have enough on his plate without worrying about the likes of us." He smiled, and it was the best smile he could manage under the circumstances. Mills did his best to reciprocate.

9

Chief Superintendent Graham Berkins sat behind his desk and gestured to DCI Tyler to take a seat.

"Jim, I have to make a statement. You know what they are going to be asking."

"I've a good idea."

"The world's changed. Those bastards who flew the planes into the World Trade Centre two years ago changed this world forever."

"And you seriously think -"

"I don't seriously think anything. The press will, though. They'll fuel enough paranoia to set this city, and the rest of the country, on fire. They will convince everyone that there is a terrorist plot afoot and likely the beginning of a fresh crusade. On top of that, we have the desecrations of dozens of churches over the past two weeks. Satanic symbols, which some will interpret as indicating a terrorist agenda, or else, God help us! - a Satanist conspiracy."

"So, what are you saying?"

"I'm saying that all sleep is cancelled until we nail ..." Berkins shook his head ... "Poor choice of words, I'm afraid. Until we *find out* who is responsible for this, and silence the rumour-mill before it has a chance to start World War Three."

"Are you alright?" asked Tyler, looking with concern at the senior officer.

"Frankly, no, I'm not. In fact, I'm a long way from alright. I need you and Mills at the top of your game. I need a break in this case and fast before the poison has chance to spread."

"We'll do our best," said Tyler. "You know that."

Berkins nodded. "I have faith in you and the team."

"I wasn't aware that the dead priest's church had been vandalised," said Tyler.

"It hasn't. St Barnabas' is one of the few churches in the area that hasn't had an issue over recent days."

"What's the latest?" asked Tyler.

"Pentagrams and inverted crosses painted on the doors of St Luke's in Stoke town centre. That was last night. And similar markings found at St Augustine's in Trent Vale the night before."

"Terrorists or Satanists?" Tyler mumbled under his breath.

"What's that, Jim?"

"Thinking out loud, that's all."

"Can't you think a bit louder?"

"Any background on the dead priest?" asked Tyler.

"As a matter of fact," said Berkins, pushing a folder across the desk. "Something else that the media will no doubt find mouth-watering."

Berkins' desk phone was ringing.

"I have to take this call. Come back to me with *anything* - and today if possible."

Tyler left the room and walked the corridors to the CID office, where Mills was winding up a call of his own.

Looking through the contents of the folder that the Chief had given him, the DCI nodded in tacit confirmation. He imagined the headlines:

Priest ritually slaughtered for abusing a choirboy.

"Anything interesting from Berkins?" asked Mills, placing the handset back onto its cradle.

"On the edge of a coronary, as usual - and at the same time wondering what the hell to say to the media."

"I don't envy him that," said Mills. "Terrorists, black magic and voodoo - the media will be loving every minute. Of course, this may turn out to have nothing at all to do with religion."

"You have a theory? Tell me more."

Before Mills could say anything further, Tyler said, "On second thoughts, let me guess: *an abused choirboy avenging the damage done*?"

"I didn't mean ..."

"Didn't mean what?"

"I wasn't suggesting ..."

"Suggesting?"

"That you were making this ... personal, sir."

"Unfinished business of my own?"

Mills started to speak, but Tyler spared him. "I was never in the choir, Danny. Though I *was* brought up in a hell-hole called St Saviour's, and at the mercy of devils dressed in black."

Mills blinked in confusion.

"We have some information," said Tyler, tapping the file that Berkins had passed to him. He threw it across the desk. "Apparently, Father Peterson left his previous parish in Stroud following allegations made against him. This was five years ago."

"I wasn't leaping to conclusions, sir. When I said this may not have anything to do with religion - the man may have had gambling debts, woman trouble or, I don't know -"

"Are you talking about the dead priest, or whoever nailed him to the cross and left him to die there?"

Mills gave it up. "I'm sorry, sir."

"For what, though? Trying, commendably, to break the gloom; or for thinking that I have an axe to grind?

And even if I did, do you for one second imagine that I would let that cloud my professional judgement?"

Tyler's eyes were glowing like coals, and Mills edged back in his seat, blasted by the intensity of the heat radiating out into the room.

"These allegations, sir?" asked Mills, cautiously.

"It's all there in the file. A choirboy named Tony Pickering. His father made a lot of noise at the time, though nothing was ever substantiated. Gerald Pickering contacted us when Father Peterson moved up to Stoke, 'alerting us to the danger'."

Mills picked up the file and began to read through it.

"I believe," said Tyler, "that we have a number of confessions in already?"

"About a dozen so far, sir. Mostly from jihadists declaring the beginning of a holy war - and a couple of born-again atheists."

"Anything credible?"

"Not yet. We do have something interesting on CCTV, though. The graffiti at St Luke's. They've got a clear image, face on; caught him in the act."

"Berkins will be over the moon," said Tyler. "He worked hard to keep those cameras active. They're proving to be the gift that keeps on giving."

As the news broke across the nation, spreading the word of what had occurred in the woods close to Trentham Gardens ... '*one of North Staffordshire's premier tourist attractions*' ... the accompanying image of a thin-faced man in the act of vandalising the exterior of a church, was presented to the public at large. Police wanted to talk to this man urgently.

13

As anticipated, the newspapers had a field day, radio and TV the same. Headlines alternated between terrorist plots and satanic conspiracies.

The experts and gossip-mongers were of one mind: there was more to this than murder.

CHAPTER THREE

Scene of crime officers dotted the woods that stretched between St Barnabas church and the rectory where Father William Peterson had lived for the past five years.

Tyler stood on the path where the jogger had first discovered the crucifixion, his back to the rectory building. Mills was coming towards him, emerging from the woods through the opened wooden door that stood curiously placed in the context of the wire fence.

"Anything to report?" he asked the DS.

Mills shook his head. "Whoever did this was careful and organised," he said. "No prints. It must have taken two people to do it, though."

"Is that the conclusion of our forensic friends?"

"It's plain common sense, sir. I can't see how one person could lift that cross with the weight of a man on it, even a frail old man."

Tyler nodded at the opened wooden door, a postcode painted across the top. "Father Peterson's private path: home to work and back."

"Nice little set up. Last place you'd expect something like this to happen."

"In some places on this sad Earth, Christian ministers have to accept crucifixion as an occupational hazard."

"Not usually in Trentham, sir."

Tyler checked his watch. "I've arranged to meet Bishop Bernard Moss. Let's see if we can get some more on the victim."

Mills drove the few miles down the A34 to the village of Tittensor. Bishop Bernard Moss, a tall, ungainly man with sharp eyes and a shock of blonde hair, was waiting on the front porch of a quaint detached cottage. He seemed young to be a bishop, thought Mills, though if pressed on the matter he would have to confess to having no idea of the age range for senior clergy in the Church of England.

The bishop's wife, Katherine, was also present at their home, and she offered to make a round of hot drinks while the cleric showed the detectives through to the study. She was an attractive woman, thought Mills, again somewhat perplexed.

He had spent little of his life in churches, and his understanding of Christian life in Britain was based largely on the negative news reports on TV. Sex abuse scandals were the usual reason for the church to make the news, in his experience, fostering in him an unformed, vague notion that the clergy comprised of lonely, celibate men not entirely to be trusted.

The detectives took their seats in the comfortable study, sitting opposite the cleric. An air of solemnity filled the room, and Tyler offered his condolences at the violent death of the man's colleague. Then he asked the bishop if he had any ideas as to who might be responsible.

Moss shook his head. "In all my years, I have never come across anything like this."

"I'm sure you're aware," said Tyler, "of the recent spate of desecrations at local churches."

"Are you making a connection between that and Father William's murder, Inspector?"

"Not particularly. I have no evidence of a connection. But I intend to fully explore any avenues of possibility. The occasional bit of graffiti isn't that unusual, but there have been a lot of attacks on local churches recently. You don't believe that might prove to be significant?"

"I've read the papers," said the bishop. "There seems to be a keen interest in pointing up an anti-Christian agenda, one way or another. I shouldn't be surprised at that. As for the emphasis on terrorism or Satanism or whatever ... I have serious doubts on the matter."

"Can I ask why that is?"

The bishop thought for a moment. "It would help, no doubt," he said, "if I gave you some background on the late Father Peterson."

At that point, Katherine Moss entered the study with a tray laden with drinks and biscuits. As she leaned over to place the tray down on the small table between the gathered men, Mills forced himself to redirect his gaze from the bishop's wife to the bookcases surrounding them. There was something particularly shameful, it seemed, in admiring the wife of a bishop, and it was not until Katherine had left the room that Mills found himself able to stop perusing the bookcases.

While Moss poured out the tea and offered biscuits, he began to talk about the late priest.

"... William moved to this area around five years ago, having served a number of parishes around the country."

"Why did he move around so much?" asked Tyler.

"It is not unusual, in our line of work. We go to where we are called, and William was called to Trentham -"

"I understand," said Tyler, cutting in, "that he left his previous parish under something of a cloud."

The bishop took a sip of his drink. "That's true," he said, looking somewhat relieved that the subject had been raised. "There were issues, though my understanding, certainly, is that whilst allegations had been made by a member of the congregation during William's previous appointment, nothing was ever substantiated."

"Could you elaborate on the nature of the allegations," said Tyler.

Mills reached for a couple of biscuits. He noticed that the bishop appeared less comfortable now, as though he had hoped that the police already knew enough to spare him from having to spell out the details.

"It involved a choirboy."

It often does, thought Mills, reaching for another two biscuits. *Here we go.*

"Accusations were made of inappropriate behaviour. The boy's father formalised the complaint and I understand that it was investigated by the police department in Stroud. The allegation was not upheld."

"There were no other incidents involving Father Peterson?" asked Tyler.

"None that I'm aware of - and certainly there have been no 'incidents' while he has been ministering to this parish."

The bishop hesitated.

Mills instinctively reached for another biscuit, but catching the eye of his senior officer, held back and instead drained his cup of tea.

"Recently William brought to my attention something that was concerning him greatly. Apparently the father of the choirboy contacted him."

"Contacted him how?"

"A phone call, one evening, out of the blue; the man suggesting that justice had not been done and that William had got away with it. He was deeply upset, naturally, and he confided in me, asking my advice on whether he should contact the police."

"Was the call threatening?" asked Tyler. "What did the caller want?"

"William wasn't sure. No explicit threats were made. It left him very anxious, wondering if there would be further calls."

"And were further calls made to Father Peterson?"

"I'm not aware that any other contact was ever made. William certainly never informed me of the fact."

"Did you advise him to contact the police regarding the phone call?"

"We discussed doing so, but in the end I believe that he had decided to hold off contacting the police unless the situation escalated."

The bishop looked questioningly at DCI Tyler.

"I'm not aware that he ever contacted us regarding the matter," said Tyler.

The bishop took another sip from his cup. "Father William was a man of the highest integrity; I have no doubt about that. He was a good priest, a good man, and a great loss to our church. When he discussed that phone call, and the allegations that had been made against him, he did not appear to have his own interests upper-most in his mind."

"Can you explain what you mean by that?" said Tyler.

The bishop appeared to think very carefully before he spoke again. At last he said, "William was a man of remarkable compassion and empathy. He was of course aware that the last thing the church needs is more scandal, and he was somewhat fearful that should the allegations become common knowledge they would likely further tarnish the reputation of the church. However, at the same time he demonstrated concern for the boy and his family. He didn't voice the specifics of that, but reading between the lines I tend to believe that he thought the father had his own agenda, and that the boy may have been intimidated into making the allegations. Or at least to re-interpret whatever had - or had *not* - occurred."

Tyler frowned. "Isn't that tantamount to blaming the victim?"

"If indeed the boy was actually a victim, then perhaps so."

Mills sensed the tension that had crept into the room. Tyler's body language suggested that he was working hard to contain his feelings. Yet the DS knew well enough the perils of leaping to premature conclusions. He knew only a little of his colleague's background; that he had gone through a dark time in childhood, experiencing at least physical abuse at the orphanage and at school. Like Father Peterson, Tyler had arrived in Stoke under a cloud, and rumours were rife that he had lost it with a colleague in London, and let some of his pent-up anger and frustration out through his fists, leading to this "exile north" as he had often referred to it. He battled his demons daily, it seemed, and when it got too much, he would run for miles around the city, burning off his rage and the temptation to drink, at times taking himself to the brink of exhaustion.

Mills wondered if a case like this was the last thing Jim Tyler needed. Except that as a senior police detective you were hardly in a position to pick and choose which cases you worked on.

Without realising what he was doing, he lifted the last biscuit from the plate, consuming it before he had even tasted it. Swallowing the last of it, he became aware of the silence, and looked up to find that the bishop and the DCI were looking at him. Smiling awkwardly, it dawned on him that they were hardly intent on chastising him for his greed; rather they were trapped in the awkwardness of the moment and wondering where to go next.

The DCI stood up to leave, and thanked the bishop for his time. On the way out the bishop's wife Katherine appeared, and again Mills couldn't help but reflect on how far the church had moved forward from the days of monastic living.

Walking back to the car, Tyler said, "Was he defending one of his own, or have I become too cynical?"

"I couldn't answer based on evidence, sir."

"Okay. I'll make an exception on this occasion, but don't make a habit of it. Let's have it, then: your gut instinct."

Mills unlocked the car, and paused. "Well, in that case ... I don't see him as the type to brush something like that under the carpet. I might be wrong, but you asked me, so there it is."

"A man you can trust?"

"From what I've seen of him. I would say so."

"He wouldn't be the first member of the clergy to cover up an unpalatable truth."

"I'm sure he wouldn't, sir."

"He didn't seem to hold much store by Satanist conspiracies either."

"Maybe he doesn't believe in the devil."

"He wouldn't have to. It's enough that those responsible do. And he wouldn't have to believe in Peterson's guilt to accept that someone else perhaps did."

Mills frowned. "I don't follow, sir."

"Ignore me. I'm scratching at things I don't understand. Anyway, how were the biscuits? I kept meaning to try one, but in the end I left it too late."

Mills was about to apologise when he caught Jim Tyler's devilish grin.

"Diet starts tomorrow, Danny?"

"It always starts tomorrow, sir."

CHAPTER FOUR

At Cedar Lane the team had been busy interviewing a string of confessors, consisting mainly of aspiring jihadists and atheist fundamentalists, none of whom appeared remotely likely for the atrocity.

Then the breakthrough came. The man, whose image had been captured on CCTV in the act of vandalising the walls of St Luke's church, had been identified as Clayton Shaw, an unemployed father of two, living in the Milton area, in the north of the city. He had been sitting at home watching daytime television when three members of Tyler's team had peered at him through his living room window.

Shaw sat silently in the interview room as Tyler and Mills took their seats opposite. Tyler introduced himself and read out the charges against him.

"So," said Tyler, "do you do this kind of thing often?" Shaw didn't respond. "I see," said Tyler. "Interesting art work, but please forgive my ignorance: what do your hieroglyphics represent, exactly?"

Clayton Shaw sneered, as though it was beneath him to explain his art to a mere flatfoot.

"Similar art works have been found at a number of other religious sites around the city. Are you responsible for those too, Mr Shaw?"

Still no response.

"It seems a pity," said Tyler, "not to have your talent given the recognition it deserves. Maybe you represent a cause of some kind. It would be a shame to let all of this media opportunity slip by, wouldn't you say?"

Shaw broke his silence. "I don't have to explain anything," he said.

"That's true. You don't. I'm not even that interested in hearing your explanations, to be honest. Graffiti is something most people grow out of by your age. Cock and balls, anti-Government slogans, favourite rock bands, satanic baloney - it's all pretty much the same thing, as far as I'm concerned."

Shaw's face became more animated.

"Pentagrams," said Tyler. "In my youth I used to love a good horror film, though I don't get so much time these days. My days get eaten up running around after dickheads like you."

Shaw's expression tightened further, and he directed a concentrated stare at the DCI.

"Please," said Tyler, "don't look at me like that. You will give me bad dreams."

"Don't mess with me," said Shaw suddenly.

"Is that a threat, Mr Shaw? What kind of threat, though? Physical violence - or do you intend to summon a legion of pixies to attack me and carry me off to the unquenchable fire?"

"You think you're clever, but you don't know what you're messing with, copper."

"Tell me, then: what *am* I messing with?"

"This is only the beginning."

"Beginning of what, exactly?"

"We are going to bring every church in this city down."

"*We,* Mr Shaw?"

"And then we will spread through the country and through the world."

"Are we talking about Armageddon, Mr Shaw? Is Armageddon scheduled to begin here, in Stoke?"

"Don't mock me, copper."

"Now, that is a challenge. Who are your friends, then, Mr Shaw?"

"We are legion."

Tyler began to laugh. "I've seen that one. And I've read the book. Before I charge you with wilful damage to property, I'd like to know whether your mission against the church extends to its ministers. In other words, you're going to have to account for your activities and whereabouts over the last few days, I'm afraid, Mr Shaw."

"Is this to do with that dead priest?"

"Now you're getting the idea. I hope you have a good alibi. I want to know where you were on Saturday evening."

Clayton Shaw was grinning. "That would be Saturday 8th November. Well, that's easy. I was at a meeting."

"Where and who with?"

"Chapter Six."

"I beg your pardon?" said Tyler.

"I'm a member of a cult," Shaw replied, proudly. "We meet up in the moorlands every two weeks. There were thirteen of us on Saturday and we were there all evening."

In the CID office the detectives sat at their desks.

"What do you make of that, then?" asked Mills.

"Not nearly as much as the media are going to. It's a story made in heaven, so to speak: *Satanists on the rampage; desecrations of Christian sites; a crucified priest.* Before the end of the week we'll have a dozen producers vying for the film rights."

"You don't believe we have our man for the murder, sir?"

Tyler eyed the DS. "About as much as you do, I suspect. Good publicity for his cause, I don't doubt - and for *Chapter Six*. But from his point of view, no more than a happy coincidence."

Mills flinched at the grim remark.

"Still, we'd better check out his alibi. And I want information on this cult, whatever it is. Get the team onto it while we're awaiting forensics."

"I'm on it," said Mills.

"And the historic complaint made against Father Peterson - the father and son in Stroud. Are we in communication with the police department down there yet?"

"We are liaising as we speak."

"Let me know when they have got their act together. I want to be there when they interview the father and son. And I want that to happen quickly, understand?"

"Perfectly, sir. But -"

"Leave the logistics to me. Berkins will authorise it. Now, I believe there is a curate at St Barnabas church who knew Peterson and the congregation well."

"Marion Ecclestone, sir."

"Is she expecting us?"

"Any time now."

"Let's not keep the lady waiting."

CHAPTER FIVE

Driving towards Trentham, Danny Mills caught himself, more than once, glancing over at Jim Tyler. An uneasy atmosphere had pervaded the cabin of the unmarked car.

The DCI had been noticeably more chilled these past months, less edgy, and Mills wondered if that had been in part down to his colleague getting used to life in a new environment, having left London under difficult circumstances. It couldn't have been easy, and while Mills loved Stoke with a passion, he was well aware that it wasn't everybody's idea of paradise.

He wondered too if Tyler had finally accepted help. He didn't expect the DCI to talk to him about such things, being far too self-contained and proud. He was a man who bottled up his emotions, his only outlet seeming to be unpredictable eruptions of anger, or else running to the point of near-collapse. Nobody, surely, could go on like that.

These last few days the edge had crept back, and Mills was concerned. Jim Tyler was as good a detective as any he had worked with, and on top of that he had become something of a friend over this past year.

Mills turned off the A34 close to the villas, following the path over the bridge towards the church where the late Father Peterson had ended his ministry nailed to a cross.

It was a shocking way to die, thought Mills, and bizarre, too, in a twentieth century backwater city in

27

England. Whoever had done such a thing had not only intended to maximise suffering, but had at the same time wanted to make a point.

Was the DCI's darkening mood simply a manifestation of the trauma of working a case like this, he wondered. Of being reminded so starkly of the evil in the world, and the seemingly desperate battle to defeat or even to contain it.

Mills parked up outside the church, got out of the car and looked at DCI Tyler, who still appeared lost in thought. "Jim, are you okay?"

"I was just wondering," said Tyler.

"Wondering, sir?"

"About church congregations, since you ask. So far, our attentions have been guided towards Satanists and terrorists and possibly abused choirboys and their parents. And we still have some miles to walk down those roads, I have no doubt. Yet even in a church of such modest size as this one, how many dark agendas might we find? Unthinkable, really, isn't it?"

"I'm not sure what you are saying."

"I'm thinking aloud, that's all."

"Are you sure you're okay?"

"Never better. Now, let's see what our curate has to say about all of this, shall we?"

While Tyler headed towards the entrance to the church, Mills approached one of the officers, white suited and on his hands and knees at the edge of the woods.

"How's it going?"

The scene of crime officer shook his head. "We're struggling, to be honest. We've been through these woods with a fine tooth comb, the rectory, too. No evidence of a struggle at either place. No fingerprints on the priest's body or on the nails or the timber. Whoever did this was careful and organised."

The evidence, or the lack of it, suggested to Mills a carefully planned murder, and not a crime of spontaneous passion. It had required thought and it had required strength. The preparation of materials. It also required motivation, extreme motivation, to carry out such a barbaric act.

"Observing shoe patterns left on the ground," said the officer to Mills, "confirms that two people were involved in carrying out the murder, or at least that two people plus the victim were present."

"One person couldn't have carried this out," said Mills.

"Almost certainly not."

Mills joined DCI Tyler and the curate, Marion Ecclestone, in the small church office located behind the choir stalls. The room was cold and the pot of tea she had made was most welcome.

The curate was a small woman, with short grey hair and the kindest face that Mills had seen in a long time. She looked tired, though, he observed; tired and somewhat dazed. It was hardly surprising.

She had last seen Father Peterson at around six pm on Saturday. There had been a late afternoon baptism, and when she left the church the priest had told her that he had a few things to clear up and that he wouldn't be far behind. He had appeared to her to have been in good spirits, and it wasn't evident that anything had been troubling him.

It seemed fairly certain that the priest's ordeal had begun not long after she had left him alone in the church. Mills tried to picture the scene.

The church was surrounded by a small churchyard, and backed onto Trentham's famous Italian gardens. Coming out of the front of the church gave the option of walking by the stream towards the abandoned stables and bell tower. But the priest would have turned left, heading back through the woods towards the rectory on the far side. It took less than a minute to enter the woods from the church, and less than a minute, walking at an average pace, to emerge on the far side, crossing the path to the rectory.

Had the killer - or killers - waited in the woods for the priest, knowing that he would be making his way from the church to the rectory? It seemed the most likely scenario, with the cross already constructed and awaiting the doomed cleric.

Marion Ecclestone had been locally ordained prior to Father Peterson arriving in the parish, and had been appointed curate soon afterwards. In her mid-fifties now, she had retired early from teaching, and lived a few miles away in Fenton with her husband, who was still teaching, and two teenage children. The curate hadn't a bad word to say about Father Peterson.

"He was the kindest man I've ever met, though my husband does run him fairly close. A very wise man, too. I never knew an occasion, be it a communion service, a funeral, a wedding or a social get-together, when he didn't have the right words to say. I don't mean that he had a store of glib phrases to dole out, that was not William at all. He could speak to somebody and, if they didn't already, he could make them believe in a loving, creator God. He had a wonderful gift. He's such a loss to us all."

For a moment it looked as though she was about to cry. Then she gathered herself and went on.

"People who are not Christians sometimes imagine that if you are a believer, and particularly if you are a member of the clergy, you don't feel sadness and grief - as though you are somehow inoculated against the effects of bereavement. I know that William has gone to a better place, but I still miss the man, and I still feel sorrow for the agony he must have endured. Even Jesus wept for his friend, Lazarus, and yet Jesus had the power to bring his friend back from the dead. But to not care about this life simply because you believe in a better one is to miss the point. William, of course, could put this far better than I can."

"I think you put it very well indeed," said Mills. "It must have come as a terrible shock."

"Thank you," she said. "It has been an awful shock for all of us. I wonder what could make somebody do such a thing."

"That's what we're hoping to find out. Do you have any ideas about who could be responsible?" asked Mills.

"I listen to the news, I occasionally read the newspapers. I know what is being said about terrorists and devil worshippers."

"And you're not convinced?" asked Tyler.

"I don't know what to think."

"And you're not aware that William was worried or concerned about anything out of the ordinary?" asked Tyler, his eyes narrowing.

"I wasn't aware," she said. "He never took me into his confidence about anything troubling him."

She looked uncomfortable, thought Mills.

"Have there been any new people attending services, or visiting the church recently?" asked Tyler. "I mean, anyone acting in a way that appeared suspicious?"

She appeared to dismiss the suggestion.

"It could be something that might seem trivial," said Tyler. "I want you to think if there has been anything that stands out in any way at all. It could be more significant than you realise."

"I will give it some thought," she said, "but really, nothing springs to mind."

Mills glanced at his colleague, wondering if Tyler was preparing to frame the question about past allegations.

He was. And he did.

The curate sighed heavily. "I am aware of all that," she said. "William talked to me about the situation some time ago. It troubled him more than he let on, I believe. He was a sensitive man. My understanding is that he fought a lot of interior battles."

"Could you elaborate?" asked Tyler.

"Nothing sinister, if that's what you mean. We can never know for sure what goes on in another person's head. But my thinking is that William was a man of empathy and compassion, and of great imagination. And with those blessings there often comes a tremendous burden of pain. He was moved greatly by the suffering of others, and frustrated that he couldn't do more to ease that suffering. I think it made him fragile, though he didn't easily show his vulnerability. He preferred, I think, to use his considerable

32

intelligence to help others rather than to dwell on his own difficulties."

"What difficulties did he have?" asked Tyler.

Marion Ecclestone smiled. "We all have difficulties, don't we? Life is never easy, even for a priest!"

Mills stifled a smile of his own, impressed at the curate's mastery of sarcasm and diplomacy.

"Have you ever felt intimidated by a member of the congregation?" asked Tyler.

"I would be lying if I said that I had never felt threatened doing my job. It was the same in teaching. Unpredictable situations can occur, and some people can be harder to deal with than others. Anyone can come in through the doors of a church, and often people come to a place like this when they are feeling stressed and even desperate. There is a vulnerability that comes with this job, and that's just how it is."

Tyler appeared ready to pounce, but the curate clearly anticipated his response.

"There is not a member of this congregation who I believe to be a danger to my well-being, or who I believe to have been responsible for killing Father Peterson, if that's what you are about to ask me. We have members of the congregation who can be outspoken and challenging in a number of ways, but no-one who I would call 'dangerous'."

"Would you tell me, if you did have any suspicions?" said Tyler, an edge to his tone.

The curate's demeanour changed in an instant, and Mills recognised that beneath the soft, soothing exterior, there was a core of iron running through this woman. She was no pushover, he thought, and likely often under-estimated.

"Do you really think," she said, "that I would protect someone who had murdered my colleague? Whoever has done this terrible thing needs to be found and brought to justice. Be assured that if I can assist in helping you to do that, I will, and without a moment's hesitation. But please, don't insult me."

"Apologies," said Tyler.

"Accepted."

Tyler and Mills made their way from the church, tracing the path into and through the woods, before emerging on the other side. The frosty weather had been replaced with a nondescript drizzle that had November written all through it. Tyler looked across the pathway to the rectory, where the priest had lived for the past five years. It was a lovely place to live, he thought, immediately catching the irony. He tacitly scribed the estate-agent blurb: *a quiet, low-crime area of the city, adjacent to impressive parkland and bordering the more formal gardens ...* One of the nicer parishes, no doubt about it. At least on the face of it. The last place you might expect something like this to happen.

Terrorists generally claimed responsibility for their actions, to promote their cause. Apart from a hatful of claims from individuals who turned out to have no credible means by which to have carried out the murder, there was nothing forthcoming. As for the Satanist conspiracy theory, they were still looking at Clayton Shaw to establish what other operatives might be in the locality.

And no obvious candidates in the congregation ... Tyler turned quickly to Mills. "Follow me," he said.

Quickly backtracking through the woods, the DCI shot back into the church as the curate was about to leave.

"Back so soon?" she said.

"One further question," said Tyler. "Who is Church Warden?"

"We have two, as a matter of fact. It's a long story. Phyllis Wagstaff and Gordon Foster."

The curate went back into the church office, returning with an information leaflet, and handing it to the detective. "All the contact details are on there," she said. "Is there anything that I can help you with?"

"No, but thank you," said Tyler.

She frowned, but Tyler had already turned to leave. Catching the curate's eye, DS Mills shrugged, before following the DCI out into the drizzling gloom.

As Mills drove back towards Hanley Police Station, Tyler again appeared deep in thought. "A penny for them, sir," said Mills at last.

"What? Oh, I see. Not sure you'd be getting much of a bargain."

"You think the church wardens had something to do with it?"

Tyler laughed. "Has your wife been reading classic detective stories to you again at bedtime?"

Arriving on Cedar Lane, Mills parked the car and the two detectives went into the Police Station, making their way to the CID office.

The team had been busy. Following Clayton Shaw from his home in Milton, officers had arrived at a farmhouse a few miles out of Leek, on the Buxton

Road. The farm belonged to Charles and Rose Blackwood, the founders of the cult whose fortnightly meeting Shaw had claimed to be present at on the evening Father Peterson was murdered.

Contact had also been established with Gerald Pickering, the father of the choirboy who had made the allegations against Peterson five years earlier. Much to Tyler's consternation, however, the local police in Stroud had already visited Pickering and his son. They had, nevertheless, established solid alibis for both, effectively eliminating them from the present enquiry.

"Looks like we're back to terrorists and Satanists," said Mills. "Oh, sorry, sir, I was forgetting: terrorists, Satanists ... and church wardens."

Tyler, in spite of himself, cracked a smile. "Did anyone tell you that your sense of humour may get you into trouble one day, DS Mills?"

"It was written on practically every one of my school reports, sir."

CHAPTER SIX

"I've contacted the wardens," said Mills. "They both live locally and are available as we speak. Any particular order?" he asked.

"Who sounds the more interesting?" asked Tyler.

"Tough call," said Mills. "I got the impression that they both had plenty to say, though."

"Church wardens generally do."

"You speak from experience?" asked Mills.

"A few cases back in London, nothing too remarkable. But if you want to know what's happening in a church; about who thinks what about who, and any hidden agendas and associated gossip, don't waste time talking to the clergy. They have higher things on their minds." Tyler looked at his watch. "But first up, we've got company. The neighbourhood Satanists are due in."

"How exciting," said Mills.

"Don't be droll."

"When you say 'neighbourhood' ..."

"I mean operating locally."

"Locally, sir?"

"You know very well, don't you?"

"Know what, sir?"

"Charles and Rose Blackwood, leaders of *Chapter Six* ... based in the Moorlands."

Mills gave a knowing smile. "In the moorlands, sir? How interesting."

"If you would like to pass comment, Danny, please be my guest."

37

"A case of not shitting on your own doorstep?"

"You don't like out-of-towners, do you?"

"That's not fair, sir. I'm an out-of-towner myself, these days. Since my wife's dream of country living got the better of us all. But like I keep telling her: nothing good can come from the countryside. It's not natural, living out in the sticks. I'm a town boy, a city dweller through and through. Stoke City football club, my local boozers, the pie and oatcake shops, and I'm happy."

"Ought we to charge them now and done with?" said Tyler, "Just for having the nerve to live outside of your beloved city?"

"It's tempting, sir."

"Come on; let's see what they have to say. And then we'll toss a coin for the church wardens."

"Isn't police work fascinating?" said Mills.

"Something like that," said Tyler.

The detectives made their way down to the first interview room, already occupied by a man with a neat black goatee beard. Charles Blackwood had a piercing, intense look about him, thought Mills. A look that was meant to be intimidating, or else enigmatic, it was difficult to tell, falling some way short on both counts.

Tyler, meanwhile, was already sniffing the air and placing what he found there in the category marked 'bullshit'. He knew from experience though appearances could be deceptive. Indeed, he had become something of an evangelist in the matter, reprimanding Danny Mills on occasion when the DS appeared to leap to premature and unsubstantiated conclusions.

"Mr Blackwood," said Tyler. "I understand that you describe yourself as a Satanist. Perhaps you could explain what your work entails, exactly."

Blackwood looked from one detective to the other, exuding a clear air of superiority and barely concealed humour. In soft, educated tones he explained the situation.

Tyler listened intently as the man gave a short lecture on the subject. It turned out that Charles Blackwood had been somewhat misrepresented, and wasn't a Satanist at all. It was a catch-all pejorative term, unsuitable for the ethos of *Chapter Six*; a term that he rejected as being simply a somewhat adversarial form of what he described as 'self-religion'. The cult he organised accommodated a number of occult disciplines, and only a few members actually called themselves Satanists, and many inappropriately at that.

"... Satanism is a misused and misunderstood term, Inspector. It doesn't necessarily involve a belief in the Satan of Christianity. It's more about affirming individual and counter-cultural expressions of spirituality. In some cases a revolt against traditional and organised religions, and often designed to merely provoke hostility in Christians and the media."

Tyler yawned

"...Of course, there are so-called Satanists who indeed worship the devil, and believe themselves tasked to prepare the way for his imminent arrival in the world."

"I see," said Tyler. "And they prepare the way by vandalising church property?"

"They would possibly call it raising public awareness."

"I'd still prefer to call it vandalism," said Tyler. "And what other methods might they use to spread the message?"

"We do not employ violence in our organisation, if that's what you are getting at."

"No violence?" said Tyler. "This devil you worship ... he's a pacifist, then?"

"Don't mock me," said Blackwood.

"Where were you on Saturday evening?" asked Tyler.

"Holding an all-nighter, actually. Our membership was gathered and everyone can be accounted for."

"That's convenient. Almost as though you knew that something was kicking off elsewhere."

The man raised a pair of monstrous black eyebrows.

"Is that gesture supposed to mean something?" asked Tyler.

"That's a matter of interpretation."

"What are you talking about? Are you suggesting that at your little get-to-togethers out in the countryside you can influence events?"

"Some believe so, yes."

Tyler took a deep breath, as though summoning powers of restraint. "I'd like you to spell that out for me, if you don't mind, Mr Blackwood."

It looked to Tyler as though Blackwood was taking to the stage. The man spoke quite eloquently about the power of numbers, of symbols, of incantations and forces of belief.

When he had finished, Tyler said, "Are you suggesting that your intended outcome that night was the death of a priest?"

The man smirked, and to Tyler it looked ugly enough to merit a damned good kick in the balls.

Tyler nodded at Mills, and the two of them went out of the interview room and stood in the corridor. Tyler's voice was trembling with anger. "What are your thoughts, Danny?"

"I bet he has fun dressing up, sir. Sounds to me like a power trip meets with mental illness. I think he's probably in need of a new hobby. Like I said before, they can be a funny lot out there in the hills."

"The other half is parked across the corridor, I understand?"

"Correct, sir. Shall we?"

The detectives entered the second interview room, where a woman dressed in black, with matching hair and an attempt at an enigmatic and intimidating stare, sat waiting.

"Mrs Blackwood," said Tyler, with an audible sigh.

The woman spoke in the same measured, educated, soft-toned voice as Mr Blackwood, and used much the same words to answer the same questions that her husband had used.

Tyler had heard enough. "You can't believe your luck, can you?" he said.

"Luck?" said Mrs Blackwood. "I'm sure I don't know what you're talking about."

"A dead priest, and not merely murdered, but crucified. Perfect advertising for your lot, except that you've made one big mistake."

"And what mistake would that be?"

"A convenient group alibi on the night when something went down. A bit too much of a coincidence, don't you think?"

41

The woman's grin was every bit as ugly as that of her husband's.

"Perhaps you need to modify your theory, Inspector. Perhaps it wasn't coincidence."

"So you are claiming responsibility?"

"Not physically, no, of course not. Not in any way that you can prove."

"Clayton Shaw," said Tyler. "He's one of yours?"

"Unfortunately, yes."

"*Unfortunately?*"

"Vandalism only gives an organisation like ours ... a 'bad name'." She began to laugh. "You think that Shaw's juvenile activities were authorised by me or my husband? The truth is, we weren't aware of what Mr Shaw was doing. We are grown-ups, *most* of us. We burn down the churches of the mind, Inspector. We don't waste our time and effort setting fire to actual buildings."

The detectives returned to the CID office to be informed that two further suspects had been brought in, both threatening imminent jihad. Both men had a history of mental health issues and each claimed to have murdered the priest single-handedly.

DCI Tyler sighed deeply. "Let's get it over with, Danny," he said.

CHAPTER SEVEN

"Do you think we can eliminate the Blackwoods and the jihadists from our investigation, sir?" said Mills, driving across town.

"I don't wish to appear flippant about any of this," said Tyler. "A man has been murdered, and in a particularly gruesome and barbaric fashion. I don't take kindly to anybody wasting valuable time and resources by falsely laying claim to being responsible. To say that those latest two 'confessors' have issues ... and the media aren't helping, ramping up the terrorism angle and bringing every fruitcake out of their bedrooms and onto the streets. Add in our 'non-violent' neighbourhood Satanists and we've barely got chance to focus on any genuine suspects."

"I wasn't aware that we had any," said Mills.

Tyler glanced across at the DS. "I still want to talk to Tony and Gerald Pickering down in Stroud. I know they have alibis. Everyone has them, apparently. But not everyone has to get their own hands dirty. I believe the Pickerings have money."

"You really think-"

"I'm not sure what to think. I'm keeping my options open, that's all. Like any good detective should. But I don't want to feed any more 'witch hunts', so to speak, just at the moment."

"What do you mean?" asked Mills.

"*What do I mean?* Calling Planet Mills, come in Planet Mills! The city is in meltdown, fearing a terrorist

43

plot or else a satanic conspiracy, in case you hadn't heard. Those are the current obsessions that the media is feeding them. And if they get their hands on the latest incidence of sexual misconduct by a priest, and child sexual abuse at that ..."

Tyler rubbed his hands over his face. "There still might be nothing to it, and that's why I want to keep the lid on. But make no mistake: I also want to investigate the possibility, and investigate it fully. Father Peterson gets a phone call five years on from an allegation made against him - for God's sake, are we anywhere near Hanchurch yet?"

"We're here, sir," said Mills, pulling the car to a halt outside a small terraced house on Willemore Street. The home of Phyllis Wagstaff, Church Warden.

The house was small, and appeared to suit Miss Wagstaff perfectly. She was scarcely five foot tall and stick-thin with it. Her distinguishing feature was a pair of glasses perched above her nose, jam-jar lenses mounted in thick black frames. Mills kept the old and well-worn observation to himself that a person would need extremely good eyesight to see though them. He also silently wondered if Phyllis Wagstaff didn't do an awful lot of reading.

The detective's hunch was confirmed on entering the small front room, which was lined almost floor to ceiling with books. When the woman offered to make a cup of tea for her visitors, the two men took their seats and spent a few minutes examining the book shelves.

"She seems to like detective fiction," said Mills, noting the considerable collection of crime novels dominating one side of the room. "I reckon she's a proper Miss Marple."

The rattle of cups indicated that the woman was coming through with the refreshments.

"Looks as though we are about to find out," said Tyler. "But a word of warning: if she brings in cake and biscuits spare a thought for your waistline."

Mills' hand rested guiltily over the expanding dome of his belly.

"I will do my best, sir."

Phyllis Wagstaff placed a tray laden with teapot, china cups, cakes and biscuits in front of her visitors. Mills tried not to lick his lips, catching Tyler's eye as he did so.

"It's a terrible business, just terrible," she said, stirring the pot. "When a priest, a member of the clergy can't go about his business without something like this happening ... they want stringing up, they really do. String them up and throw the leftovers to the birds. And that would be too good for them! It's the only language they understand. So, who's for a nice cup of tea, then?"

She looked at the detectives, who both nodded their approval.

"And please," she said, whilst pouring the drinks, "help yourselves to cake and biscuits. I'm cutting down, and this lot will only go to waste."

"Thank you," said Tyler, reaching for a side plate and selecting two biscuits, and at the same time watching DS Mills licking his lips with a desperate anticipation.

Placing the drinks in front of the two detectives, Phyllis Wagstaff looked at Mills. "There's nothing wrong with those cakes, you know. They are fresh. A working policeman needs his energy, so don't be shy."

Mills patted his stomach. "They look lovely," he said. "But I have to shed a few pounds."

"You need to keep yourself nourished, doing the job you do. You need your strength to deal with all these criminals and no mistake. I don't know what this world is coming to."

Tyler coughed, drawing her attention. "I understand," he said, "that you have been church warden at St Barnabas for a few years now."

"Fourteen, to be exact," she said. "Coming up for fifteen next year. I don't know where the time's gone."

"I expect you've seen a few changes here in that time."

"I've seen a few vicars come and go, if that's what you mean. Now, let me think. There was Father -"
"What did you think of Father Peterson?" said Tyler.

She looked again at Mills before lifting up a plate of cakes in one hand, and biscuits in the other. "Are you sure I can't tempt you?"

Mills eyed the two plates and looked about to cry. "I'm fine, really," he said, taking a slurp of tea. "Doctor's orders," he lied.

"Doctors! What do they know! Don't talk to me about -"

"Father Peterson?" prompted Tyler.

She offered the plates to Tyler, who took a cake and another biscuit, as though to break the deadlock. At this she nodded and smiled. "See," she said, looking again at Mills. "It hasn't done your friend any harm. He looks in the peak of condition if you ask me. Not an ounce of fat on him."

"Thank you, Ms Wagstaff," said Tyler, "as you were saying ..."

"Was I?"

"About Father -"

"Yes, William. A lovely vicar and a lovely man and I won't have a word said against him. He was salt of the Earth. They didn't deserve him, some of them, at any rate."

"The congregation?" asked Tyler.

"You get some funny ones. I suppose you do in any church, or anywhere else, for that matter."

"Funny in what way?"

"Don't start me on that!" she said.

"Did anyone have a grudge against Father Peterson?" asked Tyler.

The woman's eyes narrowed. "I know what you're doing," she said. "You want me to solve the case for you. I only wish I could. Do I know anyone who would have done that to him?" She shook her head. "You can't please everyone, fair enough; but I don't think anyone would have gone that far - as to kill him, I mean. Not on my life."

Tyler bit into a biscuit.

"Nice, aren't they?" she said. "Mind you, there was that Terry."

"Terry, Ms Wagstaff?"

"I'm a Miss, not a Ms! I never married and I'm proud of it. Terry ... oh, what's his name now? Banks! That's him - Terry Banks! He's been coming on Sunday mornings for a couple of months or so. He's a queer fish, that one."

Tyler asked the woman what she thought constituted a 'queer fish' exactly.

"He acts *strange*. He comes out with weird comments. He's upset quite a few of the congregation. I think Father William had to have a word with him about something."

Tyler's interest perked up. "Could you tell me more about Mr Banks," he asked her.

She betrayed a slight smile, clearly pleased that she had gained the detective's attention. Mills leaned forward, taking a cake off the plate as he did so, and taking a hefty bite before noticing what he was doing.

"It's the way he would look at you," she said. "One minute he's smiling at you like a dumb child, the next he's looking daggers, and having you wondering what you've done to upset him. After Father William had spoken to him after the service - and only a couple of weeks ago, it was - I caught Terry looking at him. Such a look it was, and he was muttering under his breath. I couldn't catch it all, but there were a few choice words in there I can tell you."

"Why did Father William speak to Mr Banks?" asked Tyler, as Mills quickly devoured the remaining evidence of his dietary lapse, licking his fingers for good measure.

"He had a go at one of our ladies."

"A *go*?" said Tyler.

"He was talking during the prayers, and it was very distracting. One of the ladies asked him to please be quiet, and he turned on her. Told her if she ever spoke to him like that again she'd regret it. And gave her one of his looks - such a look it was. She told Father William about it and he said he would have a word with him. And then, like I say, I caught him watching Father

48

William and muttering obscenities. I wouldn't put anything past him, really I wouldn't."

"I see," said Tyler, catching Mills' eye.

"And then of course there was Geraldine."

"Geraldine?"

"She had a right falling out with Father William. It came to a head one Sunday. That was only a few weeks ago, too - there must have been something in the air! Anyway, she ended up storming off, and we haven't seen her since."

"What was that about?" asked Tyler.

"Some of them reckon it was to do with Father William not agreeing to marry her son. He was recently divorced, so I heard. But because she was a regular here I think she thought she could pull a few strings, you know how it is with some people."

Tyler saw Mills eyeing the biscuit plate, and he coughed, causing the DS to edge back again in his seat.

"Anyway, she'd been out of sorts with Father William, but I think she thought she'd let things cool off before having another try. She confided in one or two of the others."

"And they confided in you, Miss Wagstaff?"

"We're not gossips, if that's what you're thinking. But when Geraldine tried again, and Father William told her 'no', she had a right flare up, cursing him so you could hear it around the church, even though they were in the office. She came out of that office swearing like a sailor and saying she'd take her business elsewhere. I ask you! Business!"

Tyler was about to speak, but Phyllis Wagstaff was on a roll.

"Then there was the Wilson family. Now, that was a sad case. Heart-breaking it was. Poor Mrs Wilson. *Marjorie*."

"What happened?" asked Tyler.

"Cancer. I know that Father William gave a lot of support. He visited her a lot towards the end, and he organised a healing service a few months before she died. Funnily enough, that was around the time when things took a turn for the worst for poor Marjorie. Her husband was broken by it. Graham. He was a lovely man. But he took it hard. He stopped coming here towards the end of Marjorie's life. I think he felt let down."

She paused for a few moments, recollecting. "He's not been back since. Didn't even have the funeral service here, yet they'd been coming to this church for years. Had a service at the crematorium and that was it. I don't think poor Graham's been inside a church since."

Tyler was again about to speak when the warden said, "And then there was Dylan Greer, of course." She said it as though she had been saving the best for last. "Now there was a character for you!"

"What kind of a character?" asked Tyler.

Phyllis Wagstaff laughed. "Now there's a tale to tell!"

Tyler waited for her to tell it.

"I don't know what went on there. Local business man - had a bit of money, so they say. Used to come here with his wife and daughter, until him and his wife split up over something. He must have had custody, at least on Sundays, because after they split up he used to bring his daughter to church and leave her in the

Sunday School group and then disappear for a couple of hours. He was using the place like a crèche, he was. It wasn't fair, and in the end Father William had to speak to him about it. And that's another one who left and hasn't come back."

Tyler sat back and closed his notebook.

"Quite a bit for you to be going on with there," she said. "And that's without mentioning ... you know."

"Know what, Miss Wagstaff?"

"Well, I don't know if you know about it. But when Father William first came here ..."

Tyler guessed what was coming. He let her say it.

"Well, there were rumours of things that had ... *gone on down south*. I mean south of the country, of course, I wasn't suggesting ... I can't imagine for a moment that Father William would get up to anything like that."

"Like what?" asked Tyler.

"You know, messing with choir boys, that sort of thing. Turns my stomach to even think about it!" She shook her head. "No! Absolutely not! Not our Father William, not in a million years. Mind you, like they say, there's no smoke without fire."

Tyler stood up. "Right," he said, "we will leave you in peace."

"You haven't made much progress with those cakes or biscuits," she said, looking at DS Mills. "Take a few with you. Keep you going through the day, they will. Please yourself. But I do hope you catch them quick, whoever's done this thing. No-one deserves that, and Father William wouldn't have harmed a fly. He was such a gentle, kind man. It's a terrible world we're living in. But go on, a cake or two won't hurt either of you."

"We could always pace ourselves, sir," said Mills, starting up the engine. "Leave the other warden for another day."

"Let's get it over and done with," said Tyler.

"As you say, sir."

Mills headed back in the direction of Trentham. As they approached their destination, he aired his thoughts to the silent DCI.

"We have a man with mental health issues, a 'queer fish' who could give you a look and mutter swear words under his breath; a woman who couldn't get Father Peterson to marry her son; a man whose wife died despite the priest praying for her and organising a healing service, and a business man told off for using the church as a crèche."

"And the winner is?" said Tyler.

Mills pulled up outside a neat semi-detached property less than a mile from St Barnabas church. A man appearing to be in his late sixties, wearing a smart suit, answered the polished front door.

Gordon Foster showed the detectives into a neat and ordered living room and offered to make a drink, which the DCI declined.

Foster, observed Mills, was a man of precise habits. He spoke in measured tones, giving everything a considerable period for reflection before commenting. Mills could see that the day was beginning to seriously try Jim Tyler's patience.

Foster asked if they planned to visit Phyllis Wagstaff, and when Mills explained that they already had done, the man widened his eyes in an attitude of questioning disbelief. "At least that saves me the time and effort of updating you on any gossip," he said.

Tyler jumped to the point, and asked Foster if he had any thoughts on who may be responsible for the death of Father Peterson.

"Doubtless Phyllis has given you a list of suspects already," he said. "She is rather prone to speculative discussions with the congregants."

He had been sharing the role of church warden for a few years now, and the matter was obviously a bone of contention, thought Mills.

Gordon Foster had been a member of the congregation for almost ten years, and spoke highly of the priest as a clever, intellectual, and humble man. He didn't once mention members of the congregation, past or present, and he had no idea why someone, anyone, would want to commit such an unspeakable atrocity on another human being.

"I read the papers, I listen to the radio and I even occasionally watch the television. I've heard all about terrorist theories, satanic conspiracies and the like, and I don't believe a word of it."

"Are you aware of anybody who had issues with Father Peterson?" asked Tyler.

A longer-than-usual pause followed.

"In a church, as in any human organisation, you have people unhappy with the leadership. It's inevitable. I have little doubt that Phyllis has filled you in with all the many 'likely suspects' who have had disagreements or harsh words with Father William. I don't believe there is anything in any of it. However ..."

Another protracted pause followed.

"I'm sure that you will be aware that William arrived here under something of a cloud. Of course, that wasn't common knowledge at the time, but in due course the *tittle-tattlers* prevailed, as they generally do."

"Under a cloud?" said Tyler.

Gordon Foster knew the full story: the choirboy, Tony Pickering, and the boy's father, Gerald. The accusations made in Stroud.

"We were quite close, actually. We had a few common interests: history, music, poetry. We would talk, and occasionally William would need to off-load. It didn't happen very often, but he knew that he could talk to me in confidence. He knew that tongues wagged, and I could be his eyes and ears. He was a man of the utmost integrity, make no mistake about that. There was nothing in those allegations, and I would stake my mortal soul on it. There was no guilty conscience there, but he was deeply hurt, all the same, naturally; he was troubled by the false accusations made against him."

"Are you suggesting that any of this led to his death, Mr Foster?" asked Tyler.

"I can't possibly know that, of course. William didn't confide to me that he was in any physical danger. There have been a few fallings out among congregants, and William could be quite a straight talker. Not everybody likes that. He wasn't intimidated by anybody that I'm aware of. His straight talking was likely the root cause of his problems in Stroud, though of course that's only my opinion."

Tyler asked Foster to clarify what he meant by the priest's straight talking leading to his problems in Stroud.

"Tony Pickering - and I only have William's word on this, you understand - Tony Pickering couldn't sing. The choirmaster had left the church following a falling out with William, and so William had taken over. He thought Pickering only remained in the choir because his father was friends with the choirmaster. Gerald Pickering, the boy's father, was also, and as far as I know still is, a local councillor, and a man of means who made significant contributions to the church funds. I understand that following William's departure from Stroud the boy continued to sing in the choir."

"Are you suggesting, Mr Foster, that not only were false allegations made against Father William because he had told the boy he couldn't sing, but that five years later, having been effectively forced from the parish, he is then murdered by ..."

"Frankly, no," said Foster. "I think that the allegations made against William are the consequence of a powerful man taking exception to a perceived slight against his son. Or that his son made up the allegations to save face and then was too ashamed to retract. I think that's highly likely, and I believe that William thought so too. I find it ludicrous that they would pursue him all the way up here, five years later, and kill him."

"Are you aware," said Tyler, "that Father Peterson was in fact contacted by Pickering shortly before he was killed?"

Foster nodded. "Yes, I was aware of that. William was deeply troubled by it and I suggested that he ought to contact the police."

"But you still don't think this constitutes a motive for murder?" asked Tyler.

"Frankly, no, I don't. If they were planning to kill him then I don't imagine they would make contact out of the blue like that and risk drawing suspicion."

Before leaving Tyler made mention of the members of the congregation listed by Phyllis Wagstaff.

Gordon Foster shook his head and laughed. "That woman ought to write murder mysteries in her *abundant* spare time. She would make a bloody killing!"

CHAPTER EIGHT

Tyler sat across the desk from Chief Superintendent Berkins. "I want to put in a request," he said.

"About this Stroud business?" asked Berkins.

"We need to eliminate the Pickerings from the enquiry."

"I take it there are no other leads emerging?"

"Not really. We still have a few people to interview this end, but to be honest, I'm not hopeful."

Berkins sighed. "The public are convinced that we're in the grip of a terrorist - or failing that, a Satanist - conspiracy, and the media are determined to feed them accordingly. Follow up what you have, Jim, no matter how thin. I'll get back to you regarding Stroud."

Terry Banks appeared terrified when Tyler and Mills turned up at the flat he was renting in Hanford. He answered the front door dressed in a grubby suit, trousers half-mast and jacket open, revealing bare feet and a matching chest.

When Mills asked if they might go inside the flat to talk, Banks snarled back, "I haven't done anything. Is this about the dead priest? Has someone said I did it?"

"There's nothing to get alarmed about, Mr Banks," said Mills. "We are simply making routine enquiries -"

"No, you're not," said Banks. "You think I had something to do with it."

"It would be better if we could talk to you in private," said Mills.

"Are you going to arrest me?"

"I would like to ask you a few questions, that's all."

Banks let the detectives inside the flat, where they were greeted with a master class in austerity. In the middle of the living room stood a single blue and white striped camping chair that had seen too much sunshine and fast food by the look of it. There was nothing else in the room, apart from the damp on the walls; not a photograph, not a cup; no sign that anyone lived there.

"Ask your questions," said Banks.

The three men stood for a few moments, and then Banks sat down on the folding chair that seemed to Mills to mark the dead centre of the room with almost mathematical precision. "Come on then, I haven't got all day," urged Banks. "I'm not working at the moment, but that doesn't mean that I can sit around talking to the likes of you lot. What do you want to know?"

Aside from attending church services regularly, it appeared that Banks found little in the way of social activity to fill his days. When asked what he had been doing around the time of Father Peterson's death, all he could say was that he had been in his flat. He hadn't had any visitors. He had been reading his Bible. He spent most of his time reading his Bible, and what was wrong with that!

Banks suddenly leapt to his feet, his face right in DS Mills. "Are you going to send me to prison for murdering him? The Bible says 'Thou shalt not kill', and I do what the Bible says. I always do what the Bible says."

Mills didn't flinch. He spoke gently to the man, inviting him to sit down, trying to assure him that no-one was accusing him of anything.

When Banks finally sat back down, Mills asked him when he had last seen any friends.

"Friends - me? You must be joking! Everyone thinks I'm mad. I see people at church. I don't need anyone else. I used to like the priest. He was kind to me. He didn't look at me like I was mad. I could talk to him. He was my friend. Sometimes he even came to see me here. Nobody else does, and I don't want them to. I'm alright as I am. I haven't got any friends now, and that's how I want it, so that's the way it is."

"Do you have any idea who might have wanted to hurt Father Peterson?" asked Tyler.

Banks shook his head. "How would I know? But I tell you this for nothing: I miss him, I really do. If you had a problem, he was someone you could talk to. There aren't many around like him. Most couldn't give a damn whether you live or die. He was different. He was my friend."

Driving away from Terry Banks' flat, Tyler said, "Loners get an unfair press. Nobody trusts them. People imagine that in their solitariness they must have something to hide. Unless Banks has an accomplice that he's keeping well hidden, I think we might have to look elsewhere."

"Who's next on the list, sir?"

"It's back to Trentham," said Tyler.

A few minutes later Mills pulled up outside a smart detached property, where Geraldine Thorpe answered the door, inviting the detectives inside her home.

She was a smartly dressed woman in her mid-forties, and she was burdened with a sarcastic grin that for some reason she seemed unable to shake. There was something distinctly unpleasant about her, thought Mills.

Leading the detectives through to a spacious sitting area that looked out on a large garden to the rear of the property, she said, "I understand that you would like to speak to me about that horrific murder. I don't know quite what you expect I can tell you, though." Her grin appeared to deepen. "Unless of course you think that I had something to do with it."

"And why would we think that?" asked Tyler.

"St Barnabas is known for wagging tongues," she said. "It's famous for it. And it's probably no secret that I left that church after falling out with Father William. I wanted him to marry my son. He wouldn't. So I took my custom elsewhere."

The woman's grin began to morph into something of a pout, thought Mills, and her eyes twinkled provocatively in DCI Tyler's direction.

"Let me guess," she said. "Phyllis Wagstaff gave me a reference."

"I'm sorry?" said Tyler.

"She has me down as the local priest killer, no doubt. She never liked me. Described me once as a man-eater, I believe. I'm not sure that's quite the same thing."

The grin was back, and her eyes widened once again in Jim Tyler's direction. "You can cross-examine me, if you wish. But you will find my credentials impeccable."

Seemingly unmoved by Geraldine Thorpe's charm offensive, Tyler asked her where she was at the time of the murder. She took evident delight in describing the romantic city break in Paris spent with a young man half her age.

"Mind you," she added, looking Tyler up and down, "though my lover had qualities that I can't deny, I'm partial to taller men. Six foot?" she asked the DCI.

Ignoring the question, Tyler asked a few more of his own. He asked her what she thought of Father Peterson, and if she could think of any reason why someone might want to hurt or even to kill him.

She answered without hesitation. "You will no doubt interpret my negative opinions on the man to be the result of sour grapes, and somewhat biased because he wouldn't agree to marrying my son. However, I have to say that there was a - how can I say this - a *creepy* side to the man."

"Creepy?" said Tyler.

"I knew about his past."

"What about his past?"

"Word gets around," she said. "People with too much time on their hands, people like Phyllis Wagstaff. I knew he'd been accused of child molesting, and frankly I'm not surprised."

"But knowing that, you still wanted him to marry your son?" said Tyler.

"A man is innocent until proven guilty. Maybe I've had time to reflect. He had a look about him. Something I didn't trust. It makes my skin creep to even think about it. You get a lot of it in the church. All of that celibacy, no doubt - it isn't healthy. And there's no need for it." Her eyes lit. "Do you reckon his death might be related to the child molesting?"

Tyler thanked her for her time.

"No trouble at all," she said, showing them to the front door. "Are you sure you won't stay for a drink?"

"We really must be going," said Tyler. "Thanks all the same."

"Glad to be of assistance. And if there's anything else I can help you with, you must call and see me, anytime. You will always be more than welcome here - *day or night.*"

As Mills pulled away in the car, he looked across at Tyler.

"Not a word," said the DCI.

A few minutes later the detectives were walking up the short driveway to the home of Graham Wilson, who answered the door looking tired and frail. His wife had died of cancer a few weeks earlier, and her suffering and eventual death had taken a grim toll on the man left behind.

He took the officers into a little conservatory built on to the back of the house, affording a stunning view across open fields all the way to the Trentham Estate a mile or so up the road.

Once the detectives were sitting down, Wilson took his seat opposite them and said, "I don't understand why you want to speak to me."

Mills took the lead, offering first his condolences at the sad death of the man's wife. "Mr Wilson, we are speaking to people who knew the late Father Peterson. I understand that you used to attend St Barnabas church."

"That is correct."

"But you haven't attended the church for a little while now."

Graham Wilson looked at the detective with an expression of disbelief. "I didn't realise that non-attendance at church had become a police matter."

"Not yet," said Mills, trying to strike a genial note. "What was your opinion of Father Peterson?" asked the DS, retreating to a more formal tone.

Wilson thought for a moment. "I always got on well with him. I never had any issues."

Mills was trying to formulate his next question, when Wilson came to the floundering detective's rescue.

"You want to know why I stopped attending the church? Perhaps you think that I may have blamed him in some way for the death of my wife. I did blame him, I suppose, at least by extension."

"Can you explain what you mean by that?" interjected Tyler.

"I can try," said Wilson. "Look, I have no doubt whatsoever that he wanted my wife to be healed. To be cured. That when he arranged the healing service, he thought it would bring comfort to dear Marjorie, and to me. I don't blame a priest because he can't cure cancer. That would be ridiculous. For a while though I blamed God. I'm beginning to see that that is a natural response to the death of a loved one, even the natural response of a Christian. Jesus wept for Lazarus. I can't remember whether Father William or Marion reminded me of that – I mean, that it's natural and good to grieve."

The detectives sat in silence while Graham Wilson assembled his thoughts.

"But I was too angry to grieve. I blamed God and so I stopped going to church. I blamed Father William because I needed someone to blame. And because, for a short time, I believed that he had made too many promises, provided too many false hopes. In retrospect I can see that may have been down to my interpretation. God heals in many ways, though he doesn't always 'cure' in physical terms. I failed to see the subtle difference, and I regret that."

"Regret what, exactly?" asked Tyler.

"That I wasn't more grateful for the comforts that he tried to provide. Marjorie was stronger than me, and I suspect that she saw a lot deeper, too. I focused on wanting my wife well again, and so deemed his efforts a failure. I was angry and I cut myself off from him and the church. He came to see me. He rang me. And I shunned him. I sent him away. I deeply regret that now."

He looked close to tears, but then suddenly he laughed. "I most certainly didn't take out my anger by nailing him to a cross and murdering him!"

The detectives were in the process of thanking Mr Wilson for his time when the phone rang. He glanced at the handset next to him on the small telephone table, before turning back to the detectives. But Tyler gestured to him to go ahead and take the call.

Mr Wilson lifted up the receiver, and after listening for a few moments, he said, "I'll call you back later. I have visitors."

Ending the call, he said, "Sorry about that. It was my son checking up on me. He rings every day, twice some days. He really doesn't need to, but I can't tell him."

"He obviously worries about you," said Mills, smiling at the old man.

"I suppose he does. I shouldn't complain. Some kids don't seem to care about their parents these days.

Jordan's always been a good lad. Marjorie was so proud of him."

"So," said Tyler as he climbed into the passenger seat, "another afternoon wasted."

Mills looked about to contradict him, when the DCI said, "It's only a matter of time before I jump in with the media and embrace the terrorist - stroke - Satanist conspiracy! Or do all roads lead to Stroud?"

Mills put the car into gear and headed back to base.

CHAPTER NINE

Back at the station, Mills had some news. "I believe that we have a development, sir."

Tyler looked up from his newspaper. "Nothing to do with growing lines of mad bastards queuing up to confess?" he said, tapping at the paper in front of him.

"Quite the opposite, actually. We've located Dylan Greer. He's waiting for us downstairs."

"Where's he been hiding?" asked Tyler, reaching for his jacket.

"Derby. Over there on business, apparently."

"Let's see what he's got to say for himself. Lead the way, Danny."

Dylan Greer was sitting in one of the interview rooms, looking tense as the detectives entered.

"You're not an easy man to track down," said Tyler.

"I didn't realise anyone was looking for me. Now that I'm here, how can I help you?"

"I understand that you used to attend St Barnabas church in Trentham."

"I did, yes. Until that vicar made it clear that the likes of me are not welcome."

"You fell out with Father Peterson?"

"I'm not sure that I would put it like that. He suggested that I was using the church as a crèche, and so I took my custom elsewhere."

"Harsh words were not exchanged?" asked Tyler.

Greer again looked nervous. "Well, maybe one or two."

"You made threats against him?"

"I may have left with a parting shot, that's how I am. I don't really mean anything by it."

"You are aware of what has happened to Father Peterson, I take it?"

"You don't think - what? That I would do *that* because ... you've got to be winding me up."

"You threatened him?" asked Tyler again.

"Like I say, sometimes I say a bit more than I should do. But you don't have to take me too seriously."

"You were angry at Father Peterson?"

"I was, at the time, yes."

"And you wanted to hurt him - to teach him a lesson?"

"No! You're trying to put words in my mouth."

Tyler asked Dylan Greer where he was the night of the murder, at which point Greer said that he wanted to speak to a solicitor.

"That is your right, of course," said Tyler. "But if you tell us where you were that evening, that may not be necessary. We can get this over with now - unless, of course, you have anything to hide? Perhaps you would like a minute or two to think about it."

Greer started to bite at a finger, looking from one detective to the other.

"I'm not a religious man," he said. "I went to church because it's what you do; keeping up appearances, you could say. I wanted to get my daughter into the church school. There's plenty that do it. But then my wife left me and I was up against it. I wanted her to go to the church so it wouldn't compromise her education, but I was so busy. I never bloody stop. I should have made more time. When the priest spoke to me - to be honest with you I thought he was going to sabotage my daughter going to that school."

"So what did you do about it, Mr Greer?"

"I didn't hurt him. I'm not a violent man. If I had wanted to hurt him, why would I have gone to the trouble of doing all … *that*? It's some religious nutcase you should be looking for."

"Is that right, Mr Greer? Or maybe you thought it would be somewhat *fitting,* nailing a priest to a cross. Do you have difficulty controlling your anger? Is that why your wife left you?"

"I've never been violent, that's not fair."

"Maybe you thought that, not being a religious man, you could take out your secular anger and disguise it as religiously motivated murder. Is that what you did?"

Greer repeated that he wanted to speak to a solicitor.

Tyler stood up and nodded to Mills. "Okay," he said. "Let's make this formal then. We'll run the tape as soon as your brief gets here."

As the detectives were leaving the room, Greer called them back. "Okay," he said. "There's no need for that."

The detectives resumed their seats.

"I can account for my actions that night," said Greer. "But does anybody else have to know where I was?"

"That depends," said Tyler.

"Depends on what?"

"On whether you were breaking the law."

Greer told the detectives that, over the past few months, every Saturday evening he had been attending the *Paradise Club* in Crewe. "I don't want this to get

68

out," he said. "I have a reputation to think about. My wife will try to use it against me. I don't want any of this to affect my daughter."

"I see," said Tyler. "Of course, we will have to verify with the club exactly what hours you kept there."

"I was there all evening. I spent most of it in the private area - I mean ... in the *guest lounge*. I was with Lydia. Luscious bloody Lydia! I didn't leave until, I don't know, it must have been kicking out time, around three."

Dylan Greer was looking at the floor beneath his feet.

"You probably just think I'm a dirty bastard, but it wasn't just about, you know - *that.* I needed someone to talk to, and I could talk to her. It cost me a fucking fortune, but she could listen like no-one else could, and I could get it out of my system."

At last he looked up at the detectives. "Does anyone else need to know about this? She'll hang me out to dry. I didn't hurt the priest, I've never hurt anybody. I love my daughter. *Please.*"

Mills emerged from the *Paradise Club* in the heart of Crewe town centre, and rang DCI Tyler.

"His story checks out, sir. The club has CCTV of him entering the club and leaving very late. He was, as he told us, in the private lounge, and with a young woman named Lydia. He has been attending the club on Saturdays for some time."

"Another dead end," said Tyler.

"He must have money to burn. I enquired about prices and it made my eyes water."

"Good job that you have your wife to go home to," said Tyler.

"Counting my blessings as we speak, sir."

"She's a very lucky woman, your wife."

"I'm no more than she deserves," said Mills.

Tyler was still laughing as he left Cedar Lane.

As Jim Tyler drove from Hanley towards his home in the ancient doomsday village of Penkhull, his laughter dried up and a more sombre mood began to settle over him. The investigation had so far yielded nothing, and the media was still piling the pressure onto the police department to unravel a non-existent terrorist plot or else construct some equally bizarre Satanist fantasy. And there was still unfinished business in Stroud that he would have given his right arm not to have to confront.

If it wasn't for the Potteries humour of DS Mills, he reflected, it might have been the perfect night to finally call it a day.

CHAPTER TEN

Early the following morning, Mills was at his desk and attempting to make an impression on the paperwork mountain, when Tyler came into the CID office looking wired.

"Any developments?" he said, throwing himself into his seat.

Mills shook his head.

"Pity. Berkins wants an update and I've absolutely nothing to give him."

Mills looked at the DCI questioningly.

As though a telepathic communication had passed between them, Tyler nodded. "There is that one avenue still to be explored," he said. "But will Berkins allow it?" He stood up, glancing at his watch. "Time to find out."

Berkins was looking tired and burdened when Tyler entered his office and took his customary seat opposite.

"Make my day," said Berkins, offering a weary smile. "Tell me that we have a breakthrough."

Tyler's pause told the Chief everything that he had feared.

"What are you proposing to do next, Jim?"

"I need to make that journey."

"I see," said Berkins, sitting back in his chair.

Tyler watched the senior man carefully. He had never been keen on authority, railing against it at every opportunity; and that attitude had got him into more than his fair share of trouble over the years. It was one of the factors that had led to altercations in his previous post, in London, and he had arrived in Stoke on Trent wondering if this was to be the end of the road, as far as his career was concerned. Yet in every sense he had been pleasantly surprised. He had come to love the area, the people, the heritage, the stunning countryside and unexpected treasures in the landscape of the city itself. He loved working with Danny Mills, who had become the closest thing to a friend that he had come across in his entire working life. And even Berkins, Chief Superintendant with too much on his plate and too few resources to deal with it - even Berkins had proved to be something of a gem.

The CS had seen the good in Jim Tyler, recognising the talent for detective work alongside an uncompromised integrity and genuine thirst for justice. CS Berkins had revealed himself as a kindred spirit, of sorts, if inhabiting a very different kind of skin. It would never get better than this, and Tyler knew it. Stress had almost killed Berkins, and Tyler had every reason to want the Chief to remain in good health and to continue in his post. From bitter experience, the alternatives could only range from the unfortunate to the potentially catastrophic.

In the heart of Jim Tyler, compassion ruled the day. Berkins was one of the good guys. He didn't deserve an early grave.

At last Chief Superintendent Berkins sat forward in his chair and nodded definitively. "Take DS Mills with you," he said. "And keep me posted."

*

Mills looked up to see the DCI approaching. "That was quick," he said. "I take it Berkins wasn't impressed."

"Berkins is always impressed. And it's *Chief Superintendent Berkins* to you! He's my new best friend. Pack your bags, Danny. We're heading down to Stroud first thing in the morning."

"He went for it?"

"Unless something turns up, we've nothing else to follow up on. What choice did he have?"

"What do they think about this in Stroud?"

"Berkins is still clearing the path, but we shouldn't have any issues, as far as I can see. That man should be working for the United Nations. I'm glad he's working for us, though. We'll meet with their CID when we get there, and then we'll get the opportunity to interview Tony and Gerald Pickering.

"Now ..." He eyed his own mountain of paper work. "Where in God's name do I begin?"

That evening, Tyler looked out from the front window of his recently purchased house on Penkhull Terrace. The view had sold the property to him; he could look out across the city and be grateful that he no longer plied his trade in the capital.

Yet that evening he couldn't settle, and for the first time in weeks he felt the old thirst calling.

Putting on tracksuit bottoms and a sweat top, he set off into the darkness, running down the hill from the village centre, heading towards Trent Vale and Oakhill, before reaching the A34. From there he ran in the direction of Trentham, tracing the route that the jogger had taken when she discovered the body of Father Peterson.

Once Tyler had reached the path from which the woman had spotted the crucifixion in the woods, he stopped running, and stood gazing through the wire fence into the pitch-dark woods; the place where the priest had died. He tried to imagine what could bring someone to cause such suffering to another person. What in the world could lead to someone nailing an old man to a wooden cross, and watching him die in agony?

Sadism, he knew, took many forms; and not all of them necessarily fatal. He had himself fallen into the hands of bullies and sadists over the years, though none of his memories of such monsters were more vivid than those from childhood.

Breaking off the train of thoughts racing through his head, he began to jog again, past the now unoccupied rectory, looping back around at the entrance to the golf course at the top of the lane, before returning to the point from which the jogger had seen the aftermath of the crucifixion. His thoughts flicked over the faces and voices of the people he had recently interviewed, and over the hysterical reports in the media about terrorists and devil worshippers.

He thought of his imminent visit to Stroud. *Tony Pickering, abused choirboy, allegedly; and his father, Gerald.* They had alibis, apparently. But what if they hadn't? Could what happened to Tony Pickering, if indeed anything had happened to him - could that have led to what had taken place in these woods? And what if Father William Peterson had been an abuser, and possibly a serial abuser? What if he had hurt someone else, someone in this area, during his five years here? What if that person, or persons, had taken the ultimate revenge?

74

There had been no formal allegations made against the late priest, apart from the historical ones made by Pickering. But then some people chose to seek justice in other ways, leaving the police out of it altogether.

What did he hope to find in Stroud? A guilty father and son who had extracted a belated justice of their own?

No, that was too easy.

Perhaps he would unravel a clue revealing the exact nature of an old priest's predilections ... a clue that might point in the direction of other victims who may have been responsible for killing him?

Tyler began to run again, picking up speed as thoughts of the present case began to morph into old memories. The demons were gaining strength once more, chasing Jim Tyler as he made his way back towards the ancient village of Penkhull.

He reached the village exhausted, and even the lights of the pubs in the square failed to entice him.

He made his way from the square down to Penkhull Terrace, where for half an hour he stood under the shower, letting the hot water scald the fatigue and rinse away the remnants of a multitude of dark thoughts.

It was getting late when he finally climbed into bed, almost convinced that he had done enough to earn a night's rest. But despite falling into a deep sleep almost as soon as his head touched the pillow, peaceful slumber was to elude him. He was back at the orphanage, and then at school, alternating back and forth between the two circles of hell. In both places demons dressed in black, devils draped in midnight gowns, were tormenting him. Brandishing their weapons of war they had prepared him half naked to take out their angst and pleasures on rebellious flesh.

Tyler woke up sweating, his throat parched, yearning to drink deeply from the bottle, to quench a thirst that mere water could never entirely alleviate. Still, he tried, getting out of bed, running the cold tap and drinking a pint straight down before returning to his bed.

Sleep was elusive, and when it did come he was back in the dormitories, and then walking the dimly lit corridors that led to frightening doors on the other side of which stood grinning devils in black gowns wielding their instruments of torture.

Tyler was again sitting bolt upright on his bed, his thirst raging out of control.

Donning his running clothes for a second time that night, he set off once more into the darkness.

CHAPTER ELEVEN

The journey to Stroud started early, in the company of the dawn light. The detectives were sharing driving duties and it was Tyler's shift. Mills could see how frazzled the DCI looked and asked if he was okay.

"I'm not going to doze off at the wheel and kill us both, if that's what you mean."

"That's very re-assuring, sir. Thank you."

"Don't mention it. Any further questions?"

"Are we nearly there, sir?"

Despite the friendship that had grown between the two officers, Jim Tyler still rarely talked of his personal life. It always seemed to Mills to be a closed door to which entry was routinely denied.

Danny Mills filled some of the gaps in the conversation, telling Tyler how much he still longed to move back to the city. "I'm a town dweller, that's the nub of it," he said. "I'd move back in the blink of an eye. But she's still in love with country living, and reckons the kids are settled at school now. I tell you, I've no chance."

Mills talked about how he was rarely getting to any Stoke City football matches these days, and how tough the job was becoming with staff shortages and rising crime that the government seemed in permanent denial of. At some point he asked Tyler if he was planning on making Stoke his permanent home.

"I've no plans to move at the moment," said Tyler. "I'm done with the bright lights of London, that's for sure. But who knows what life might throw up?"

"That's true enough," said Mills. He hesitated. "You know," he said, "I moan on about my better half dragging me out into the sticks, but I wouldn't be without her, not for the world. Doing this job, well, some days you need a friendly face waiting for you at the end of it."

Tyler turned to Mills. "Go on," he said. "Spit it out."

"Sir?"

"Don't come the innocent," said Tyler. "I know where this is heading."

"I'm sure I don't know what you could possibly mean, sir."

"You think I need the love of a good woman. And you may be right. The trouble is finding such a creature. Most of us only get one chance. Anyway, thanks for your concern. I'll let you know if there are any developments."

Tyler had been married once, and most days he still believed that the break-up had been entirely his fault. He had put his career before all else and convinced himself that he deserved to be alone. He had said as much. In rare moments, fragments had come out, and most of them in the company of Danny Mills. And Mills had always treated such outpourings with due respect and absolute confidentiality, talking of these sacred titbits to no-one apart from his wife, who was unanimous in her verdict: *"the man needs to move on"*.

Mills knew that Tyler had seen the woman from the school a few times, though that appeared to have fizzled out for some reason. He had also let slip that he was seeing a stress-counsellor, or therapist, on the advice - *or was that on the command*? - of CS Berkins.

The DCI had anger issues and a drink problem, and Mills was well aware that keeping dark stuff stored up inside you could be a recipe for disaster. They'd told him that on the *Stress Awareness* course, and these days, whenever he had been feeling particularly stressed out, he applied the wisdom of not bottling up his feelings. It helped that his wife always knew when something was wrong, and he had given up trying to hide his anxieties from her. It felt quite liberating getting it off your chest, and he suspected it would help Jim Tyler too. The difference was that the DCI had issues that stretched way back into his past, into his childhood, and the experts reckoned that sort of thing often required long-term professional help.

Mills reflected on the journey they were making; travelling down to Stroud to interview a young man who claimed to have been abused by Father William Peterson. How close to home was all this for Jim Tyler? He had been far more edgy again recently, and this case, this aspect of the investigation, was likely weighing heavily.

Yet how to raise the subject was another matter. Mills had had his head bitten off once already for making such connections. All he could do was keep a watchful eye, and be there for his colleague if and when he was ready to talk.

He wouldn't hold his breath though.

At the central police station in Stroud the detectives were taken through to meet the local officers who'd interviewed Tony and Gerald Pickering. DI Kathy Bunt and DS Ian Raskin introduced themselves and Bunt presented the visitors with the file.

As Tyler flicked through the pages, Bunt said, "I'm still surprised that you've come all the way down here to interview them. There's nothing to follow up that we can see. Tony Pickering is adamant that the incident took place, and his father is still very angry about it. But both have solid alibis and no convictions whatsoever."

Tyler continued to look through the file.

Raskin and Mills made small talk while Bunt eyed Tyler with evident fascination.

At last Tyler closed the file. Then he looked at DI Bunt and said, "I assume that Gerald Pickering has considerable means."

"He's a wealthy man, yes."

"The wealthy don't have to get their own hands dirty, if they choose not to," said Tyler.

"That's very true," said Bunt. "But those kinds of people often make a habit of it, and end up with a record. Gerald Pickering is as clean as a whistle. We've tapped into various associates of his, some of whom he may have crossed over the years, and ready to dish the dirt."

"And?" asked Tyler.

"While not everyone thinks of him as a saint, no-one has given us any cause for concern."

"Too good to be true?"

Bunt laughed. "You don't give up easily, do you? No, I wouldn't say 'too good to be true' at all. He has a temper, does Mr Pickering, and he can be obstinate in the extreme. He's not a particularly likeable man, in many ways. He likes to have things his own way, in my opinion. Overbearing, a bit of a bully, most likely - but there's absolutely nothing that gives us grounds to be suspicious."

She smiled at Tyler. "I can see you're not convinced. You need to see the man for yourself, and do things your way. I suppose that's why you made the journey down in the first place." She stood up. "This way, when you're ready."

"I want to see them separately," said Tyler.

"Your wish is our command," said Bunt. "Who would you like to see first?"

Tony Pickering was nineteen years of age, fourteen when the alleged assault took place. He looked timid and shy, and far younger than his years.

Tyler sat down opposite and explained the purpose of the interview. Mills took a seat and smiled toward the young man, while Tyler watched Tony Pickering smile back at DS Mills. A smile that said, *I want to be liked. I want to be believed.*

A smile that rang a bell deep inside the DCI, causing a wave of self-loathing to almost overwhelm him; smashing against everything that he preached in his professional life. But the battle was a vain one; gut instinct was ruling the day, and he knew that Tony Pickering, even before he had spoken a word, was lying.

The rest, for Jim Tyler, was merely going through the motions.

He asked Pickering to explain exactly what had taken place. What had Father William Peterson done to him five years ago?

He watched and listened as the young man went through his long-rehearsed tale. It was credible in presentation and detail. But it was lies.

Tyler could never have explained to another person how he could know with such assurance; he didn't understand it himself. His work depended on evidence, facts and proof, and he proclaimed that creed at every opportunity. Mills himself had been on the receiving end of those very sermons.

When the interview had been concluded, the two detectives stood out in the corridor for a few minutes before going to see the young man's father, Gerald Pickering.

"Thoughts?" asked Tyler, inwardly demanding more of the DS than he was expecting from himself.

"A very believable account," said Mills.

"It was," said Tyler. "But do *you* believe it?"

Mills thought carefully before answering. He knew only too well that Tyler was not a detective who tolerated his officers jumping to premature conclusions. Gut instinct was one thing, and it had its place, though it could only ever be a starting point.

"My instinct," said Mills, choosing his words carefully, "my gut instinct suggests ..."

"Yes?" prompted Tyler, impatiently.

"I'm really not sure, sir. It's not obvious to me that he's lying. But that doesn't mean that he's telling the truth, either."

"That's very helpful," said Tyler. "I hope you're not just playing it safe. I'm not testing you out, believe it or not."

"I think we should hear what Gerald Pickering has to say," said Mills.

Gerald Pickering was a man Jim Tyler had seen many times, though in different guises. He was a small man in stature, with piggish eyes that oozed aggression; he appeared to manifest every hallmark of the bully. Tyler found himself secretly reflecting that the man would have made a successful member of the senior ranks of the police force, and no doubt any large hierarchical organisation that quashed individuality and rebellion with militaristic discipline, for that matter. Tyler's dislike for Gerald Pickering was immediate, and in an instant he saw the cowering son doing the father's will.

He listened to what Gerald Pickering had to say. And when the man had finished ranting, Tyler asked him for his thoughts on the death of the priest.

The question appeared to wrong-foot Pickering. Taking a moment or two to steady himself, he said, "My alibi has been established already."

"That's not what I'm asking," said Tyler.

The piggish eyes blinked. "I'm not for a minute saying that I wanted him nailed to a cross for what he did to my son. Metaphorically, perhaps, but not literally. If you think I had anything to do with his death, then you are wrong."

"Do you have any theories on what might have led someone to kill Father Peterson?"

"Of course I do! He likely interfered with someone's son who was less law abiding than me! That type tends to keep doing their seedy, filthy business until they are caught. It's like a disease with them. So, for what it's worth, I reckon he picked on the wrong one and got his come-uppance."

There was a look of victory on Pickering's angry face. The truth here would never be proven; Tyler had little doubt of that. But he would stake a detective's pension that the alleged episode down here in Stroud had gone like this: the priest had been too honest about Tony Pickering's singing and ousted him from the choir. You didn't do that to the son of a man like Gerald Pickering, and a price had to be paid. Then, for the sake of appearances, his false 'pursuit of justice' had to be maintained - either that or his anger at Peterson rejecting his son had gone too deep to be let go of.

Was Gerald Pickering capable of digging so far into his well of anger as to arrange the death of the priest, and by crucifixion? He had the anger and the resources to accomplish the task, but five years on?

On balance, it seemed highly unlikely, though true psychopaths were always apt to surprise you.

"You contacted the priest recently," said Tyler. "What was your purpose in doing that?"

"I what?" said Pickering.

"Are you denying that you made contact with -"

"Yes! I am damn-well denying it! Who told you that?"

"Have you ever tried to make contact with Father Peterson since he left this area?"

"Absolutely not! Why would I? Look, are we finished? I do have other business to attend to."

Tyler looked at Mills, to query whether the DS had any further questions to ask. When the DS indicated not, Pickering said, "Peterson was not the man many thought he was. He was a clever trickster, who doubtless abused others, and probably on your own patch up there in Staffordshire, too. Whether that's what got him killed, who knows. That's your job to find out. But I'll tell you this for nothing: if you come back here trying to dig up dirt on me and my son again I'll make it a legal matter next time."

Tyler thanked the man for his time, allowing the sarcasm to ring loud and clear through the interview room before he began tracing the corridors back out towards the fresh air.

CHAPTER TWELVE

On the journey back to Staffordshire, Mills, taking his turn behind the wheel, asked the DCI if he intended pursuing the Stroud angle any further. For a while Tyler didn't respond. Then at last he said, "What galls me the most about this, Danny, is that Gerald Pickering may yet turn out to be right."

Mills turned to look at Tyler, holding the look for a few moments.

"That doesn't mean that I think he is right," said Tyler. "And by the way, you might want to keep your eyes on the road ahead. I may only be a middle-aged detective, but I'm not quite ready to die."

"Sorry, sir," said Mills.

"Whoever did that to Father Peterson planned it," said Tyler. "And whoever it was sustained their anger long enough to carry it through. This case doesn't add up to terrorism, or Satanism, but neither does it add up to the work of Gerald Pickering, though it might add up to somebody very much like him."

Tyler rubbed at his face with his hands and sighed wearily. "No, Danny, I'm not pursuing the Pickering angle further. We have no evidence whatsoever that Pickering's allegation has any substance. No-one else in Stroud came forward with allegations or backed up those made by Pickering. And no-one in Staffordshire has come forward with allegations against Father Peterson either. There's no motive for murder there, just too much macho pride and loss of face. But I'm still intrigued as to why Peterson thought Pickering had contacted him if in fact he did not."

Tyler fell into a prolonged silence as Mills plunged further into the darkness, heading north.

It was late when they arrived on Cedar Lane, and the place was buzzing with activity. It didn't take the detectives long to ascertain the reason for all the excitement.

A priest had been attacked on the outskirts of Hanley. Father Reece Mathews, from St John's church on Aslington Road. He'd been rehearsing and preparing for a baptism service with a young family. The family had left and the priest had been clearing up when a man appeared at the back of the church. The priest had asked the man if he could help him and had then been assaulted for his trouble.

Father Reece Mathews was taken to hospital with minor injuries and concussion. He had been conscious throughout his ordeal and he was able to give basic information to the police officers at the scene and later at the hospital. It was reported that the priest's knuckles appeared grazed and swollen; and there was blood on his shoes that may not have been his own.

"Looks to me like he gave as good as he was getting, or possibly even better," said Mills. "Some local druggie no doubt hoping to rob the collection plate, and thinking that all priests are pacifists."

"I doubt the media will see it like that," said Tyler, "given the current climate. If they're keeping him in overnight we'll let him get some rest and visit in the morning."

*

The following morning, and living up to expectations, the media was featuring the attack on Father Reece Mathews. It was also milking the conspiracy angles. Two serious attacks on members of the church; Satanists and terrorists were back in fashion again, at least on the streets of Stoke on Trent.

Already there had been calls coming in claiming responsibility for the fresh attack, all of which would require checking out.

Mills, contacting the hospital early, established that the priest was being kept under observation for another day, and the detectives set off for the City General Hospital, finding Mathews in a side ward. The priest was in his early fifties, with a mess of grey hair making him look much older. His face still bore marks from the attack of the previous evening, and his knuckles too, noticed Tyler. He reminded the DCI of someone, though he couldn't place him.

Mills introduced them and asked the priest how he was feeling.

"I'll be better when I get out of this place. I spend too much time here as it is doing my job."

"A dangerous occupation these days," said Mills, without thinking.

"Indeed," said the priest. "That wasn't what I was getting at though. Visiting the sick is a large part of my working week."

"Of course," said Mills, blushing slightly.

He asked the priest if he was up to answering a few questions, and Mathews gestured that he was. The DS noticed that Tyler had gone quiet and wore an expression that didn't bode well. Putting his observation to one side, he began questioning the victim.

Prompted by Mills' questioning, the priest went over the events of the previous evening, concluding that it was almost certainly an attempted robbery.

"It was very brave of you to fight off the robber," said Mills. "Most people in your position would have let him take a few quid. Was there much money kept in the church?"

The priest shook his head. "Not a great deal, no. But, still, it's money given by people who don't necessarily have a lot to start with. Perhaps I was a little foolhardy, but there it is."

"You have no idea who the person who attacked you could be?" asked Mills.

"I've not seen him before."

"Could you give a description?"

"It all happened so fast. I turned around and there he was. I acted on instinct. I didn't get chance to study my assailant, I'm afraid."

His tone was somewhat dismissive and curt, thought Mills. He looked again at DCI Tyler, who appeared to be chewing something over.

The detectives left the hospital. On the way out Mills said, "Are you alright, sir?"

"Any reason I shouldn't be?" asked Tyler.

"You seem a bit quiet, that's all."

"Possibly I have a lot on my mind: murder enquiries, that sort of thing."

"I'm sure you have a lot on your plate, sir."

Tyler looked at the DS, and appeared about to say something. But instead he fell silent.

They were almost at the car when Tyler said, "Does any of this strike you as odd, Danny?"

"How do you mean?"

"Someone comes into the church hoping to steal a few quid. He gets battered by the priest. All very heroic, and it might make a nice story in the press once they get their minds off devil-worshippers and religious fundamentalists."

Mills frowned. "What are you suggesting, sir?"

"Oh, I don't know. That Father Reece Mathews has the kind of face that someone might want to punch just for the hell of it?"

Mills appeared shocked. "Is something the matter, Jim?"

They had reached the car, and Tyler turned to face his colleague. "Yes, I think there might be. I promised that I would get myself some help. I haven't. But I'm going to. This can't go on. It isn't fair on you, the team, and quite possibly the likes of Father Reece Mathews. I see a face, I hear a voice ... one that reminds me ... and I lose all self-control. I keep making appointments and then cancelling them or else turning up and not saying anything. There's a space open this evening and I'm going to take it."

Mills smiled. "Good for you, Jim."

Later, as good as his word, Jim Tyler sat in a small room opposite the therapist who had already endured four sessions of near total silence and a dozen cancellations.

This time, sitting opposite the small, fragile-looking woman with the bottomless gaze and seemingly infinite stores of patience, he began to tell the story of what happened at St Saviour's all those years ago.

CHAPTER THIRTEEN

Ralph Elsmore, arrested for the assault on Father Reece Mathews, sat in the interview room facing the two detectives. Mills noted that the man looked angry, belligerent even, though not the least bit afraid. He was a plasterer by trade, and currently working for a local company. He had two young children and a common-law wife, and no previous history of assault.

"I intend to press charges," said Elsmore. "I want this taking all the way."

"Are you saying that you were attacked by Father Mathews?" asked Tyler. "That you walked into the church, minding your own business, and he leapt out at you?"

"You can take the piss. That's why people don't come forward."

"Perhaps you would care to tell me what happened," said Tyler.

Elsmore told his story, which started when he attended St John's church, aged twelve. He had become a regular. Until one time, following Sunday school, he had been waiting for his mum to pick him up as usual. He was the only child left behind that day, and the priest had sexually assaulted him.

Tyler leaned forward. "This is a serious allegation, Mr Elsmore," he said.

"It was a serious thing he did! He had hold of my genitals and he said I should come around to the rectory after school one afternoon. Dirty bastard! I was shit

92

scared. I stopped going to church and my mum gave me hell about it. I couldn't tell her what happened, she wouldn't have believed me. She would have skinned me alive for telling lies."

"So why now?" asked Tyler. "Why attack him now?"

Elsmore looked uncomfortable. The bluster had disappeared.

"Mr Elsmore?" prompted Tyler.

"It's difficult to explain."

"Try your best," said Tyler, trying to reign in the sarcasm.

"I'll be honest, then," said Elsmore. "It's with what happened to that other priest."

"What other priest?"

"You know - the one who was killed."

"You attacked Father Mathews because another priest was murdered? How does that work, exactly?"

It took Ralph Elsmore some considerable time and effort to frame his words; to get right the thing that he was trying to untangle. The upshot was that hearing about the murdered priest had acted like a trigger. He had wondered what could have made somebody do something like that, and then he remembered how he had felt after Mathews assaulted him at Sunday school all those years ago.

"I thought what happened to me was nothing compared with what's happened to some poor sods. The church is famous for it, and it covers it up. Everybody knows that. So I reckoned someone had paid him back, and it got me to thinking. I didn't think I'd have the guts to do anything, but that evening I was in the pub. I'd had a few pints and I couldn't get it out of my head. What he'd done. And that no-one would listen, not after all this time.

"I was walking home, close to the church, and I saw the door was open. And I thought to myself: I bet he isn't even there, it will be someone else. I went inside, like I was going back in time, and there he was. I couldn't believe it. And I just - I flipped and I went for him."

"Did you confront him about what he'd done to you?" asked Tyler.

"I wanted to, but in the end I said, 'You won't even remember me, you dirty bastard' - or something like that. Then I went for him, like I said."

"Are you intending to make a formal allegation against Father Mathews?"

"You just try and stop me. I bet dozens of people will come forward and make complaints of their own. It just takes one, and it's about time I got the ball rolling."

"That is your prerogative," said Tyler. "However, you still entered the church building and attacked him physically, causing actual injury."

"I did. Maybe I shouldn't have done, but I'm glad I did. If I hadn't have done that, I wouldn't be sitting here now telling you about the far worse things he did to me and God knows how many others. He wants locking away. I've stayed quiet too long."

"Mr Elsmore," said Tyler, "where were you on the evening of Saturday 8th November?"

"I was coming back from Spain," said Elsmore. "I haven't got a tan because it was pissing it down the entire week. Just my bloody luck!"

*

Tyler was busy typing out a report when Mills came into the office.

"It looks like Father Mathews has had a few allegations made against him over the years, sir."

"Interesting," said Tyler, continuing to type away furiously. "Anything recent?"

"It was all back in the 80s. Four incidents reported around the time Elsmore reckons he was assaulted. All the allegations were similar; and all the complainants were boys aged around twelve."

Tyler stopped what he was doing. "Were the allegations fully investigated?"

"Looks like a couple of them were, sir."

"Nothing substantiated?"

Mills shook his head. "One of the allegations was more serious. But nothing was proven and the cases were eventually closed."

"He hasn't a cat in hell's chance of proving anything now," said Tyler. "The vicar gets you alone, grabs hold of your balls and makes a dodgy invitation to come around to his place ... where's the evidence for something like that?"

"Elsmore still wants to make a noise about it," said Mills. "And I can't say I blame him."

"That's fair comment. If there's any justice to be had, and if what he reckons was done to him is true, he's not going to find that justice through the courts. Not a chance. Not for an unwitnessed assault that took place almost twenty years ago. Not unless the vicar confesses."

"There's more chance of Stoke City winning the treble, sir."

"Not an optimist, are you, Danny?"

"More a realist, I would say, sir."

"That's as maybe. But Ralph Elsmore still has a charge to answer. You don't just go blundering in, taking the law into your own hands."

"You certainly don't, sir."

CHAPTER FOURTEEN

Mills was lying in bed next to his wife, going back over his notes on the case, while Mrs Mills read a magazine and tucked into a box of peppermint creams. She looked over at her husband, watching him as he lay frowning into his notebook.

"Anything I can help you with?" she said.

"It's this case. It's doing my head in. You know what the media are saying, but it's bullshit."

"It generally is," she said. "That's why I stick to magazines."

It had worked for Mills in the past, running investigations past his wife. Telling someone else, someone outside the job, had the curious effect of clarifying things in his own mind. He was free to spell it out in simple terms, and at the same time able to try out the most unlikely hypothesis just to hear what it sounded like in a conversation. On a few occasions it had produced the most unexpected results.

"If we take out the theories about Satanists and terrorists," he said, "this is what we have left."

He paused a moment, thinking about something.

"Go on," she said.

"I'm probably wasting both our times."

"Well, with that attitude you'll never know, will you?"

"Okay. So ... Jim thinks there's some mileage in the idea of a revenge killing."

"Revenge for what?"

"Child abuse, most likely. He's got a bee in his bonnet about it. But that's another story. Anyway, the case down in Stroud. If there were others, other victims, and one of them -"

"But I thought that was years ago, Danny."

"It was. There could have been other incidents more recently, though. And even more serious assaults than the one alleged in Stroud. If the church covered this up, somebody might have their own ideas about justice."

Mills' wife gave the idea some thought, but didn't seem convinced. "I've seen stuff like that on TV," she said. "I mean, in detective dramas. But even then, I mean to say - *crucifixion?* What other theories have you got? I mean, to do something like that you've got to be seriously deranged."

"Well, we have got someone with mental health issues who fell out with the priest. And then there are a couple of other people who fell out -"

"Fell out! You don't nail someone to a cross and watch them die in agony because you *fell out* with them. Not unless -"

"You're *seriously deranged*?" said Mills. "We have a man who stopped attending the church because his wife died, and the priest failed to heal her."

"Is he ... 'seriously deranged'?"

"Look, if you're not going to be serious -"

"Grief can do strange things to a person, Danny. You shouldn't underestimate the effects of grief."

Mills thought for a moment. "He's an old man. He's quite frail. I don't see him doing anything like that, no matter how badly he was grieving."

"Is he rich?"

"How do you mean?"

"He could pay someone."

"Will you be serious," said Mills. "This isn't Saturday night at the movies. This is real life. This is my case!"

"Just a thought," said Mrs Mills, returning to her magazine.

"Sorry," he said.

"For what?"

"You're trying to help."

"You're the detective."

"Don't be like that. I didn't mean to sneep you."

"You didn't. I've got broader shoulders than that. I need to have."

"What's that supposed to mean?"

"Look, you're tired," she said. "Maybe things will be clearer after a good night's sleep."

He laughed. "Sleep! Chance would be a fine thing. I can't get any of this out of my head long enough. Sometimes I wish my head was plugged in at the mains, and I could switch it off at bed time."

"I reckon we could all do with that sometimes." She placed her magazine down on the bedside table and turned back to her husband. "Start off by putting that notebook away," she said. "And then move a bit closer. I'll give you something else to think about."

Danny Mills lay listening to the soft snores coming from his wife's side of the bed. The distraction from his labours had been a welcome one, and he could stand plenty more of it, given the opportunity.

He thought over his lot in life: a loving wife, two wonderful kids; a job he enjoyed and that took him back daily into the city he loved. He thought about Jim

Tyler, and hoped to God that Jim could find some peace of mind. He was by far the best officer he had ever worked with; less pre-occupied with unnecessary procedure and process, a man with a heart who had been badly hurt early on in life. And this wretched case was taking him back into that damaged past, and hardly bringing out the best in him. Mills had read somewhere that what didn't kill you made you stronger, and he was inclined to agree. Tyler would come through this, and shine even more brightly as a result.

Danny Mills started to drift into sleep when a memory came into focus, a recent one. Sitting in the living room of Graham Wilson's home in Trentham, wondering what it must be like to lose your wife, and finding yourself alone. Did having faith make it any easier? Knowing one day you would be back together? But Graham Wilson had left the church, apparently disillusioned when the healing service organised by Father Peterson had failed to deliver; had failed to save Marjorie's life. The prayers, the promises ... did that make it all the worse for the likes of Graham Wilson? That wasn't how it was supposed to work, surely to God!

The thoughts were spinning around in the mind of DS Mills, finding their rhythm as he gave thanks, in his own way, for the blessings that were his, and that he knew were beyond anything he had ever done to deserve them.

Sleep was coming down, blurring the edges, when he remembered, again, the phone call. *Mr Wilson's son.*

He muttered something, and his wife stirred. But a minute later they were both fast asleep.

*

Jim Tyler was once again putting on his running clothes. He had lain on his bed, tossing and turning, the case running riot through his head and leading nowhere. But still it was better than reliving the memories from the past; the dark dormitory, the visits to sombre rooms at school and in the orphanage, where men dressed in black gowns ruled the roost, brandishing sticks and unforgiving eyes.

His next appointment with the therapist was in two days, and it was like a stepping stone beyond his reach. Another opportunity, if he could take it, to cut out more of the cancer that had been eating him alive for decades.

He set off into the darkness, pounding the streets of Penkhull until, beneath the relentless rhythm of his feet, the borders blended and gave way, becoming the streets of Hartshill, Shelton, Basford, before bringing him, an hour later, wearily back to his home to stand beneath a scalding shower and beg for release.

CHAPTER FIFTEEN

It was late the following day when the DCI sat once again across the desk from the Chief Superintendent.

Berkins looked as tired as Tyler felt.

The DCI came straight to the point. "I'm not pursuing the Pickering case," he said. "Not because I have any better suggestions, I haven't. We've turned up nothing credible and we need another appeal to the public."

"I see," said Berkins, looking unsurprised. "Of course, we can organise that." He leaned forward. "Jim, you are no doubt aware that we've had a spate of attacks on clergy overnight and three more earlier today. The nature of the graffiti has changed somewhat. We appear to have lost the occult symbols in favour of references to sexual abuse by priests – and all painted large through the city for everyone to see."

"I'm well aware," said Tyler. "It might explain why people have stopped coming in claiming to be terrorists and devil worshippers. The new pastime is kicking the shit out of the vicar and proclaiming it was done in the name of historic abuse."

"Indeed," said Berkins, raising his eyebrows at the turn of phrase. "Anyway, the media are switching focus. They're dropping their obsession with terrorism and suchlike, at least for the time being. They want interviews about church cover-ups. The news tonight is going to be full of it, and not just locally. Stoke is going back on the map." He sighed. "And to think this place used to be world famous for its ceramic industry!"

Berkins sat back, watching the DCI carefully. "I want to ask you something," he said. "Not so long ago you were sitting here telling me that you were seeking help."

Tyler held up a hand. "I did say that. But are you suggesting that I'm not performing to the best of my abilities?"

"I'm not suggesting anything of the sort. If that was the case, we would be having a very different conversation. Be in no doubts about that. You're more edgy than I've seen you for a while, Jim. I know you were reluctant to accept counselling support, but you were acknowledging that you needed to address certain *personal issues*. I've supported you in your move here, and I have no regrets whatsoever in that regard. You are one of the best DCIs I've ever encountered, and that's straight off the bat." He smiled, warmly. "I want to support you in any way I can. I hope you understand that."

"That's appreciated," said Tyler.

Berkins twitched. The famous catchphrase was coming. The CS hadn't used it for a while, but here it was, in all its splendour.

"In a nutshell, Jim, if there's anything about this case that's troubling you ... I mean in the sense of causing you difficulties ... personally ... I mean to say ..."

Tyler had never seen the CS so tongue-tied. He tried not to smile.

"What I'm trying to say, Jim ... in a nutshell ..."

The nutshells were falling thick and fast, as though making up for lost time.

103

Tyler rescued the drowning man. "There's nothing I can't handle, Derek, though I appreciate your concern. I'm getting help. But as far as this case goes, without a break, someone coming forward, I don't know where to go next, and that's the truth of the matter."

"I admire your honesty. Like I say, I'll go public with an appeal. But my guess is that we'll get an avalanche of crusaders on a mission to bring down the church, so be warned."

Tyler shrugged. "The Satanists and terrorists have had their time in the sun. It's about time others had their turn."

Berkins blanched at the dark turn of phrase, and looked to be scrambling around to find one of his own.

"In a nutshell ..." he started, before abandoning the sentence, as though recognising that an old habit had resurfaced, if not quite sure what it was.

Mills was in the CID office when Tyler walked through.

"We'll be watching the CS again as we devour our evening meals," said Tyler.

"He's agreed to another appeal?"

"I'm fairly certain it was already planned. He just wanted to be certain we weren't already sitting on the solution."

"There have been more attacks, sir. Two reports just in."

"Anything serious?"

"Nothing life threatening, as far as we know. But still nasty enough if you happen to have been on the receiving end."

"I told Berkins that we're not pursuing the Pickering case. I think he was relieved to hear it. I get the feeling that some people around here think I have a personal agenda. Am I giving that impression?"

Mills cleared his throat unnecessarily.

"Well, if I did have an issue with the church, Danny, this would be the case for me. The thing is - I don't. And that's the truth. I have an issue with anyone who abuses their position of power and authority. I don't care whether that's a teacher, a politician, or some jumped up bureaucrat on our own beloved payroll. I don't like witch hunts, I don't like people who jump on bandwagons, and I don't like anyone who tries to exploit a situation for their own selfish ends."

Later that evening Mills and his wife watched CS Berkins' appeal on TV.

"No further forward, then?" she said after the appeal for information had been delivered and the brief Q and A session completed.

"Not a bloody inch," said Mills. "I think the clergy are going to have to start going around in plain clothes if these attacks continue. And they will continue, no doubt. The public love a new fashion to engage with, and priest-bashing is becoming all the rage."

His wife made a hot drink and Mills brought in the biscuit box. As he opened the store of supper treats his wife pulled a face at him.

"Don't you start," he said. "Just a couple, that's all."

"It's not only your brain that doesn't have an off switch, Danny," she said. "That stomach of yours is developing a mind of its own. And it's a yard ahead of you these days when you walk through the door."

105

"I lost two pounds last week."

"Is that like the guy who lost a pound and found a fiver?"

"What are you suggesting?"

"You're in denial, sweetheart. You're officially getting fatter. I still love you, but the scales don't lie and your pants are bursting at the seams."

"Only with love for you, my sweet."

He put the biscuit box down. "You're right, though. The diet starts … now."

She ran a hand over his cropped bristle-cut. "I'm thinking about your health, that's all. I don't want to be raising our kids on my own."

Mills kissed her.

She smiled. "Of course, there's the exercise issue, too."

"You're feeling ... energetic? Two nights in a row?"

She smacked his arm. "What I was thinking was you could ask Jim to start taking you on some of his marathons."

"Don't push it. I've not done cross country since I left school, and I've no intention of starting again now."

"He's still as keen as ever?"

"I've been getting reports, sightings of him out running all hours of the night. It's never right."

"You're worried about him?"

"I am a bit. I think this case has got to him a lot more than he's letting on. He reckons he's getting help, so we'll have to see. He's said that before."

"These things take time. He never talks to you about his problems?"

"I get glimpses here and there. He had a rough time growing up in that orphanage in Leicester. I think that's where most of it comes from. It was run by the church. His school was, too, I think. He wasn't happy there either."

"You think all that is affecting his judgement?"

"I'm not a psychologist. But what if he's become obsessed with, oh, I don't know - with an outcome that ..."

"Reflects his experiences?"

"Ignore me. I'm talking rubbish."

"Are you? I'm sure that things like that happen. They can happen to the best of us, if we're under too much pressure."

"He'd never admit to anything like that."

"Of course he wouldn't. He might not even recognise it in himself. That's what therapists and counsellors are there for. They help coax it out into the light, and then you can deal with it."

"You sound," said Mills, "like you know what you're talking about."

"Maybe I just read too many magazines."

"I'll invite him round for dinner, and you can set to work on him."

"I didn't think he did socialising."

"He doesn't, generally."

"Anyway, he needs professional help by the sound of it, not his mate's wife looking for a new hobby. What happened to that woman he was seeing?"

"Alison," said Mills.

"Headmistress at the school in Penkhull, wasn't she?"

"She probably still is. He saw her a few times. I don't know what happened. He never talks about it."

"What does he talk about, apart from police work?"

107

Mills' silent response seemed to echo around the room.

"He sounds like a sad, lonely man to me, Danny."

"I don't think he ever got over his divorce, back in London."

"Life has to go on. You have to get on with it or else - or else it kills you, eventually."

"You sound like you're talking from experience," said Mills.

"No, I've been lucky. I've been blessed, and I thank God every day for you and the kids."

She switched the TV off. "These attacks on the clergy are worrying, though," she said. "Maybe there's something in it. Maybe the priest was killed because of something he did, back in the past or even recently. Jim Tyler could be right, and this was revenge. I just hope he's not going to start joining in."

"How do you mean?"

"I mean attacking members of the clergy."

"Don't even joke about things like that."

"Sorry," she said, yawning. "Well, I think I'm done."

"I'll be up myself in a minute," said Mills. Then he caught his wife's grin. "What?" he said.

Her gaze fell on the biscuit box. "I'll have to start counting them."

After his wife had gone up to bed he lifted up the box of treats. "I thought you were my friend," he said. "And all this time you've been conspiring against me. Perhaps I loved you too much. We're going to have to cool it for a little while, let things calm down, and then we'll see where we go from there. It won't be easy for either of us, but it has to be done. I hope you can see that. I hope this isn't the end; we've shared some wonderful times together, some beautiful moments, my gorgeous bevy of beauties, my cheeky little band of digestives and bourbons and custard creams ... and we might still have a future ... one day ... we'll have to see."

He kissed the box and rattled the contents a final time, imagining a fake tear in his eye. "But now I have to see another. She lies waiting, and I cannot, I will not, let her down. She has made herself beautiful, and my passion must go where it is called. Goodnight, my sweet ones."

Mills climbed the stairs to the bathroom and attended to his ablutions. Sparkling now with new-found energy and zest he entered the bedroom to find his wife asleep beneath the subdued lighting.

He lay beside her, far from sleep, listening to the faint rumblings of an un-suppered belly. Reviewing the past days and recalling again the visit to Graham Wilson, and the phone-call from Mr Wilson's son.

CHAPTER SIXTEEN

Tyler went into the small room and closed the door. He sat down opposite the woman. He didn't try to make small talk. He didn't even try to smile at her. In every other encounter of this kind there had been a dance, of sorts; a ritual, of a kind. This was different. Everything stripped down to nothing.

Neither spoke or needed to. Tyler was under no pressure to say anything, or conform to anything. He caught her eye when he felt like it, and looked away when he felt like it. No prompt was given, the session not confined by the ticking fingers of a clock set for fifty minutes. An open session, a clear and full morning if necessary, with the option to stand up and walk out at any time, returning if the inclination was there. The police department could not be expected to pay for such luxuries. Tyler had paid, and he was there on his own time. If it didn't work out, he could book again and keep on booking until his pockets were empty and his boredom threshold finally breached.

Six minutes in he started to cry. The woman didn't try to stop him, and neither did she encourage him. Jim Tyler cried for twelve and a half minutes, intermittently, and then he spoke.

In the long minutes that followed, he detailed the worst things that happened to him, and how it had made him feel then and how it made him feel recalling it now. Twice he was sick, vomiting into the bags provided, wiping his eyes and blowing his nose on the tissues.

When he had finished, he stood up, silently, and went out to wash his face and use the toilet. Then he returned and sat down again. This time, he looked the woman straight in the eye, and he thanked her. Only then did she speak, asking him how he was feeling.

Tyler thought about the question, and then he repeated what he had said earlier, focusing on the worst of the worst, homing in on the horror like a surgeon taking the blade into the heart of the tumour. He was sick again, and he cried again, though less violently this time. Following another visit to the bathroom he again took his seat. "There's nothing left to come up," he said. "It's out now. It's done."

The woman asked him a series of questions, and he answered them, hiding nothing from her, or from himself. He didn't feel in the least exposed. He had not the least sense of shame, or fear, or anger. He knew that those feelings would return, as part of being alive. But they would no longer rule the roost or appear as abnormal extremes bent on shaking him loose. It was alright to feel anger, and okay to be afraid; and at times perfectly normal and right to burn those devils dressed in black, setting them alight in the fire of his imagination.

To nail them to the crosses I have made for them. Yes, even that.

He stood up finally and shook the woman by the hand, thanking her. She suggested that he had done it all himself, and that she deserved no thanks at all. She reminded him that she was there any time he needed her.

There was nothing more to say.

Jim Tyler left the room, left the building, convinced that he was ready to get on with living the rest of his life.

DS Mills parked up outside St Barnabas church. Marion Ecclestone had agreed to meet him before the mid-morning service.

He sat in the small office and shared a coffee with the curate, asking her how things were going in light of the current wave of attacks. "I haven't had any problems personally," she said. "But these are worrying times."

"Particularly given what happened to Father Peterson," said Mills. The curate's eyes widened. "Not that I'm suggesting that such a thing is likely to happen to anyone else, of course," he said quickly, before burning his mouth on an overly zealous slurp of coffee.

"Are you alright?" she asked, Mills' eyes watering, breathing hard to try to cool the fire in his mouth. "Can I get you a glass of water?"

"I'm okay," he spluttered. "But how are you coping without him?"

"The parish have been mucking in as best they can. We are managing, and the congregation have been helping out too. I suppose it's the trench mentality. When the chips are down, that old war-time spirit kicks in. People rally round."

"It's good to hear that," said Mills.

"Are you any closer to finding the person responsible?"

"I must admit, we're struggling a bit. You haven't thought of anyone else who might have reason?"

The curate shook her head. "The media appears to have changed its tune: revenge rather than devil worship or whatever." She looked questioningly at the DS.

"At the moment it's hard to know what's going on," said Mills.

"That's not very re-assuring," she said, finishing her coffee. "Though I do find your honesty most refreshing."

"That's my problem," he said. "I'm too honest."

"Can you be too honest?"

"You can in this line of work. Those at the top seem to think so, anyway. You're supposed to give the impression that you're on the brink of solving every case. The fact of the matter is that we're no further on than when we started." He eyed her for a moment. "I visited Mr Wilson."

"How is he?"

"He looks frail," said Mills. "It must have hit him hard, what happened to his wife."

"It did. I think he was looking for someone to blame. It's not uncommon. You blame God and then you start blaming his representatives. But Father William had broad shoulders. He wouldn't have given up on Mr Wilson, in fact he didn't. He absorbed some harsh words, but he still tried to contact him. He wanted to be there for him. He was such a compassionate, kind, loving man."

"Did you say that you met Mr Wilson's family?"

"I met his son. Jordan. He attended the healing service. He wasn't a regular here. I don't believe that he lived locally."

"Did you meet him after things took a turn for the worse?"

"I did, yes. I visited Graham at his home and his son was present. They were both angry, inconsolable. I didn't stay long. It was clear that I wasn't welcome. "

"Did Jordan Wilson speak to Father William?"

"I'm not aware that he did. He probably did, because William would have done everything he could to offer support. He never mentioned Jordan specifically." She looked at Mills questioningly. "You don't think ..?"

"I don't know what to think. Killing a priest because he couldn't save a loved one seems a bit far-fetched to me," said Mills, watching the curate closely.

She nodded. "I would agree. But to do what was done for *any* reason seems far-fetched. I mean, to torture and kill somebody like that ..."

The curate looked at her watch.

"I'd better let you get on," said Mills. "Your flock will be arriving."

As Mills walked out of the office and back through the church, he noticed the two church wardens. Gordon Foster, engaged in conversation with an elderly lady at the back of the church, didn't appear to have seen him; but Phyllis Wagstaff had clocked him and she was making her way over at some speed.

"Good morning, Inspector," she said. "How's your investigation going?"

"You've just promoted me," said Mills.

"I'm sure you deserve it. Have you had any joy yet, I mean, in catching the killer?"

"We're working on it."

"Were any of my suggestions helpful?"

The woman was digging, and Mills was careful not to feed her insatiable imagination. "We must all keep our eyes and ears open," he said, heading for the door.

Outside the church Mills looked across to the woods where the body had been found, casting his gaze to where someone, more than one person, had been waiting, with a cross already fashioned and ready. It could only have been done out of revenge, or from pure hatred. No other motive made any sense in a case like this, surely, he thought. And apart from Tony Pickering, no-one had accused the priest of abuse. That didn't necessarily mean that there wasn't someone out there with claims to having been abused by Father William Peterson, or acting on behalf of someone who had been.

Mills scratched at the back of his head, as though the action might funnel a thought into focus. He could see well enough why abuse would be a major theme to be explored in the investigation, with all the recent attacks on clergy – and even the nature of the graffiti had changed, moving in that direction.

And yet ...

He thought again of Mr Wilson. The phone call from Mr Wilson's son.

It was bugging him. He had to put his mind at rest.

Graham Wilson answered the door. "What do you want?" he asked. "I've already answered your questions."

A shadow appeared behind him. "Who is it, Dad?"

"You'd better come in," said Mr Wilson.

In the hallway Mills was confronted by a smartly dressed man, a younger version of Graham Wilson. He glared at Mills but didn't say anything.

The three men went through to the living room, where the son immediately opened fire. "Is this the one who came last time?" he asked. Graham Wilson nodded. "Why are you back again harassing my dad? He's already answered your questions. He's still grieving, for pity's sake. We all are."

Mills held out a hand to the man and offered his condolences. But Jordan Wilson refused to take the proffered hand of the detective, again demanding to know why his father was being 'harassed'.

"I'm making routine enquiries," said Mills.

But Jordan Wilson quickly cut in. "Routine? So, you call harassment *routine* now, do you?"

"We are investigating a serious crime."

"And - what - you think my dad had anything to do with it? That priest was a phony. He shouldn't have been in the job, making promises he couldn't keep; exploiting our hopes. We're angry, yes, we're fucking angry. But that doesn't mean we go around killing people!"

"Perhaps you could tell me where you were and who you were with on the evening of November 8th," said Mills.

"I don't believe this," said Jordan Wilson. "You seriously think ... you can go to fucking hell, that's what you can do. Don't you think my dad's been through enough without all of this crap? Look, I'm warning you: get out of my father's house before I say something I shouldn't."

"Like what, Mr Wilson?" asked Mills.

116

The man's fists were clenched, his eyes swollen crimson with thundering rage. "I said get out before I fucking well throw you out!"

CHAPTER SEVENTEEN

"It seems that I can't leave you alone for five minutes," said Tyler as the two men walked down to the interview room where Jordan Wilson was waiting. "He's made an official complaint against you."

He stopped walking and looked hard at DS Mills. "A second visit, Danny? For the purpose of asking a 'few more questions'? A bit thin, I have to say, though I don't imagine for a minute that the charge of harassment will be upheld, and neither should it be. You were acting in good faith. You never act otherwise."

"Thank you, sir."

"On the other hand, I don't see what you hoped to achieve."

"I was acting on a hunch, sir. That phone call from Wilson's son, when we visited."

"Translated, for the purpose of answering the complaint: 'I was wishing to clarify a couple of points, *sir*,'" said Tyler. "You wished to ask questions which 'might relate to other persons of interest and which cannot be divulged at this time'. Berkins, bless him, will be nothing but supportive. It's no secret that I'm generally not a fan of senior bureaucrats, but that man is truly one in a million. We can tidy this mess up and give the Chief one less headache to take his tablets for."

"I appreciate it," said Mills.

"I wouldn't have said that you had anything to go on. And no reason whatsoever to make that visit. But now I'm not so sure."

"Sir?"

"Earlier today I learned some valuable lessons about myself. About unhelpful 'defence mechanisms' that I have employed for far too long. It seems to me that Jordan Wilson has likewise shown a tendency to over-reaction. Does he have something to hide? Let's see if we can find out, shall we?"

Jordan Wilson was looking sharp in a mustard suit, and sitting next to his solicitor who was decked out in sober grey. The same belligerent attitude that had been apparent when Mills visited was back in spades.

Tyler began by offering his sincere condolences for the death of Jordan Wilson's mother, but Wilson didn't even acknowledge the DCI's words. Instead he launched into an angry tirade about the bullying tactics of a police force that needed to get its act together and catch real criminals instead of harassing law-abiding citizens.

When the tirade had finished, Tyler said, "So, thank you for coming in today. I want to ask you some questions about your whereabouts on the evening of Saturday, November 8th."

Wilson looked set to react again, and his solicitor urged calm. Then the solicitor asked Tyler if his client was being interviewed as a result of making a complaint against Detective Sergeant Mills.

"Your client is voluntarily answering questions as part of an investigation into the murder of Father William Peterson. He is free to leave at any time. No charges have been made against your client." Then, turning his attention to Jordan Wilson, Tyler said, "Mr Wilson?"

Wilson turned to his solicitor, who nodded.

"My father," said Wilson," was staying with me and my family at our home in Nottingham. On the evening you mentioned we went out for dinner."

"We?" asked Tyler. "Can you be more specific?"

"My father, my wife and our two children. We were booked in at 7pm and we left around 9pm."

Wilson gave the details of the restaurant.

Tyler asked Wilson what he did for a living. Wilson told him.

"You strike me as a man who is used to having people do a job exactly the way you want it doing," said Tyler.

"What's that supposed to mean? What are you trying to suggest?"

Tyler assumed an expression of innocence. "I'm not suggesting anything, Mr Wilson. What do you assume that I was suggesting?"

The solicitor twitched, but Wilson answered. "I have high standards, I don't deny that. You have to, when you run a business. Everything I do is above board, in case you're looking to dig up any dirt."

"There is enough dirt out there," said Tyler, "without me having to dig for it."

Jordan Wilson started to react, leaning forward, his fists tightening, when his solicitor again urged caution.

"I can see that you have a temper," said Tyler.

"Has my client answered all of your questions?" asked the solicitor.

"We're getting there, slowly. Are you afraid your client might *fly off the handle*?"

"What exactly are you trying to insinuate? Mr Wilson has been through an extremely difficult time. He is still suffering the trauma of losing his mother; the effect that has had on the rest of his family has been extremely detrimental, and the last thing that my client needs at a time like this -"

"I appreciate," said Tyler, "that it has not been an easy time for Mr Wilson. For the record, I am not accusing your client of anything. I have a job to do, and that job involves asking difficult questions. If I was not concerned with a murder investigation I might wish to delay asking those questions until a time better suited to your client. I'm afraid I do not have that luxury."

The interview was terminated without any relaxation of the bad vibes circulating the room.

While Berkins and Tyler discussed the complaint against Mills, the DS checked out Jordan Wilson's alibi. It proved to be solid. He was well known at the restaurant, a regular who frequently visited with his family. The party had all arrived together, at the time Wilson had suggested in the interview, and they had left together around two hours later. There was timed CCTV evidence of their collective arrival and departure.

Later that day, the detectives compared notes in the CID office. "Berkins played a blinder," said Tyler. "You have nothing to worry about." Mills didn't look convinced. "It doesn't change anything, does it?" said Tyler.

"No," said Mills, as though acknowledging a dirty secret.

"A hunch is a hunch, Danny. If you believe the man is guilty, then you can find a way to make it fit. But that's not your style. You're not a vindictive man, and you have no reason to go after Wilson. There's no agenda, and they haven't a hope of making a harassment charge stick."

"Thank you, sir."

"But now I'm intrigued. Paying others to do your dirty work is one of the oldest stories in the book, and one of the most difficult to prove. Unless someone leaves a loose end and the whole thing unravels. Wilson has motive and means, and he's a very rich and a very angry man."

Tyler stopped talking and appeared to be thinking deeply.

"My hunch, for what it's worth: they'll prefer to leave it hanging over our heads as a kind of security rather than go ahead and blaze a trail that risks drawing the wrong kind of attention. Wilson's something of a hothead at the best of times, I suspect, and this is hardly the best of times for him or his family. But his solicitor knows his business. When the lady protests too much, as Shakespeare once suggested, we smell a rat. On the other hand, if we continue with this line of enquiry, they will use every means available to them."

"I wonder," said Mills, "if there could be someone else who blamed the priest for the death of a loved one."

Tyler laughed. "So now you want to keep the template and fit it with a different face? If nothing else, this needs putting to bed. Let's pop round to the church. That curate seems to practically live there."

"... Of course," said Marion Ecclestone, as she sat in the church office with the two detectives, "over the years quite a few congregants have died. We have an older population here, on the whole. Most churches do, apart from some of the more evangelical ones, perhaps. I think the youngsters prefer the music provided at the more charismatic venues. But here at St Barnabas I've seen a lot of bitterness. When somebody dies, many people feel the need to find someone or something to blame.

"I will be honest with you, Inspector. I don't believe I've seen such anger turned towards the church as I witnessed from Mr Wilson and his son, and particularly from the son. They took poor Marjorie's death so hard. She suffered so terribly towards the end. Father William I'm sure tried his best to offer what comfort he could. His compassion was astounding; a remarkable man. Whatever was thrown at him in the course of his duties, he didn't flinch; he never took anything personally."

The curate looked curiously at Tyler, as though the shape of the DCI's questions had suddenly been revealed. "They were angry, as grieving people often are - but no, not like that. They were hurting, yes, terribly - but no, not in a million years."

"You sound very certain," said Tyler.

"Grief can do strange things to people, we're agreed on that. I can only speak as I find." She looked shaken. "No," she repeated. "*No*."

*

123

The detectives left the church. The day was overcast and rain was threatening from the west. The two men looked over instinctively towards the woods where Father Peterson's body had been found nailed to the cross. Though neither spoke, the thoughts of the two officers flashed respectively through their minds: theories, suspicions, hunches and dead ends.

They were heading towards the unmarked police car. In the days that followed they would come to remember that moment. Everything was about to change. All their thoughts on the case about to be blown sky high; all lines of enquiry up to that point about to seem redundant, desperate and strained. A dark light was waiting to explode, ushering in a bolder, stranger, and more deadly reality.

Mills saw the phone flashing on the dashboard, and he quickly opened the car door. Tyler stood behind him, listening as an unfolding truth began to make its presence known.

CHAPTER EIGHTEEN

The woman had been found nailed to the church door. The doctor at the scene told Tyler that the woman had been dead for a few hours at least, though he was unable at that point to be more specific.

St Bartholomew's church in Baddeley Green, a few miles from the centre of Hanley, had seen its congregation dwindle in recent years. That fact was hardly unique; it was becoming something of a trend for the church in general throughout the UK. St Bartholomew's was rarely used at all during the week, and did not have its own priest. It shared Father Malcolm Reed with five other churches in the parish.

The church was situated a little way back from the main road. The doors to which the woman had been nailed faced out on a wooded area, and were not visible from the thoroughfare that ran past towards Leek Road. Father Reed had been popping by to retrieve some notes that he had left there at the weekend, when he made the discovery.

Tyler approached the shaken priest, and asked if he recognised the woman. He said that he did not. "Should I recognise her?" he asked.

"Not a congregant?" asked Tyler.

"I've never seen her before."

He asked the priest when he had last been to the church, and if anyone else had access to the building.

"I was here a couple of days ago," he said. "A few other people do have keys." He gave the names of the church warden, the verger and the organist. "I'm aware, of course," he said, "that there have been a number of attacks on members of the clergy recently, including the tragic murder of Father William."

"Did you know him?" asked Tyler.

"We met a few times over the years. I didn't know him well."

"How did you find him? Was he well liked?"

"As far as I know he was liked. He struck me as a caring, devoted minister. As in most professions, there is a grapevine, and not all priests are particularly well thought of. Personally, I never heard anyone speak of him in anything other than glowing terms. Are you any closer to finding the culprit?"

The word jarred, causing Tyler to conjure images of teenage boys stealing apples from a church orchard. It didn't seem anywhere near adequate in describing some sadistic fiend capable of nailing living flesh to a cross of wood, and watching a man die in agony.

"Do you think this latest killing is somehow related?" asked the priest.

"It's too early to make any assumptions," said Tyler.

"I noticed that the poor woman has some interesting adornments."

Tyler had noticed them too, and wondered about them. He asked the priest if he was familiar with the items that the woman wore on her clothing and around her neck.

"They clearly denote an interest in the occult," he said. "I'm no expert, but the symbolism she has chosen is hardly obscure. There have been a lot of desecrations of Christian sites lately, I'm sure that you're aware of that. I suppose I'm trying to be an amateur detective, and I ought to leave it to the professionals."

"Not at all," said Tyler. "Any theories will be gratefully and carefully considered."

"Well," said the priest, "the symbols suggest an interest in Satanism."

"Interesting," said Tyler.

"I suppose the media will have another field day. I've read some of the previous speculation; about satanic conspiracies and the like. The trouble with this kind of thing is that it can so quickly catch fire. Before you know it ..."

The priest waved his hand. "I'm sorry, I ought to let you get on with your own investigation and stop interfering."

DS Mills came over and took details of the other people who had access to the building, while Tyler approached the scene of crime officers already working the scene. He wanted to know if the person responsible for the death of this woman had also murdered Father Peterson. The response was non-committal: as soon as that could be established he would be the first to know.

Later that day a call was received by the duty officer at Cedar Lane from a woman named Faye Winkelman. She was concerned that her friend, Jane Hopkins, was missing, and aware that a woman had been found murdered in Baddeley Green. Her friend, she said, lived close to that area. Faye Winkelman had then given a description of her friend, and it was later confirmed that the dead woman was indeed Jane Hopkins.

When officers asked Winkelman when she had last seen her friend alive, she said that it had been at a recent meeting that she had attended on Saturday, 8th November, at a farm outside Leek belonging to Charles and Rose Blackwood.

"A dead priest and now a dead Satanist," said a rather sombre looking CS Berkins.

"You're not suggesting that war has broken out between the factions?" said Tyler.

Berkins looked at the DCI but didn't respond. It was a look suggesting that jokes in bad taste were not helpful and far from welcome, regardless of rank.

"We're rounding up members of the cult," said Tyler. "We had them down as a harmless group of somewhat peculiar hobbyists who watched too many horror films. We're also waiting for forensics to confirm that the same person, or persons, killed Jane Hopkins and Father Peterson."

"On what grounds are you basing your assumption?"

"Very similar modes of execution, primarily. On the other hand, given that Hopkins was a self-proclaimed Satanist, possibly someone in the Christian community killed her as a revenge attack for what was done to the priest."

Berkins looked at Tyler as though scanning for evidence of sarcasm.

"Then again," said Tyler, "she might have been killed by another member of the cult, for some other reason. We'll see what forensics say. I can't give you anything concrete just yet."

Berkins eyes narrowed as he leaned forward in his chair. "What is it, Jim?"

"I'm not sure," said Tyler. "But there's something bubbling just below the surface. I can't quite see it yet."

"You think Jane Hopkins was silenced by another cult member?"

"It's a possibility."

Berkins was about to say something when his phone rang. He picked up the receiver and listened, looking at Tyler as he did so. When the call ended, he said, "Well, it seems that at least part of your hunch was bang on the button."

"Forensics by any chance?"

Berkins nodded. "We're looking for the same killer."

CHAPTER NINETEEN

At the end of a long day Tyler and Mills sat together in the CID office going over their notes. They had interviewed James Grocott, Evie Ryles, Faye Winkleman, Toby Smee, Patty Gide, Al Cooke, Ian Curtes, and re-interviewed Clayton Shaw, and Charles and Rose Blackwood. All members of the *Chapter Six* cult.

"Notable lack of pithy arrogance from Charles and Rose Blackwood," said Tyler. "Less chirpy when it comes to the death of one of their own."

Mills nodded silently. Even Clayton Shaw had seemed more subdued this time around. But no-one had been able to suggest any clues at all as to why somebody would wish to nail Jane Hopkins to a church door, let alone who had actually done it.

Hopkins had been thirty two years old, and she had lived alone in a large detached property in Stockton Brook, just a few miles from where she had been killed. Her parents had died a few years previously, and as an only child she had found herself the sole inheritor of the property, along with the considerable savings that her parents had accumulated. They had both been academics, sociologists, and their only daughter had followed suit. They were senior lecturers at universities in the West Midlands, while their daughter taught Social Sciences at a local college. Her parents had died in a boating accident in France during the summer four years earlier.

Jane Hopkins wasn't known to have any friends to speak of, keeping herself very much to herself. Even Faye Winkelman appeared to have used the term rather loosely; 'acquaintance' might have been more accurate, according to Winkelman, when pressed on the matter during the course of her interview. It wasn't known that Hopkins had been in a relationship recently, or that she had ever had a serious relationship.

"She was an intense and very private young woman," Charles Blackwood had told the detectives. She had joined the cult three years ago and appeared committed.

Tyler couldn't help wondering about the timing of that. "Her parents died in an accident, and a year later she joins a Satanist cult," he said, addressing Blackwood. "What was her motivation for joining your group?"

"She was clearly fascinated by the occult. Satanism was of particular interest to Jane, though, as I have said before, our group is not exclusively made up of members comfortable with that designation."

"Apologies," sighed Tyler, without conviction. "Do go on, please."

"Jane had a deep academic interest in such matters, specifically Satanism, and she was extremely well read."

"But she wouldn't have needed to join your cult in order to study the subject in a purely academic sense?"

"No, she would not. Jane wanted to explore *ritual* in its fullest sense. That requires numbers of people. There is a deeply practical aspect to any study of the occult that requires membership of a suitable group of likeminded individuals. Of course, other groups may

131

have catered for her specific interests more generously. Perhaps she was a member of a Satanist group also. If so, she never divulged. I suspect that she was drawn to *Chapter Six* at least in part as a social activity."

"Even though she was something of a loner?" said Tyler.

"That is also true. But, you see, she understood the necessity of self-discipline. It may well have been a challenge to her, having to share time and space with people who she wouldn't usually choose for company."

"The likes of Clayton Shaw?" said Tyler.

"Our group was, and still is, extraordinarily diverse. That is part of its strength. I think that Jane would have easily recognised that the strengths of membership in a group such as ours would outweigh the challenges and inevitable frustrations."

"Did Jane ever speak about her parents, about their deaths?"

"Not at length. I knew a little."

"Were her parents Satanists?"

"On the contrary - they had been practising Christians."

Tyler's eyes lit and he glanced towards DS Mills, who was now leaning forward with interest.

"Had Jane been a Christian?"

"I believe so," said Blackwood.

"Was her 'conversion' somewhat sudden, do you know?"

Blackwood grinned. "If you mean: did Jane reject Christianity because of the deaths of her Christian parents - I would have to say no, not at all."

"You seem sure of that," said Tyler. "After all, a year after her parents died suddenly, she joined a cult, declaring an interest in Satanism."

"I didn't know Jane until she came to us, so of course I can only go on what she has told me. But it seemed evident that she became disillusioned with the Christian faith a long time before her parents died. I would suggest that she had been searching for a group like ours for a long time, and if the death of her parents was at all significant it was in the sense of liberating her. What I mean to say," said Blackwood, "is that Jane was a very sensitive person. She doubtless recognised that her Christian parents might have been hurt to discover that their daughter was worshipping Satan."

Rose Blackwood offered a similar picture of Jane Hopkins to the one her husband had provided, and was equally dismissive of Tyler's suggestion that grief had led her to join the cult.

"We are somewhat particular in who we accept within our group, Inspector. Sometimes people come to us when they are really searching for something else entirely. Should someone come to us because, for example, they are grieving the loss of a loved one, in whatever form that grief is taking, we would be cautious in the extreme. One might of course say the same about the church taking on a candidate for ordination. A grieving soul looking for comfort may not be suitable material for the priesthood, and I would expect any organisation of substance to share our caution. But none of that is relevant in the case of Jane Hopkins. She was deeply keen to explore aspects of the occult, including Satanism, in practical, ritualistic terms as well as academically."

James Grocott, Evie Ryles, Patty Gide, Ian Curtes and Al Cooke offered little that the Blackwoods hadn't already provided. It struck the detectives what a diverse group they were. A financier, a singer with a funk band, a supermarket checkout assistant, a double-glazing salesman and a swimming instructor; some of them married, most of them not; ages ranging from mid-twenties to late fifties, and two of them parents.

Clayton Shaw, who appeared to have been the only one of the group interested in desecrating Church buildings, was somewhat sheepish this time around. He offered nothing that further illuminated the life of Jane Hopkins, but at the same time it didn't seem apparent to the detectives that he was hiding anything either.

"Which brings us to Toby Smee and Faye Winkelman," said Tyler, drumming his fingers on the desk as he looked again at the notes in front of him. "One of their own has been killed, murdered in a sadistic fashion, and everyone is scared. That's natural enough, unless of course they all conspired to kill her. Frankly I doubt that. On the other hand, they may be wondering who's next."

Mills' eyes widened at the suggestion. "Thinking that the killer plans to pick them off one at a time?"

"Just a thought," said Tyler. "Smee and Winkelman, though ... those two know something."

"There could be a conspiracy of silence," said Mills. "I'm not certain I trust any of them."

"That's because, like me, you had a good Christian upbringing."

The darkness in Tyler's tone brought DS Mills up sharp. "We didn't do church in our house, sir."

"It's about all we did do in mine," replied Tyler. "But that's another story, and it needn't concern us today. You don't think that there was something less, should we say, *forthcoming* about Toby Smee and Ms Winkelman, then?"

"I think they seemed frightened."

"More so than the others?"

"I would say so, yes. Apart from Clayton Shaw."

"But not holding back, particularly?"

"Hard to tell, sir."

Tyler's thoughts drifted around his impressions of Smee and Winkelman: Smee, a short, stocky man of twenty six; Winkelman, an oddly attractive, distinct-looking woman only slightly older. Smee had blazing blue eyes, and an affable nature; a clerk working for a team of solicitors in Leek. Winkelman, with blue-tinted black hair, was a curious hybrid of new-age hippy and professional business-woman, and ran her own small business selling occult paraphernalia in a moorland village. Both were articulate, and both seemed afraid.

"And they're both," muttered Tyler, as though inadvertently voicing the thoughts in his head, "holding something back."

The detectives were about to wrap it up for the night when Tyler took a phone call.

His expression quickly became animated, and after a few moments he nodded to Mills.

"We can come straight away," he said, ending the call.

CHAPTER TWENTY

Mills drove. The sleet was coming down hard, announcing for the still unconvinced that winter was now official. The road out towards Leek passed close to Baddeley Green, where the body of Jane Hopkins had been found nailed to the door of St Bartholomew's church. Faye Winkelman lived out beyond Leek, and Mills reminded the DCI that the weather was usually a good deal worse in the Staffordshire Moorlands.

"Are you suggesting that we postpone our visit until the spring, Danny?"

"Forewarned is forearmed, sir. That's what my mother used to say, God rest her soul. Faye Winkelman said it was urgent, then?"

"Not life threatening. She didn't say very much, but I got the idea that it couldn't wait. Besides, I was intrigued. I think she's been wrestling with something. She wanted to talk earlier but couldn't for some reason. Maybe she's been talking it over with someone."

Mills drove on, the wipers struggling now to cope with the sudden deluge. "I said it gets worse the farther out you are from the city, sir."

"Yes, you did, didn't you? And the necks get redder and the eyes further apart and the knuckles start to drag along the pavements."

Approaching Leek town centre Mills took a rabbit-run through a maze of side streets, emerging onto Ashbourne Road before heading for the small settlement of Onecote where Winkelman lived.

"Animal and child sacrifice country, eh, Danny?"

"I'm not sure they always go that far, sir. I did once spend an evening in one of the villages close to the Derbyshire border. I don't like to talk about that, though, sir."

Tyler grinned. "You still can't convince your wife to move back to the Beloved City?"

"Not in this lifetime. Her childhood dream has come true."

"It wasn't to marry a man like you?"

"You can't win 'em all, sir."

They turned left at the crossroads and pulled up outside a small row of terraced cottages. Mills caught the movement in the downstairs curtains, a face peering out. A moment later the front door opened and Faye Winkelman ushered the detectives into her home.

The front room, at least, was not as Mills had expected. He had assumed that every room would be adorned with occult reference; esoteric symbolism painted straight onto walls, bookcases stuffed with satanic baloney and witchcraft manuals.

The front room comprised of two sofas, a footstool and a small bookcase peppered with a few items of the arcane. Most of the books reflected a general academic interest in philosophy, religion, psychology and science.

The detectives commandeered one of the sofas, and Winkelman sat opposite them. She appeared fraught, far more so than she had done earlier in the day, down at the police station. Mills sensed that what she was about to say was coming at a considerable cost, one way or another, and he tried to ease the tense

137

atmosphere by small-talking about the weather conditions in the moorlands.

Winkelman didn't appear in the mood to engage. Even before he had finished his summary of climactic variance in Staffordshire, she said, "Things have got heavy lately."

The detectives waited for her to say more. She seemed to be still weighing something up.

Was she referring to the death of a cult member, wondered Mills, or about her life in general? "Take your time," he said at last.

"I'm leaving the group," she said.

Again the detectives waited, and again Winkelman paused. And then it all poured out in a rush - how she had been disillusioned with membership of the cult for some time and was no longer sure that the group was right for her.

Mills tried to tease out what was troubling her. It seemed that she was unhappy with the behaviour of some of the other members.

"Can I ask who you are referring to?" asked Tyler.

"Well, it's no secret to you what at least *one* of the members has been up to," she said.

"Clayton Shaw?" said Mills.

"He deserves everything he gets. I didn't sign up to be part of a gang of vandals going around daubing graffiti everywhere."

"You don't get on with Mr Shaw?"

"The man's an idiot. He hasn't the first clue what the membership is about. But until a replacement is available they don't wish to compromise the numbers."

"They?" said Tyler. "You are referring to Charles and Rose Blackwood, I take it?"

138

She nodded. "I think they find Shaw an embarrassment. They ought to."

"Do you think," said Mills, "that Clayton Shaw might be responsible -"

"For killing Jane - or the priest? I shouldn't think so. Graffiti's more his level. He enjoys being a part of something subversive, but he's not really hardcore. I can't see him being violent. I think he wants to belong; needs a surrogate family. He likes being around women with a common cause, as he sees it. He can be a bit creepy at times, but he's hardly a killer as far as I can see."

Tyler said, "Miss Winkelman, I'm sure that you didn't invite us out here so that you could rehearse your resignation speech to Charles and Rose Blackwood. What are you frightened of?"

She swallowed hard, her eyes moving between the two detectives.

"Do you fear that you might be next?" asked Tyler. "That whoever killed Jane might be planning to work their way around the membership?"

She shook her head. "I would have left the group anyway. If anything, all of this has delayed my departure. What I mean is, I want to be seen to be leaving for the right reasons, and not because I am fearful for my own safety. But there is something that's worrying me, and that's why I wanted to talk to you."

"Then please go ahead," said Tyler.

"I was talking to Toby earlier," she said.

"Toby Smee?"

"I'm a little closer to Toby than I am to the others. I believe he shares some of my disillusionment."

She broke off. "I'll stop beating around the bush. After we left the police station Toby and I got talking, you know, about everything that has been happening lately, and particularly in the light of what happened to Jane. I'm not sure that I would have thought of it myself, but for some reason Toby mentioned someone." She took a deep breath. "It was someone who joined the group a short time ago."

"Go on," said Tyler.

"I didn't like the guy from the start. He only came to a few meetings and to be honest I was glad to see the back of him. If you think Clayton Shaw's weird and creepy ... but anyway. He criticised everyone and everything. It was clear to me that he wanted to take over, and have things done his way. He was so intense it was scary just being in the same room. Then he stopped coming, but even then I was worried that he might come back."

"What's his name?" asked Mills.

"Luke Summers."

"How recent was this?" asked Mills.

"We usually meet fortnightly. He didn't come to the last meeting, but he attended the two previous to that."

"So he may turn up again?" said Tyler.

"Well, I suppose ..."

"It's just that you seemed to suggest that he won't attend again. Has someone said as much?"

"Actually ... Toby told me. I assumed Charles and Rose spoke to him and told him Summers wasn't welcome."

"And you've not seen him since?" asked Mills.

"No."

"Has anyone mentioned him?"

"No, apart from Toby. Perhaps they're all as relieved as I was that he had moved on."

"Do you know where he was living at the time?" asked Mills.

"I know very little about him. He was very private, secretive. One thing I do remember, though."

"What's that?" asked Mills.

"When his name came up in the conversation ..."

"Yes?"

"It was like Toby had seen him, or had contact - though he didn't elaborate. It got me thinking."

"What exactly is on your mind, Miss Winkelman?" asked Tyler.

"Toby's more frightened than he's letting on," she said. "Something's bothering him. I think you need to talk to him."

"Do you have any idea where we would find Mr Smee at this hour?" said Tyler, checking his watch.

"He should be here any time now," said Winkelman.

CHAPTER TWENTY ONE

Faye Winkelman made drinks, and a few minutes later a car pulled up outside the property. Tyler asked her if Smee was aware that police detectives would be at her home waiting to speak to him, and she said not.

"How do you think he will react?"

"Toby trusts me. He knows I would never do anything to hurt him."

"You don't think he might be angry?"

"Why would he?" she said. Then her expression changed, and it appeared to the detectives that at last the penny had dropped. "You think he'll feel he has been tricked, lured into a trap?"

"He might see it like that," said Tyler.

"Toby has nothing to hide, as far as I know. He'll understand. He'll know I'm only doing this because I don't want him to come to any harm."

She answered the knock at the door, and was in the process of planting a kiss on Toby Smee's lips when he caught sight of the two plain-clothed officers sitting in his girlfriend's front parlour.

His shock was entirely understandable, thought Mills, beginning to feel like he was part of a reality TV show himself. He watched Smee enter the room, looking back at Winkelman as he did so.

"What's going on, Faye?"

"Sit down, Toby," she said.

Smee didn't look ready to sit down. "I don't understand. Has something else happened?"

142

Tyler explained the situation, but Smee was looking at Winkelman, as though for corroboration, or else for a translation into a language he could get his head around.

"I'm worried," she said.

Smee placed his arms around her. "About what happened to Jane? What - you think you're next?"

"I don't know. When we were talking, earlier ..."

"I don't understand."

"You mentioned Luke Summers."

"You think he's something to do with this?"

"You've had no contact with Mr Summers since he left the group?" said Tyler, cutting in.

"None at all," said Smee.

"Can I ask how his name came up, Mr Smee?"

Smee looked at Winkelman, as though trying to work something out. "I don't know," he said. "We were just talking - talking about the group, about what happened to Jane. About what kind of maniac would do something like that. I suppose we recalled that guy coming."

"And?" said Tyler.

"Well, nothing, really. It's a bit of a leap to say that someone who came to two meetings would start killing us off, if that's what you're thinking." Again, he looked at Winkelman.

"So why bring him up at all?" asked Tyler.

Smee looked back to the detectives.

"If you know anything, Mr Smee, I suggest that you tell us, and tell us now."

"I don't know anything about him."

"Are you afraid of him?" asked Tyler.

*

The sleet had stopped falling as Mills pulled up outside the home of Charles and Rose Blackwood. Tyler thumped on the front door, and after a couple of minutes a light appeared in the porch.

Charles Blackwood looked unimpressed. "I take it this isn't a routine visit?" he said. "It's gone midnight."

"Can we come in?" asked Tyler.

Rose Blackwood was waiting in the hallway as the detectives entered the property.

"Sorry for the lateness of the hour," said Tyler. "But this is a murder investigation, and needs must."

The detectives were led through to the lounge area.

"So, how can we help you *now?*" said Charles.

"I want to know about Luke Summers," said Tyler.

Charles and Rose Blackwood appeared to blink in unison.

"Anything that you can tell us about Summers would be appreciated," prompted Tyler. "We know that he was a member of your group."

"Briefly, yes," said Rose, and Charles nodded in agreement. Then he left the room, returning with a laptop computer. "Let me consult the oracle," he said.

"Have you had any contact since he last attended one of your fortnightly meetings?" asked Tyler.

"None," said Charles.

Rose, as though sensing that they were off the hook regarding whatever business the detectives were concerned with, offered to make drinks. Tyler declined.

Charles had found what he was looking for.

"Luke Summers attended two meetings." He gave the dates.

"What can you tell us about him?" asked Tyler.

Charles Blackwood continued to consult the oracle for a few minutes. "We have very little information on Mr Summers. He asked to join us and he appeared to share our interests. I recall him as being a somewhat disruptive individual."

"In what ways disruptive?"

"In every way," laughed Charles. "Nothing was ever as he would have liked. I couldn't help but wonder why he didn't set up his own group. He wanted to take over, that was obvious enough."

Rose concurred. "I recall a rather disturbed young man, actually," she said. "I think he would quickly have alienated the rest of the group, which then likely wouldn't have survived."

"Wouldn't have *survived*?" said Tyler. "An interesting word, in the circumstances."

A pause followed, and everyone present appeared to wait for someone else to make the next move.

At last Rose Blackwood broke the deadlock. "I didn't mean literally 'survive', Inspector," she said. "Are you suggesting ..."

"Suggesting what?" asked Tyler.

"Are you suggesting that this man was responsible for killing poor Jane?"

"We are just making enquiries at this stage," said Tyler. "Do you have any contact details for Luke Summers?"

Charles shook his head. "Unusually, no. But then everything about that man was unusual."

"Do you have any background information at all?" asked Tyler, impatiently.

145

"I'm afraid not. I'm sorry that I can't help. Summers was not suitable for our group, and it was with some relief to us all, I believe, when he stopped attending."

"You didn't tell him that he wasn't welcome, then?"

"I would have done, in the interests of the group. But in the end it wasn't necessary. He clearly decided that we weren't right for him."

"He told you so?"

"He did indeed."

"One thing I do recall," said Rose, and all eyes were suddenly on her. "It was before the start of one of our meetings. Summers was talking to Toby Smee, and I recall Toby saying something that made us all laugh. We'd speculated about where the devil would be raised if he became incarnate as a child. Toby said - I can remember it so well - he said it would have to have been in his old orphanage."

Mills could see the expression on Jim Tyler's face from the corner of his eye. With an effort of will he kept his eyes on Rose Blackwood.

"Smee was raised in an orphanage?" Tyler asked her.

"Care home or orphanage, something like that. Anyway, he hated the place. 'Religion forced down your throat night and day'; that was how he put it. He joked that it was enough to make an angel fall from grace."

Rose Blackwood appeared lost in memory. "We all laughed at that," she said. "But Summers didn't laugh. It was the look on his face. I've never seen anything like it." She patted at her heart. "I'm not easily rattled, but it still gives me the shivers thinking about it now."

146

CHAPTER TWENTY TWO

The graffiti through the city had gravitated wholeheartedly to the corruption of the clergy, and the cover-ups perpetuated by the church. The focus was on child sexual abuse and the media were running full speed ahead with it.

Tyler was at his desk when Mills walked in, throwing down a saturated jacket. "Here comes the afternoon shift," said the DCI. "My powers of deduction tell me it's wet out there."

"Cats and dogs," said Mills, "or as we say round here: pissing it down. Is Berkins playing ball?"

"I've told you. Berkins always plays ball. He thinks I've started messing with a Ouija board to get answers though."

"This would be the case, sir."

"Whether it's down to the conjunction of the stars or not, I've had a surprisingly successful morning."

"You've found Luke Summers?"

"I went to see Toby Smee."

"Couldn't you sleep?"

"I never sleep. I work around the clock and you should know that by now."

"I'll make a note of it, sir."

"I caught him as he was leaving for work. I asked him which orphanage he met Luke Summers in. It was like pulling teeth, but we got there in the end. There's a story to tell but I haven't had a hot drink yet this morning and so my storytelling powers are not at full tilt. I don't know what this operation is coming to."

"We can soon remedy that, sir."

Mills made a hot drink and placed it down in front of the DCI. Then he took a seat. "I'm all ears, sir."

"That's merely an illusion caused by having your hair cut to within an inch of its life. I digress." Tyler took a sip, savouring the tea in exaggerated fashion, and nodding approvingly. "You are coming along nicely, DS Mills. This is the stuff of promotions."

"All in a day's work," said Mills.

"It wasn't an orphanage, as it turns out," said Tyler, "it was a care home in Blythe Bridge. Smee had been there for a couple of years, and he was fourteen or so when Summers was admitted. He was the younger by a couple of years, and according to Smee he was a strange one even back then."

"He befriended Smee?" asked Mills.

"Not really. And before you leap to any further conclusions, let me put your mind at rest about something. You're likely imagining that the home was run by a band of religious maniacs who abused both boys, turning them into raving Satanists, at least one of them going on to crucify priests in his spare time."

"I was thinking nothing of the sort," said Mills.

"That surprises me, because I certainly was. I couldn't help myself. I've always been a sucker for the nice, easy, simple explanation. Pity that real life is rarely like that."

"So what happened?" asked Mills, reaching for the biscuit tin stored above the mountain of paperwork adorning his desk.

Tyler laughed. "You look like a man about to settle down for a cosy tale with tea and biscuits. You are not at the cinema."

Looking instantly guilty, Mills resisted the call of the sacred tin, pushing it towards the DCI, who shook his head.

"There's nothing very cosy about this particular tale, I'm afraid to say."

"I can take it," said Mills. "Stokies are built to withstand pretty much anything."

Tyler told how Smee had painted a picture of a caring environment in which he had largely thrived, despite a harsh past that had preceded it. Religion hadn't been forced down anyone's throat, and Smee hadn't come to his interest in the occult through over-zealous or abusive clergy. "Quite mundane, that part of the story, actually. Smee had a love for horror films, initially, which he reckons led to an interest in various forms of occult literature. He met Faye Winkelman some years later, at the group run by Charles and Rose Blackwood. They shared a mutual fascination with the arcane, the gothic, and basically anything that involves dressing up in black. Smee regards himself as something of ... how did he put it, now? A *tourist,* that's the word he used: *going along for the ride.*"

"Faye Winkelman being a part of the ride, so to speak, sir?"

"You're getting the picture."

"What about Luke Summers?"

"That's where things start to get interesting."

Tyler watched the fingers of Mills' right hand inadvertently reach again for the forbidden tin.

"Control yourself, Detective Sergeant Mills!"

149

Mills snatched back his hand, and Tyler continued.

Summers had been admitted to the care home late one night, occupying the room adjacent to Smee. The grapevine at the home had kicked in immediately, with most of the kids being aware of the dramatic late-night arrival of the new boy, and naturally wondering what his story was. Most new arrivals' stories came out eventually, voluntarily or else under duress. With Luke Summers it seemed that everything was somewhat different.

"Human nature being what it is," said Tyler, "the less you know the more curious you become."

"A bit like this case," said Mills.

"Indeed."

"So Summers became something of an enigma?"

"Smee thought Summers enjoyed being of interest; having an air of mystery around him, making him seem more interesting to the other boys. But where usually a boy's silence would make him vulnerable to pressure, no-one seemed overly willing to push Luke Summers."

"They were afraid of him?"

"Smee suggested that there was what he described as an 'unnerving aspect' to the young man, and he depicted Summers as having 'a look that you didn't want to mess with'. Anyway, after a few weeks at the home Summers, on his own terms, began telling stories about his past, and about what had led to him being admitted into care. Smee said that he thought a lot of the stories were just that: flights of fantasy told by an attention-seeking youngster to amuse himself and to gain an audience."

"What kind of stories, sir?"

"Well, top of the bill was the one Summers told them about how he had killed both his adoptive parents by setting fire to the house while they were asleep in bed. Asked why he would do that, he told his young audience: '*Because I could. I was bored.*'

"That's how Toby Smee remembers it. He reckons Summers had a stockpile of stories, and that they often involving death and suffering. But that one was the most memorable."

"Did he believe Summers?"

"He thought he was just trying his best to shock everyone. That killing your parents would make you top dog in the tough guy stakes; or in the 'I'm the most interesting child in here' stakes, depending on how you decide to look at it."

"Was any of this ever substantiated?"

"Not that Smee was aware of. He said that Summers was only at the home for a matter of a few months, and he never saw him again until he turned up one evening for a Blackwood meeting."

"I see," said Mills, looking somewhat deflated by the apparent anti-climax.

"That's not all," said Tyler. He gestured. "Go on," he said. "I think you might need a chocolate digestive to help you get through this part."

Mills needed no second invitation, scrambling immediately for the tin.

"Sitting comfortably?" said Tyler. "After I left Smee's house I checked out the care home in Blythe Bridge. I had to play a bit rough to cut a few corners, and there's been quite a turnover of staff over the years, which is hardly surprising doing a job like that.

151

Anyway, the upshot is that Summers' adoptive father was a *priest*."

"Really?"

"And Summers was admitted into care following the tragic deaths of his adoptive parents."

"So Summers really did kill his parents?"

"Let's not jump to conclusions."

"How did they die? Was it a fire?"

Tyler sat back in his chair and delivered the punch line. "The house - the rectory - burnt down. Luke Summers was the only survivor."

CHAPTER TWENTY THREE

"Okay, Jim, let's hear it."

Tyler, sitting once again across the desk from CS Berkins, gave the details.

Luke Summers was moved from the care home in Blythe Bridge to one 'more suited to his particular needs.' The home had not been a happy experience for Luke Summers, according to the records. He always seemed to be in trouble, usually for fighting, lying, bullying or stealing. The police were never involved. The home enforced its own discipline but in the end the youngster was moved to a 'more robust establishment able to cope with severe and challenging behaviour.'

Tyler, during the telling, conjured a reflection of himself as a youngster: resenting authority, hating those who tried to impose their will on him. But where he had moved on to college, university, and eventually a career in the police force, Summers had graduated from care homes in and around Leek to a psychiatric hospital in Cheddleton.

The doctors assigned to Luke Summers uniformly suggested that early childhood trauma had been responsible for the young man's problems. The death of his natural parents, under appalling circumstances, compounded by the later dramatic and traumatic deaths of his adoptive parents, had caused the youngster to be wrenched from two loving environments into the vagaries of a care system that had not the slightest notion of how to provide for such a damaged individual.

Berkins interrupted Tyler. "Was it ever suggested that Summers might have been responsible for the fire at the family home that fateful night?"

"The cause of the fire was never established. Doubtless there were no grounds for suspecting the twelve year old son of a priest - a man of God, and his loving wife - of being anything more than a tragic victim."

Tyler continued, telling the CS that there had been nothing among the many reports on Luke Summers stating that he had ever claimed responsibility for killing his adoptive parents. The alleged 'confessions' made by Summers were unique to his relatively short stay in the original care home and were apparently never repeated. Or at least there was no documentary evidence to indicate that they had ever been repeated. Most of the children privy to those candid outpourings no doubt saw them as tall tales meant to shock and impress, and that was how Toby Smee had seen them.

And Smee had then apparently forgotten all about Luke Summers and his wild tales, until Summers had rocked up one evening for a meeting at the home of Charles and Rose Blackwood.

Berkins asked about Faye Winkelman.

"Smee and Winkelman are an item," said Tyler. "She noticed that the two men appeared to know each other, and Smee told her about Summers staying at the same care home. Winkelman checked newspaper archives and found that Godfrey and Rachel Berrington had died in a fire at their rectory home close to Cheadle.

She also noticed that Father Berrington and his wife had left behind a son who had survived the fire.

"Luke Berrington. Birth name: Luke Summers."

Winkelman had wanted to speak to Charles and Rose Blackwood about this, but Smee had urged caution, saying that it was none of their business. And then Summers had disappeared from the group almost as suddenly as he had arrived. Smee said they had been relieved that he had stopped attending, due to his menacing persona and generally disruptive personality, and felt it was no longer necessary to talk to Charles and Rose. So the matter was dropped until Faye Winkelman again brought it up.

"Do we know how the fire started?" asked Berkins.

"The report was inconclusive."

"And Summers has no criminal history?"

"None whatsoever."

"So, in a nutshell, there's no reason to assume that Luke Summers is actually involved in any of this."

"We could do with eliminating him from our enquiries at the very least," said Tyler.

"And if you do, what will that leave?" Berkins sighed. "Follow your instincts, Jim."

The CS indicated a selection of newspapers piled on his desk.

"The media are giving terrorist plots a rest for the time being. It's a toss-up this morning between revenge attacks for historical sex abuse perpetuated by members of the clergy, and revenge for satanic abuse. God help us! Maybe we ought to sit back and let the media pick out the bones and solve the case for us."

"Give me twenty four hours."

"That's a long time in politics and police work," said Berkins.

"Luke Summers is key to solving this."

"Have you been consulting the Tarot, Jim?"

Berkins face broadened into a smile, the first that Tyler had witnessed on the face of the CS for some considerable time.

He didn't envy the man. He respected him, and someone had to do the job. But quite why anyone would want to do it was beyond the DCI. All of that stress and responsibility and the shit that went with it; still, it was better that a man like Berkins had stepped up to the mark than another of the bureaucratic bullies that the Force appeared to churn out on a regular basis, and that had proven to be so popular down in London and in every other department through the land. You had a guy like Berkins, who would support you and not spend all of his time looking out for himself and furnishing his own nest - well, you learned to count your blessings.

The two men looked at each other and unspoken respect flowed between them.

"Tarot aside, the busy bees in white suits are suggesting that the same person was responsible for the two murders," said Tyler at last. "And that two people were responsible for the murder of the priest, though not necessarily for the murder of the woman."

"You think we would be better off sitting in an armchair, decked out with a deerstalker and a pipe, and content ourselves with puzzling it out?"

Berkins sat back with a half grin hanging uncomfortably from his face.

It was getting late in the day for someone in the rank of Chief Superintendent to start trying to be funny, thought Tyler. But let the man have his moment. He worked hard enough. He deserved it.

"Yes," said Tyler, getting up from his chair. "Some days I do."

The consultant psychiatrist at Cheddleton Hospital, Doctor Winston James, had written in the patient report that Luke Summers had been originally admitted following an attempted overdose of a Class A drug. In the months following that original admission, and over subsequent years that saw him admitted to the hospital on numerous occasions, Summers had revealed 'a consistency of unpredictability' along with a 'complex web of issues'. Notably, he had displayed long periods of almost catatonic behaviour, often, but not always, followed by explosive outbreaks of mania. At times he was bedridden, at other times requiring sedation and one-to-one specialist input around the clock. At yet other times his functioning had met the threshold for independent living. He had settled into an eventual pattern of voluntary admission followed by sustained periods in the community, including regular employment.

Following Tyler's surprisingly fruitful phone call to Doctor James earlier in the day, the consultant psychiatrist had agreed to meet up. Tyler had his own theories on the reason for the good doctor's unprecedented levels of helpfulness, and he wasn't shy about sharing them with Mills on the journey over.

"The man's an unadulterated careerist and he wants to get on the new MDPT."

"MDPT! No kidding," said Mills.

"That's the Multi-Disciplinary Project Team to you," said Tyler, helpfully.

"I suspected as much," lied Mills. "Lucrative, is it?"

"Not so much for the other members I suspect. The nurses and social workers will no doubt fail to see so much as an extra 'thank you' in their pay packets. But a few hours a month will I'm sure prove to be time very well spent for the good doctor. Still, we don't get paid for making snide, cynical remarks born out of envy, do we?"

"We don't, sir."

"Come on, Mr Sarcasm. Let's take advantage while we can."

Doctor James looked to be in his late fifties. His beard was grey while the hair on his head was clinging to the remains of a youthful style, and was a resolute natural jet black. The detectives took a seat while the psychiatrist opened up a thick file, eventually handing a photograph over the desk to the DCI.

"That's the most recent we have," said Doctor James.

"When did you last see Mr Summers?" asked Tyler, still looking at the photograph.

"Two years ago. The photo is from around that time. I'm not aware, speaking to other health care professionals who have maintained contact with Luke, that his appearance has radically changed."

As he said this his eyes narrowed. It was a questioning look that asked what business the detectives were really there to discuss. But Tyler didn't take the bait. He wanted to know what contact the

158

hospital, or at least the psychiatric services, had maintained over the past two years. It didn't appear that there had been a great deal.

"Mr Summers has proven to have been something of a success story, actually." Again, a questioning look, as though the boast demanded that any contradiction be made clear. And again Tyler passed over the invitation to clarify precisely the nature of the sudden interest in Luke Summers.

The two men, thought Mills, were acting like grand masters in a chess game; each trying to read the others' mind.

Tyler asked about Summers' background, his time in care homes, the death of his parents; the doctor's responses seemed generic and not helpful in the slightest. Then Tyler tried to insinuate a note of suspicion about the tragic deaths of Reverend Berrington and his wife; but the doctor was clearly not the type to be easily drawn into idle speculation. At some point he checked his watch, and looked about to indicate another appointment, when Tyler said, "Do you have any reason to believe that Summers might be a danger to the public?"

The doctor didn't hesitate, shaking his head. "None of us can ever give that kind of promise about anybody, even ourselves, for that matter." He appeared to snigger to himself at the remark. "Like you, I can only go on the evidence available, and on the basis of that I have to say that there has never been any indication that Mr Summers is a danger to anyone apart from possibly himself. A Community Psychiatric Nurse remains involved, and she will of course update you should you require that. Otherwise, Summers has been discharged from my care. Of course, he would be re-referred should his situation change and concerns arise regarding his wellbeing."

"You mean a suicide risk?" asked Tyler.

"A crisis of any description," said the consultant.

Tyler looked again at the photograph. It revealed the face of an unremarkable man who you might pass in the street without giving a second glance. An almost bland example of humanity, he thought. No distinguishing features whatsoever.

"Any further questions?"

"You mentioned a CPN," said Tyler.

"Back along the corridor; third door on the left."

CHAPTER TWENTY FOUR

The detectives entered the administration office and asked to speak to the Community Psychiatric Nurse assigned to Luke Summers. After consulting the database the secretary made an internal call. She informed the detectives that Arlene Mitchell would be through in a moment.

As good as her word, a woman appeared, introducing herself as Arlene. Tyler asked if they might talk somewhere privately, and the CPN led the detectives through to a small room adjacent to the main office.

"I must apologise," she said, as soon as they were all seated. "I've been off on sick leave for a few weeks and I'm still catching up."

The woman appeared bright and helpful, thought Mills, if somewhat nervous. Being visited by detectives wasn't most people's idea of fun, he reflected. A nice balance of professional and affable, and he could stand half an hour in her company, particularly if refreshments were in the offing.

Tyler explained the purpose of his visit.

"I'm a little overdue to see Luke," she said, apologetically.

"Long overdue?"

"A few weeks."

"He's not a priority case?" asked Tyler.

"Luke has been on an even keel for a while now. I would still like to see him soon though. I wouldn't like to let things drift. He's done remarkably well. I'm quite proud of him, actually."

"Any reason why things might drift?" asked Tyler.

"Can I ask why you are interested in Luke?" she asked the detective.

Mills smiled to himself. This woman was no fool, he thought, enjoying the contest.

"Routine enquiries at this stage," said Tyler. "Nevertheless, we would like to speak with him as soon as possible."

Arlene Mitchell frowned. "Routine enquiries ... and at the same time 'urgent?'"

"I didn't say *urgent*, exactly."

"How soon do you need to speak to Luke?"

"Today, ideally."

"Quite urgent, then?"

"None of your colleagues have been in touch with Mr Summers during your absence?" asked Tyler.

"Wouldn't that be nice!" she said. "I'm afraid staff shortages mean that anything that isn't *strictly* urgent has to wait these days. I can ring him now. It's a good time of day to catch him. When he works it tends to be late evenings or nights."

She left the detectives in the room, returning a few minutes later.

"No joy I'm afraid," she announced. "I can try again later."

"Can you let us have Mr Summers' contact details?" asked Tyler. "Home address, telephone number."

A look of concern shot across the CPN's face.

"Is something the matter?" asked Tyler.

"It's just that Luke can be a very sensitive individual."

162

"Sensitive?"

"The police suddenly turning up at his flat - I think it might spook him. It would certainly spook me."

"I can't imagine that you would have anything to hide," said Mills, regretting the remark the moment he had uttered it.

"I would like to be there to support him, if that's okay," she said.

"Might he not be at home now?" asked Tyler. "I mean, does he always answer his phone? Some people don't, in my experience. Myself included, when I'm not working. We do need to speak to him today. I'm more than happy for you to come along. It might prove helpful, a friendly face."

Arlene Mitchell seemed uncomfortable. "Can I speak to my manager?" she said. "I won't be a moment."

When she had again left the room Tyler turned to Mills. "Was that thunder outside or did I catch your belly rumbling?"

Mills glanced out through the small window. "It does look a bit uncertain out there," he said. "She seems nice enough," he added, awkwardly.

"Nice enough for what?"

"Helpful, I mean."

"Let's hope so," said Tyler. "That's the way it's supposed to work." Footsteps were sounding outside the door. "We are about to find out."

The CPN returned to the room looking flustered. "I've spoken to Luke's landlord. His rent is overdue and the landlord hasn't been able to contact him. He was about to visit Luke's flat. We can meet him there in half an hour?"

163

Mark L. Fowler

Tyler sat in the passenger seat next to her, Mills following behind in the unmarked police car. Luke Summers had been renting a flat in Sneyd Green in the north of the city for the past couple of years. According to Arlene Mitchell, he had not previously been behind with his rent and there had never been a complaint of any kind from his landlord.

Tyler noted that the CPN appeared tense as she drove. He wondered if she had been off work with a stress-related condition. Most of the public services' staff seemed to suffer from nervous conditions at some stage in their careers; too much pressure and too few resources, that age-old story; and little sign of things improving anytime soon, he had no doubt.

Attempting to ease the tension in the car, Tyler made small talk about the weather and the state of the NHS. But small talk was not something that Jim Tyler was practiced in the art of, and quickly he was out of his comfort zone. The conversation turned back to Luke Summers, Tyler asking about the man's early life, and the CPN remaining cautious, giving little away. He tried another approach, asking what hobbies and interests Summers had. At this Arlene Mitchell seemed to flounder. Luke, she said, had never really discussed any particular passions or interests.

It could be murder getting information from fellow public servants, thought the DCI. Everyone was terrified of breaching confidentiality these days, protecting their own little files of information. He didn't blame her. Like everyone, she was doing her job. He sensed too that she was protective of her client, and he applauded her for that.

164

As they approached Sneyd Green, she said, "I'm not trying to be elusive. I hope you understand that. It might be helpful if you asked, well, more direct questions, perhaps."

He liked this woman. There was a sharp intelligence that sat alongside her undeniable loyalty to her client. Not the frequent glib insistence on hiding behind bureaucratic protocol that marked his dealings over the years with too many public sector professionals.

"Would you say that Luke has any particular interest in the occult?"

"That's an interesting question. Really, I have no idea. I take it that isn't an idle enquiry just to kill time?"

"Do you read the newspapers?"

"Only at weekends," she said "The arts section mainly."

"The rest of it might give you bad dreams."

"I do occasionally catch the headlines. I'm aware that a priest was killed in Trentham. I watch the TV occasionally, too."

"The last time I looked it was full of crime dramas," said Tyler.

"They're my favourites. So, naturally I'm curious."

"About who killed the priest?"

"As long as it doesn't turn out to be anyone I know."

"Do you know anyone who might be of interest?"

She glanced across at the detective. "I believe absolutely in client confidentiality. But if I suspected anyone of committing a serious crime ... I have no interest in shielding a killer."

"I understand that Luke has never been known to be violent. That no-one has ever pointed a finger at him for the death of his adoptive parents."

165

"Why should they?"

"Have you ever found him intimidating?"

She turned into a side street and waited for the council wagon to make its slow way past her car.

"Luke has a lot of issues. In his manic states he can become, should we say, rather inventive. He has at various times laid claim to killing his parents, and to killing other people too. Those claims have been checked out. There has never been any evidence that he has harmed anyone. On another day he has no memory whatsoever of having made those claims."

"Has his manner ever frightened *you*?"

"Luke can be intense when he's in one of those phases. It usually doesn't last. I suppose that, if you were not used to him, and you found him in a manic state that you would naturally be unnerved. The greater fear, the greater likelihood, in my opinion, is that he might harm himself, and that could include self-neglect."

"Has he ever harmed himself?"

"Not substantially, no. I believe that he has sufficient insight into his condition to summon help. So far that has proved to be the case."

The dustbin lorry finally moved past and Mitchell drove the last few yards before pulling up outside a shabby block of flats. "This is it," she said. "Number Seventeen. Luke rents the upstairs flat."

Tyler peered through the dismal rain at the closed curtains of the room upstairs indicated. "Perhaps he's having a lie-in," he said.

He caught the look of sudden trepidation on the face of the CPN.

166

A van pulled up opposite. "That's Mr Richardson," she said.

"Come to check on his investment?" said Tyler.

They watched Mr Richardson get out of his van. He was a large, round man, with a bald head and a quick stride. He fairly marched around to the side door, which gave direct access to the upstairs flat.

Tyler got out of the car. Mills was parked up behind and likewise got out, joining the DCI on the pavement. They watched the landlord disappear inside the building.

"Let's give him a minute, Danny."

Arlene Mitchell joined the detectives as they waited. Then Mr Richardson re-appeared, wearing a grim expression, marching over towards them. He acknowledged Arlene Mitchell. "You'd better come in and see this for yourself, love."

They followed the landlord up the staircase to the floor above. A narrow hallway led to a kitchen, bathroom, living room and bedroom. Mr Richardson pointed to the bedroom. "I've never seen anything like that before in my life."

The detectives and CPN went into the small room, which consisted of a single bed and side table. The walls and ceiling had been vividly painted with weird symbols and strange hieroglyphics. Hanging suspended on strings above the bed was a papier-mâché model of an animal's head; a goat's head.

"And that's just for starters," said Mr Richardson. He led the party through to the other rooms, similarly decorated with vivid art of an occult nature. Hardly an inch of wall or ceiling space had been left unadorned.

In the kitchen Tyler checked the fridge. Half a bottle of sour milk and a lump of mouldy bread suggested that Luke Summers hadn't been in the flat for some time.

"When were you last here?" Tyler asked Mr Richardson.

"Four or five weeks ago," said Richardson. "I mean, this sort of thing isn't on," he added, looking at the CPN. "Late paying his rent and now all this! I tell you, I'm not putting up with it. I mean to say, who's going to pay to have this lot repainted?"

They wandered back through the flat to see if anything had been left that suggested Summers intended returning to the flat. But apart from the items in the fridge the place had been stripped bare.

Outside, having extricated themselves from a still fuming Mr Richardson, who was demanding to know when he would get his money as well as having his flat redecorated, the detectives got into the CPN's car.

"Has Luke Summers done anything like this before?" Tyler asked her.

"Not that I'm aware of. Like I said, there have been no problems with Luke for some time. He's been paying his rent and working hard."

"Where has he been working?"

The CPN looked awkwardly at the detective.

"The warehouse where Luke's been working haven't seen him for a couple of weeks now. I checked before we left. They ought to have made contact. They assumed he was off sick."

"The symbols, the goat's head?" said Tyler. "An interest in the occult ... has that not been evident?"

168

"Not to me," she said. "There's nothing in the files. It's not something that Luke has ever mentioned to me."

"Might we assume that he has entered another manic phase?" asked Tyler.

"I think," said Mitchell, "that we need to find him as quickly as possible."

"Does he pose a danger to the public?" asked Tyler.

"I still think he's more likely a danger to himself," she replied.

The detectives got out of the car and watched Arlene Mitchell drive away.

"Time for Berkins to play ball again," said Tyler.

"Another appeal to the public, sir?"

"You mind reader you."

CHAPTER TWENTY FIVE

It was late in the day when Mills came across something that he thought Tyler ought to look at. A history of Luke Summers had been put together, documenting all his placements in care along with hospital admissions. One of the homes that Summers had attended, Deep Vale House, just outside Leek, had been burned down in a suspected arson attack a year ago. No-one had been charged or even apprehended. Miraculously, there had been no casualties, but all the young people had needed to be resettled, scattered between various care homes throughout Staffordshire.

Tyler contacted Arlene Mitchell and informed her that an appeal had been issued in the hope that Summers could be located. She sounded grateful for the information. He asked her for precise admission and discharge dates over the past twelve months, double checking against the information that he had already gleaned. She confirmed what Tyler had suspected. That Luke Summers had not been in hospital around the time of the arson attack.

"Are we leaping to conclusions?" he asked Mills. "Luke Summers' parents died in a fire. One of the homes that Summers was placed in as a child was razed to the ground twelve months ago. Summers' adoptive father was a priest. A priest has been crucified, and fellow occultist, Jane Hopkins - who Summers met at the Satanist's fortnightly bash - has similarly been murdered by being nailed to a church door."

170

Mills remained circumspect. "We need a motive for the murders of Jane Hopkins and Father Peterson," he said. "If that points to Luke Summers, then maybe we are onto something."

"You don't say!"

"Nothing's come in from the appeal for information?"

"Give it time. You can run in this city, but you can't hide."

Mills looked quizzically at the DCI, who held his look for a few seconds. "I've been waiting to deliver that line since I got here," said Tyler.

"It has been well worth the wait," said Mills.

The following day brought no new information about the whereabouts of Luke Summers. Speculation was growing that he had fled the area. A nationwide appeal for information was repeated but still nothing was coming in.

Then Tyler received a call from Faye Winkelman.

She had heard the appeal, and sounded anxious, close to tears. "What if he killed Jane and now he's coming after me?" she asked Tyler.

"Why would he kill Jane?" Tyler asked her. "And why would he want to kill you?"

"I'm frightened," she said. "I think he's going to kill all of us."

She was already on the doorstep waiting when the detectives pulled up outside the property. They went inside and took their customary seats in the living room, while Winkelman remained standing, appearing too full of nervous energy to sit down.

171

"Have you heard from Summers?" Tyler asked her.

"No," she said, as though answering an accusation.

"So why do you imagine that he's going to come after you, or any of the others? Look, if you know something, now's the time to spit it out."

"I've been talking to Toby," she said.

"And what did he tell you?"

"I suspected … I *knew* something was going on."

"Miss Winkelman?"

"He's confessed to having an affair. He was seeing Jane."

The detectives traded confused looks while Winkelman continued.

"Jane contacted Toby. She told him that Summers had been in touch and wanted to meet up with her again. Back when he was attending the meetings a few of us thought he had the hots for Jane. But she never said anything about it. When she spoke to Toby she said that she'd seen Summers a few times."

"*Seen* him?" asked Tyler.

"Do you need it spelling out?"

"I'm afraid I do. In a murder investigation we can't afford to misinterpret any information provided. So," said Tyler. "Seeing Luke Summers in what sense?"

"You know. They got together. Romantically. Boy and girl!"

Mills grinned, but it was quickly contained when he caught the DCI's eye.

"What did she think about him getting in touch?" asked Tyler.

"Toby said that she wasn't keen. That Jane had found him weird back then and was relieved when he left the group."

172

"If she found him weird," said Tyler, "why did she agree to see him outside of the group?"

"I think Jane had her own problems. I think she was looking for something, and maybe she thought she had a connection, you know, with Summers' interest in the occult. I don't know, I'm guessing. Jane could change in the blink of an eye. Monday Jane and Tuesday Jane could be two entirely different people. But it sounds like she started to worry about what she was getting into. They saw each other a few times and then one night he turned up at her house. No warning, he just arrived, out of the blue. She told Toby that Summers had changed; that he was different."

"In what way different?" asked Tyler.

"He was unkempt for one thing. At the meetings he was always smartly turned out. Always meticulous; precise about everything. But she said he seemed all over the place and looked like he hadn't shaved for days; that his hair was a mess and his clothes looked dirty. *He* looked dirty."

"But Jane invited him in?"

"I think she was shocked and didn't have time to think. He didn't stay long. He was freaking her out."

"Can you be more precise?" asked Tyler.

"He was banging on about End Times. Prophecy, and all of that; but not making any sense. He was rambling on, talking non-stop about Satan's arrival on Earth, and the role that he was being asked to play. Like he was going to be pivotal, and his destiny - most of it was incoherent and Jane wasn't sure what he was talking about. She made an excuse about being tired and she told him that he would have to leave."

"Did he threaten her?" asked Tyler.

173

"Not directly, as far as I know. But she felt threatened all the same. He was still ranting when he left. Jane wondered if he was ill, and she thought about calling the police. But he hadn't actually made a threat against her, and so she didn't say anything. She expected him to turn up again, but he didn't make any further contact. She was going to mention it at the next group meeting, but in the end she confided in Toby."

"And you say that Jane and Toby were having an affair? How long had this been going on?"

"Toby said he had been seeing her for a while, a few months. I wasn't surprised to be honest. He was sniffing around someone else in the group a while back, and I think that's why *she* left. I sometimes wonder if he didn't join up just to meet other women. I mean, that's how he met me, after all."

"He confessed to his affair with Jane?" asked Tyler.

"He said he was afraid, and that he couldn't keep it to himself any longer. He thought Summers might have killed Jane because she snubbed him. A day or so before she was killed she saw Toby, and said she thought someone was following her. That's when she told him about Summers making contact."

Winkelman started to cry. "He's scared that Summers knew about him seeing Jane, and that he killed her and may be planning to kill him too. But when I told him to speak to you ... I don't know why he won't. He said that he didn't want to put me at risk, and that we shouldn't see each other anymore."

"Otherwise he might have kept the affair a secret?"

"I don't know. Like I said, I've had my suspicions, and there are probably other affairs that I don't know about. I've had it with the cult and I've had it with

174

Toby Smee. When I heard about the appeal for information, I started putting it all together, and I thought: what if Summers isn't satisfied with killing Jane Hopkins?"

"We don't know," said Tyler, "that he has killed anybody."

"He's had a disturbed past, from what Toby's said."

"That's as maybe. Not everyone who has suffered in the past turns out to be a killer," said Tyler pointedly. "What did he tell you about Luke Summers?"

Winkelman told the detectives what Smee had told her, about Summers' parents dying in tragic circumstances when he was very young. About him being moved endlessly around the care system and having a rough time of it. "Toby was in care himself and met Luke Summers there. He recognised Toby when he attended the group."

"Is that how Summers came to join in the first place - through Toby Smee?"

"I'm not aware of that. I understood it to be a coincidence. I don't want to stay here on my own."

"Is there anywhere else you can stay?" Tyler asked her.

"I'm going to stay with my mum until you've caught him."

Tyler asked for a contact number, and she wrote the details down on a scrap of paper and handed it to him.

The detectives got back into the car.

"I think we need to have another chat with Mr Smee," said Tyler.

Mills drove.

CHAPTER TWENTY SIX

"I don't suppose he'll be too pleased to see us," said Mills as he sped through the gloom towards Toby Smee's house.

"I don't suppose he will," said Tyler. "If he wants to avoid us knocking on his door at a godforsaken hour, then he will have to learn to be more open with us when he has the chance."

The house was in darkness, and the car parked outside suggested that Smee was at home. "Looks like he's already tucked up in his bed for the night," said Mills. He wondered with whom, now that Faye Winkelman and Jane Hopkins were out of the picture, one way or another.

Mills knocked on the front door. There was no response, and Tyler was about to go around to the rear of the property when a light came on upstairs. A few moments later the front door opened.

"Sorry to disturb you so late," said Mills.

Smee looked at his watch as though to emphasise the lateness of the hour. He was wearing a dressing gown and pyjama bottoms, and from the look of him he had just woken up.

"We need to ask a few questions," said Mills.

"It can't wait until daylight?"

"Not really. If you don't mind."

Smee gestured to the detectives to go inside.

"Would you like a drink, seeing as you are here?"

"We don't want to put you to any trouble," said Mills, unconvincingly.

Smee switched the kettle on, and the three men sat around the kitchen table.

"We understand," said Tyler, "that you spoke to Jane Hopkins recently about Luke Summers."

Smee looked at the detectives as though for clues.

"Have you been talking to Faye?"

"We understand," said Tyler, ignoring Smee's question, "that Jane Hopkins informed you that Summers went to see her recently. And that prior to her murder she told you that she thought she was being followed."

The kettle was coming up to the boil. Smee looked at it as though unsure what to do next.

"Do you recall having that conversation with Jane Hopkins?" said Tyler.

"Something like that, yes," he said at last, getting up to make the drinks.

"*Something like that*?" repeated Tyler. "But you didn't think to mention it the last time we met?"

"I ..."

"Mr Smee?"

"I was having a relationship with Jane. I panicked. I didn't want to hurt Faye. I was afraid I might be under suspicion. I was with Jane the night before she was killed. I'm sorry, I should have said something."

"I'm inclined to agree," said Tyler. "When *precisely* did you last see Jane Hopkins?"

"I left her place for work early that morning. I didn't kill her. I left her and I went to work." He turned his back on the detectives. "Tea or coffee?" he said.

"What aren't you telling me?" said Tyler.

177

Smee didn't respond.

Tyler repeated the question.

"*Luke Summers,*" said Smee.

"What about him?"

"He contacted me."

"When and how exactly?"

"Did you say tea or coffee?"

"I didn't," said Tyler.

Smee turned back around. "I went up to Hanley to get something. When I pulled up on the car park he came out of nowhere. He got in my car with me before I even realised it was him. He said if I spoke to the police about Jane ... he said I'd be next."

"When was this?"

"I was on early that day, like I said. I was in town by mid-afternoon."

"The day Jane was killed?"

"Yes."

"You didn't tell us about Summers contacting you and contacting Jane Hopkins, yet you told Faye Winkelman about him making contact with Jane?"

"I was full of guilt."

"Guilt for what?"

"Being unfaithful to Faye. I wanted to come clean. I wanted to warn her about Summers. I didn't know what to do."

"You must have realised that Faye would be frightened. And that she would speak to us."

"I wasn't thinking straight. I said I'm sorry. I should have come clean before."

"Luke Summers threatened to kill you if you spoke to us about Jane - what did you think he meant by speaking to us about Jane? That he had already killed her?"

"I didn't know what he meant. I didn't know she was dead. I found out later, when it was on the news."

"And still you didn't tell us about your conversation with Summers and your suspicions that he had killed Jane Hopkins?"

"I was scared."

Tyler shook his head. "You think he's killed someone, that he may be planning to kill more people, and we have to come and bang on your door in the middle of the night to squeeze this information out of you?"

"Like I said -"

"Yes, you were scared." Tyler stood up. "You were in care with Luke Summers. You remembered him?"

"Not until he told me who he was. But he remembered me. When he first attended the group he told me that he had been at one of the care homes."

"You didn't introduce him to the group?"

"No, I didn't. I hadn't seen him since we were kids."

"How did he find out about the group?"

"His interest in the occult, I suppose. It's all underground of course but if you know where to look you can find like-minded people. And people leave, so maybe he knew someone who had left the group, I don't know. But I didn't introduce him."

"And you haven't been in touch with him since he left?"

"No. Until he came up to me on the car park I hadn't seen him."

"Why would he kill Jane Hopkins?"

"I don't know."

"Because she was having a relationship with you?"

"Possibly. I think he's crazy enough."

"I'm struggling, here," said Tyler. "You think Luke Summers killed Jane Hopkins, and that he might be coming after you and Faye Winkelman and God knows who else - and yet rather than tell us of your concerns, you put the fear of the devil into Miss Winkelman before settling down for a good night's sleep. Can you see why I'm struggling?" Tyler took a long, deep breath. "I want to know what time you arrived at work on that day, what time you left and who you were with. I want you, Mr Smee, to account for every single minute after you left Jane Hopkins."

The detectives headed back towards the city. Tyler was brooding over the facts of the case, such as they were, and listening to the groaning sounds coming from DS Mills' stomach.

At last he gave it up. "It sounds like you haven't eaten for days. Do you think you will make it back to base?"

"Touch and go, sir, but I've got to lose weight if it kills me."

"Doctor's orders or your wife's?"

"Both, but mainly my wife."

"What do you make of Toby Smee?"

"I don't trust him. But if his alibi checks out ..."

"I've no doubt it will. We need to find Luke Summers. We need a break in this case."

As the car plunged on through the dark, cold night, heading for the lights of the city, the detectives kept their silent premonitions to themselves. Mills had an uneasy feeling that something was about to happen, while for Tyler the foreboding was even more nebulous, manifesting in a vague sense of undefined panic that seemed to generate from his core.

They arrived on Cedar Lane to find that there had been a fatal fire in the Longton area of the city. DS Mills' old stomping ground. The body of a young woman had been found, or what remained of it.

Tyler asked for the address, and turned to Mills. "Evie Ryles," he said. Another member of the *Chapter Six* cult had perished.

CHAPTER TWENTY SEVEN

The following morning CS Berkins made a fresh appeal to the public for urgent information about the whereabouts of Luke Summers, this time making it crystal clear that Summers was wanted in connection with several recent murders. The man was not to be approached by members of the public, who were instead to contact the police immediately.

Forensics were trying to gather whatever evidence the fire hadn't destroyed, and Tyler was eager to hear from the pathologist once the post mortem was completed.

Mills asked the DCI, "What are you thinking, sir? That this wasn't murder?"

"I'm interested in the fact that Evie Ryles wasn't able to get out of the house. She may have been drunk, stoned, on medication, sleeping tablets - who knows. The house was badly damaged, but from where she was found it seems odd to me that, awoken by a fire in the house, let's say, she wasn't able to get out through the front door. The worst of the fire spread through the back of the house first."

"Are you saying that she got drunk and left the grill on, sir?"

"I don't know what I'm saying. She may have been smoking in bed. Let's see what the pathologist comes back with."

The fire had started around midnight as far as the fire investigators could tell. "We didn't leave Smee's place until after that," said Mills. "If he's picking off members of the cult -"

"Why would he do that? There's a personal connection with Jane Hopkins, fair enough. I don't trust him, but ..."

"What is it, sir?"

Tyler thought for a moment. "I want to speak to Faye Winkelman again," he said. "Call it a hunch, for want of a better word. We need to be doing something."

Faye Winkelman's mother lived close to Cheadle, and only a few miles from where DS Mills and his family had relocated. "We're doing a tour of your past and present," said Tyler as they headed out.

"I've always wanted to be on *This Is Your Life*, sir."

They passed through the crossroads at Cellarhead close to where Smee lived. Tyler looked about to say something, before falling back into reverie.

Audrey Winkelman lived a few hundred yards from the town centre, and Mills parked outside a small detached property. "On the whole," said Mills, "Satanism seems to favour the reasonably well to do middle classes."

"Rubbish," said Tyler.

"Sir?"

"For one, who says the middle classes are well to do these days, and two - why are you assuming that the mother has the daughter's interest in the subject?"

"Point taken," said Mills.

"Which one?" asked Tyler.

"Both, sir." Then, "Are you okay, Jim?"

Tyler sighed wearily. "Any reason I shouldn't be?"

"You seem a bit -"

"*Edgy*? You seem fond of that tune."

"Think of it as the favourite song of a concerned colleague and friend."

"If I wasn't 'edgy' I wouldn't get out of bed in the morning. But I'm okay." He smiled at Danny Mills. "There's something just out of reach and it's doing my head in. However, you'll be glad to know that I'm not thirsting for the bottle, and neither am I aching to put my fist through the face of every second person I meet."

"Good to hear that, sir. All in all, it sounds to me like a clean bill of health."

Tyler gave him a look. "I've found a listening ear and its beckoning me to talk."

Mills eyes lit up, but the DCI quickly responded.

"No, I've not met anyone, not even the woman of my dreams; so you can cut the speculative gossip before it starts. I don't get it for free, this listening ear; I pay for the privilege, and it's worth every penny. A form of prostitution, you could say. I've come across men over the years, and from all walks of life, who will pay to be with a woman, and all they want to do in their company is talk all night. Someone, a stranger, who won't judge them, but who has enough understanding of this world to actually hear what's being said. It's a rare gift, Danny, and without meaning to be rude, it is, in my experience, generally at a premium with women. They are the best listeners. Perhaps they have a more developed sense of empathy. I don't know. I can talk to you, Danny, but not like I can talk to her. No offence meant."

"None taken, sir."

Tyler got out of the car. "Anyway, we have more pressing business to attend to."

He walked to the front door and knocked gently.

A woman answered, nervously, through a narrow gap provided by the security chain.

"Who is it?"

"Detective Chief Inspector Tyler. I would like a word with Faye Winkelman, please."

The door closed again, before opening fully. The woman answering the door looked drained. "I'm Audrey Winkelman," she said. "I'm Faye's mother. Would you like to come through?"

Audrey was smaller than her daughter, and her clothes less esoteric. Her voice was soft and she appeared to virtually hover as she walked.

She led the detectives through to a comfortable sitting room, very Laura Ashley, thought Mills. Faye was sitting on a long sofa, a magazine next to her, the TV on but muted and showing a nature programme.

Tyler asked Faye if she had heard from Luke Summers, and she said that she hadn't. She looked tired; both women did, as though they had been up all night. Talking about men, thought Tyler. *Luke Summers; Toby Smee.* He asked if she was alright, and she nodded in response. Then he asked her if Smee had been in contact again, and when she failed to respond, her mother cut in.

"For goodness sakes, Faye, do yourself a favour. Tell them!"

Faye issued a thin smile at her mother, and then she said, still looking at her, "Toby called."

185

Audrey Winkelman looked over at the detectives and appeared to groan with exasperation. "Do I have to tell them, Faye?"

When she still didn't respond, Audrey said, "It wasn't a very long visit, and not a very pleasant one. Tell them, for God's sake!" She shook her head at the detectives. "Right, if you won't -"

"No, Mum, I can speak for myself." She looked at Tyler. "There's not a lot to say. Toby came here earlier. He'd been trying to contact me at home, and when I didn't answer the door or my phone he came here. He's been here before."

Audrey caught the eye of DCI Tyler. "You don't approve of Mr Smee?" he asked her.

"Frankly, no, I don't. I think Faye is better off without him. But she's old enough to choose her own boyfriends, so I try to stay out of it."

Tyler looked back to Faye. "What was the purpose of his visit here today, Miss Winkelman?"

"Go on then, tell him!" urged Audrey. "It was a warning, that's what it was."

"A warning?" Tyler asked Faye.

"He told me that the secrets of the cult have to remain secrets."

"And if they don't?"

"He said I would be placing myself in danger."

"He was threatening you?"

"I don't know."

"Of course he was!" chimed in Audrey. "How can you interpret it any other way?"

Faye Winkelman shook her head. "He probably meant that there is an occult danger, not that he's planning on doing me any harm, Mum."

Audrey rolled her eyes. "You're well out of that cult. I told you that you shouldn't mess around with people like that."

Tyler asked if Smee had made it clear what kind of secrets she was being warned not to share.

"If I told you what the secrets were they wouldn't be secrets," she snapped.

"What I am asking," said Tyler, through gritted teeth, "is this: are you being asked to conceal anything illegal? Information about a crime that has been committed, for example?"

Faye shook her head. "There's a confidentiality agreement that you have to sign when you join. It basically means that you can't go around telling non-members what you get up to at the meetings, or reporting on what other people might be saying."

"But supposing that someone confessed to a crime during a 'meeting'?" said Tyler. "Or proposed to commit one - would the confidentiality agreement cover that?"

"That's never happened. I never once heard anyone say that they were going to do anything illegal. Or confess to a crime."

"Not even Clayton Shaw?" said Tyler. "Desecrating church buildings?"

"I never heard that discussed," she said. "It would not have been condoned, I'm certain of it. He's off his head. He hasn't the first clue about anything."

"Was Toby Smee present throughout the meeting on the evening that the priest was killed?" asked Tyler.

Faye Winkelman hesitated.

"Yes or no?" pressed Tyler.

"I'm not certain."

187

"Was he there at all?"

"He was there, yes. He may have arrived late. I'm not certain of the exact time."

"He was *definitely* late?"

"Yes. But you can't think that Toby ..."

"We're exploring all options at the moment," said Tyler. "On the day Jane Hopkins was killed, Toby Smee claims that after he finished work he went to town and then visited you."

She nodded, while appearing distant, as though pondering something.

"What is it?" asked Tyler.

"Probably nothing," she said.

"Say it and let me be the judge," said Tyler.

"It's just that ... when he came round that day ..."

"Yes?"

"Thinking about it, it seems contrived."

"You think he may have been using you to provide an alibi?"

"It doesn't make sense," she said. "That suggests that he knew something was going to happen. That someone else was going to kill Jane."

Audrey showed the detectives to the door. Before they left she stepped outside onto the pavement and said to Tyler, "Do you think he might be involved?"

"Like I said earlier," began Tyler, but Audrey Winkelman finished his sentence for him. "I know," she said. "*Just routine enquiries at this stage*. I don't like that man. There's something about him."

Mills drove back towards the city while Tyler sat next to him, brooding once more over the case. "Who is Faye Winkelman really afraid of?" he said at last. "If

188

Smee's already been to Audrey Winkelman's house, it can hardly be Toby Smee she's hiding from, can it?"

"Unless she imagines there's safety in numbers, sir. You never can tell with some people. Or maybe she's afraid of Luke Summers but pissed off with Smee for being unfaithful."

"The more we find out, the less I'm certain of," said Tyler.

"I've been saying that for most of my working life," said Mills, "my married life too. Particularly the married life, now I think about it."

"That's a very helpful observation," said Tyler. "We must be nearly there?"

CHAPTER TWENTY EIGHT

A call came in. A man answering to the description of Luke Summers had been spotted in a derelict property in Penkhull.

Tyler entered the CID office shaking his head. "Five minute walk from my house," he said to Mills. "The woman who rang in said she thought a tramp was living there. She was getting around to ringing the council, saw the photo of Luke Summers this morning in her husband's newspaper, and called us. She sounds certain it's the man in the photograph."

"Do you know the property?" asked Mills, concealing a faint smile.

"I've run past it at least three times this week!" said Tyler. "Thank the Lord for nosy neighbours. Anyway, we've sent out officers to keep an eye on the place."

Mills frowned. "We're not going straight in?"

"That's what Berkins wanted. But the woman thinks the man has been at the property for a few days; and she hasn't noticed him leaving or returning. I want to see if anybody else is interested in that derelict house."

"Taking food in, sir?" Mills' expression brightened further. "An accomplice?"

"Let's not get over excited at this stage. None of this may prove to have anything to do with any of the murders. On the other hand, we are looking for two people for the crucifixion of Father Peterson. So let's see. I'm curious to know if anyone turns up at the property. If it is Summers in there, he won't be going anywhere. We've got the place covered."

Tyler picked up the phone and asked to speak to Arlene Mitchell. Then, placing the phone back down, he shook his head. "Out doing good in the community." He stood up. "If that phone goes, I'm back in with Berkins."

He hadn't even reached the office door when the phone rang.

Tyler spoke to the CPN, telling her that it was possible Luke Summers was living in an abandoned property in Penkhull village, and at the same time picking her brains, trying to establish if there could be anyone who might be taking him provisions.

She wasn't aware of anyone who Luke Summers particularly associated with. He wasn't a man who appeared to make friends.

Tyler ended the call and turned to DS Mills. "She asked to go with us. Apart from the obvious risks to her safety ... but on the other hand," he said, thinking aloud, "she's worked hard to build a good professional relationship with Summers. That relationship might yet prove invaluable."

You didn't get that from your average detective, thought Mills. For most officers - those he had come across, at any rate - it was all about the arrest; solving the case, and prosecuting the crime: Getting the killer behind bars. And most of the time it had to be that way.

Tyler looked at Mills. "What?"

"Nothing, sir."

"Are you sure about that?"

"Positive, sir."

191

Tyler didn't seem convinced. "Anyway, Berkins won't let me hold back for long. At the end of the day all eyes are on him." He was scrutinising the DS when the internal phone rang. Mills picked up, grateful for the distraction. "Talk of the devil," he said, covering up the mouthpiece.

"Tell him I'm on my way."

Berkins was looking harassed. He gestured for Tyler to take a seat.

"In a nutshell, Jim: I can't buy any time on this. I've tried, but the pressure upstairs, you wouldn't believe it."

Tyler did believe it, and he understood entirely.

"I'm sending them in," said Berkins. "I can't take any chances."

Tyler took a different tack. "If you can't buy time, at least allow me to go in."

"This isn't the time for heroics, Jim."

"I'm not interested in heroics. You know me better than that. Look, we don't have to take any chances. We maintain backup, and plenty of it, but I give it a go first. That way we have nothing to lose."

Berkins considered it. "On the other hand, Jim, what do we have to gain? It's not like you've met the man. You've nothing to build on. Is there something you're omitting to tell me, by any chance?"

"I've been in contact with Luke Summers' CPN."

"And ...?"

"She's willing to come along -"

"Absolutely not! No chance, Jim. You can't risk the life of a civilian!"

"I thought you might say that. I had to ask."

192

"Well, you've asked and you've had my answer: categorically -"

"I wouldn't place her at risk, of course; she would be outside the property. I could tell Summers that she was there, and that she was concerned for him. Re-assurance. But she wouldn't be face to face with Summers until we had the cuffs on him."

Berkins sat back. At last he said, "You've not let me down yet, Jim."

"Thank you," said Tyler.

"Is there anything else?"

"I still believe we should hold fire and see if there's any further activity at the property."

"Don't push it."

As Tyler was leaving the room, Berkins said, "It will take you a few hours to set things up I dare say. You've got until dusk."

Tyler asked Arlene Mitchell to come over.

As soon as she arrived at Cedar Lane, he briefed her on the situation. She would stay behind the lines until Summers was brought out of the building safely. Then she could travel onward with him. That was the deal and it was non-negotiable. He asked if she had any questions.

She looked at the DCI with a mix of surprise and admiration. "I've worked with the police quite a few times over the years," she said. "I've never worked with anyone quite like you before though."

"Your lucky streak was bound to come to an end eventually."

"How certain are you that it's Luke in there?"

"One concerned member of the local community. Or a nosy neighbour, if you'd prefer. It sounds like she doesn't miss a trick, and I'm only concerned that she failed to spot the likeness earlier. After all, that photograph has been in circulation now for at least twenty four hours. She needs to tighten up her act!"

"I realise of course that you're treating Luke as a murder suspect. But do you really think that he's responsible?"

"We need to eliminate him from our enquiries. Okay, my honest answer is that at this stage I really don't know. Given the circumstances, we have to talk to him. We have no evidence that he's killed anyone. It's another reason why I don't want to go in heavy handed."

"I appreciate that," she said.

The time was drawing near and Arlene Mitchell travelled in the car with Tyler and Mills, parking at a discreet distance from the property. The surveillance around the house was equally discreet, and it would take a trained eye to realise that there was anything out of the ordinary going on that wet November afternoon in the quiet streets of Penkhull.

Mills had ascertained that there had been no activity in the property since the surveillance had been put in place. No sightings of anyone in the property at all. No clue that anyone was even in there.

Dusk was beginning to fall and everyone involved had taken up their positions, with roadblocks secured at both ends of the short street.

Tyler asked Arlene how she was feeling.

"I hope Luke's okay," she said.

He could see that she was nervous, and he doubted that it was on her own account. He knew empathy and compassion when he saw it, though it was often in short supply. But it was here in spades.

He checked his watch and nodded to Mills. Then the two detectives moved to the door at the rear of the property.

The front door had been boarded up, as had the front windows. There was no access currently through the front of the building. The back door was broken and flimsy, and Luke Summers, or else somebody mistaken for him, had been seen briefly exiting and then entering by the rear door, for whatever purpose. The neighbour had only caught a glimpse, though it had left her in no doubt that this was the man in the photograph, the man that the police wanted to speak to urgently.

There were two windows boarded at the rear of the property, leaving one, upstairs, with the pane broken. There was a straight drop beneath it, a potential escape route though hardly a very practical one.

A section of the backup squad positioned themselves with the rear of the property visible; the thickening darkness providing adequate cover. It was time, as Mills put it, *to boogie.*

"Let's keep in mind," said Tyler, "that if that is Luke Summers in there, we have absolutely no evidence whatsoever that he has committed any crime at all."

"Hearing you loud and clear," said Mills. "But be careful, sir."

The detectives went into the small back yard, Mills stationing himself a few feet from the broken back door.

Tyler entered the building.

195

CHAPTER TWENTY NINE

The door opened without offering any resistance, and Tyler edged his way into the property, peering cautiously into the cold, damp gloom. He listened carefully, before feeling his way in slowly, allowing his vision to adjust to the darkness. Mills followed on behind, ready to provide immediate support.

Tyler checked the back kitchen. The small fridge was out of action, unplugged at the wall, and when he opened it he found nothing inside. He moved methodically through the downstairs rooms; neither the larger back room nor the tiny front room revealed any signs of recent life.

Arriving at the foot of the stairs, he looked upwards to observe that the room at the top was seeping a dim light from beneath an ill-fitting door.

He started to climb the narrow staircase, one painfully slow footfall following the other, when he heard a splintering sound from behind him. He turned around quickly as Mills cursed under his breath. Then a voice above shouted, "Who's that? Who's there?"

"Sorry," whispered Mills.

"Those damned biscuits," whispered Tyler. "I said they'd be your downfall."

The detectives waited. The door at the top of the stairs was slowly opening. Two frightened eyes peered down the stairs. "Who is it, what do you want?"

"Are you alright?" asked Tyler.

"Who are you?"

"I'm here to help you."

"I don't need your help."

"Mr Summers? Luke?"

"I don't know you."

"Come downstairs, Luke. Nobody's going to hurt you."

The man's shoulders were moving, and then a gentle sound of sobbing issued.

"Luke?" said Tyler. "Let me help you."

"No-one can help me."

"Are you hungry, thirsty?"

"For what I've done there's no help. When you're in league with the devil there is no help. I killed them - I killed them all!"

"Luke, no-one's going to hurt you. Please, come down the stairs. Have you eaten today?"

"I killed the priest. I nailed him up on a cross. Do you want to know why?"

"Luke, it's freezing in here. We can go somewhere warm, somewhere safe."

"I'd never met the priest. He'd done nothing to hurt me. He was the symbol of light that must be vanquished to make way for the arrival of the Dark One. And those so-called Satanists, their insincerity will be punished in the flames of hell. They were not fit to serve the Dark One. But take heed: my work isn't finished. There are others to be taken down and punished. You must go now. I still have work to do and the time grows short."

The upstairs door closed.

Tyler turned to Mills and gestured for him to radio in the backup. Then the DCI made his way up the few remaining stairs.

At the top he listened outside the door. He could hear the sounds of sobbing interspersed with what sounded like feverish prayer. Already the backup team had assembled at the foot of the staircase, and Tyler gestured for them to hold off.

He waited for the prayer to end and then he slowly opened the door.

The man was cowering against the wall; not looking at the door, but looking up towards the ceiling, and mumbling some inaudible incantation. His features were still recognisable as those of Luke Summers, despite the wild stubble and manic, staring eyes.

"We are here to help you," repeated Tyler. "I'm going to take you where they can make you well again."

The incantations continued, and then Summers abruptly stopped, turning his head, staring at Tyler. His expression was vacant, as though he wasn't seeing the detective, but merely responding to the sense of a presence in the room.

"I have to stay here," he said. "I have my work to do."

"Arlene's worried about you. She wants to help you; we all want to help you, Luke."

"I killed all those people."

He was starting to sob again. Tyler edged closer. The sobbing stopped and suddenly Summers looked up, his eyes blazing. "I haven't finished I haven't even started they'll pile them high in the streets blood will drown the world I'll kill I'll kill I'll kill them all ..."

He was shaking, frothing at the mouth.

Mills moved in closer, but Tyler, sensing the movement behind him, motioned for him to stay back.

198

Luke Summers' eyes, like red hot coals, began to cool, and the tears came, the sobs building, heaving out of him in violent spasms. "Help me!" he screamed, and then the screaming gave way to gentle sobs, like a broken child, lost and frightened.

"Come and speak to Arlene," said Tyler.

"She can't help me."

"She wants to help you. She's here for you, Luke."

Tyler placed a hand on the man's shoulder. "Come on, let's go, shall we?"

He helped Summers to his feet and keeping hold of his hand aided him down the steep staircase. Mills had discreetly alerted backup to stay out of sight and not unnecessarily spook the man.

Tyler escorted Luke Summers out through the back yard and along the path towards the waiting car.

Arlene Mitchell stepped out of the shadows, startling Summers; until recognition brought with it the first faint signs of relief, struggling into the ghost of a smile.

They took him to the hospital. He would spend the night on the secure unit and the consultant would see him first thing the following morning. The consultant would confirm that Luke Summers had undergone a manic episode, the most extreme recorded on the patient so far. In the grip of his mania he would likely have acted irrationally, out of character; he would have displayed abnormal energy and strength and yes, it was entirely possible that he might have acted violently, though there were no marks of violence on him. He might, in the grip of such an extreme episode, have done almost anything at all, including killing people and quite possibly having no memory of what he had done. And, indeed, when Tyler and Mills were finally able to question Luke Summers about his activities on the dates of the murders, they would discover that he had no recollection of having hurt anybody, recently or in the past. Neither did he have any recollection of having confessed to murder.

Whatever the man had done, or hadn't done, his conscience appeared to be clear.

CHAPTER THIRTY

Arlene Mitchell, in the days that followed, spoke to Jim Tyler on a number of occasions regarding Luke Summers. The man was beginning to make good progress. He was eating, communicating coherently, and appearing less agitated. Yet he continued to have no memory whatsoever of living in the derelict house or decorating the walls and ceilings of his flat. The suggestion of his recent activities appeared to come as a complete surprise to him, and Arlene Mitchell was convinced that he was telling the truth as he saw it.

There were no plans to release Luke Summers back into the community, and no evidence on which to charge him with any crimes. There was no evidence at the scene of any of the murders implicating him, or anyone else, for that matter; no witnesses, and no clues.

"And yet he was aware that murders had been committed," Tyler told the CPN at a meeting at the hospital. "He even confessed to them."

"He didn't name any of his victims, though. It could have been a generic confession prompted by the approach of the police."

"Is that likely?" asked Tyler.

"It's possible. Nothing so far indicates that Luke is hiding anything. He's intelligent enough to fool me, I don't doubt that; but my instincts suggest - and I've known Luke a long time and I've seen most of his moods and phases by now - my instincts are telling me that he really doesn't remember very much at all."

"It's possible he could have committed murder and has no memory of doing so?"

"Yes."

"Though virtually impossible to prove," said Tyler.

"It's hardly a way of getting away with murder. Instead of life imprisonment it's the prospect potentially of life in a secure mental institution, where life will almost certainly mean life. If there was any history of violence on Luke's part I might have greater reservations. But there isn't any."

Tyler went quiet. After a few moments the CPN asked him if he was alright.

"I'm just wondering where to go next with my investigation."

"I wish you luck. It seems to be an unusual case."

"My cases often are. I think they must reserve them for me."

"You do a difficult job."

"We both do."

"Undervalued but luckily overpaid," she said, and they both laughed.

"I don't believe I've come across a priest being crucified, except in horror movies. The same goes for nailing people to church doors. I don't envy you."

"Thanks," said Tyler. "Let me know if there are any developments your end."

"Of course."

There was an uneasy pause, and her smile was beguiling before becoming consumed in unfettered professionalism. He returned the smile and she assured him that if she had any doubts whatsoever, or reasons to be less certain about Luke Summers, that she would not hesitate to make contact. In any event she would be in touch.

The moment hovered, and then, almost as though performing a highly choreographed dance routine, the two of them turned away to go about their business.

From the car Tyler contacted Mills, who was back at the station going over statements and reports.

"Did you get a signed confession from Summers, sir?"

"He doesn't recall a bloody thing! Listen, I want you to go back over the statements from Smee - any inconsistencies that we might have missed. And start digging into that man's past. The homes he attended. Reports on him from staff at the homes and from any other professionals involved. I have a private appointment and then I'm heading back to base. See what you can turn up, Danny."

Jim Tyler sat opposite the woman. The pressure had lifted and he spoke openly and without hesitation. He was running for pleasure these days, and not fighting the urge for the bottle every night. The devils from his past had been burned out of their hiding places; talking had done it, lifting the veil. Their power over him had been diminished to the point where he could merely relate the facts of the matter, without making a fist, and without shedding a tear. He was close to feeling sorry for them now, the sad monsters of yesteryear. None of them had ever done anything that they had not, at some level, been authorised to do. Inflicting pain and fear in measures once condoned and now condemned. That some had taken pleasure in it ... but how could that ever be quantified, proven in a court of law, all these years on?

The past was dead and buried, and Jim Tyler was singing over the ashes.

And the woman listened; and he knew that in her cold detachment she cared and heard and that was enough. He would not need to come here again, paying his money to be listened to and in his own way absolved for making himself a martyr.

At the end of the hour he shook her hand and walked out into the cold rain, fresh and alive; his only remaining torments residing in a case that he was born to solve.

Except that Jim Tyler had never believed in fate.

Mills greeted him with news. The DS had been doing as instructed and he had just come off the phone following an illuminating conversation with an old key worker once assigned to Toby Smee.

"Dan Fairbrother, sir. He worked at the care home where Smee spent five years of his childhood."

"He's still there?" asked Tyler incredulously.

"Due to retire next year. Sounds like one in a million."

"I'd like to meet this one in a million ... *though the odds sound stacked against it,*" said Tyler.

"Very amusing, sir. He's there for a few hours yet, though, so if you fancy ... *defying the odds and backing a rank outsider ...*"

"You can take a joke too far, do you know that, DS Mills?"

"I'm learning, sir." Mills looked curiously at the DCI. "Are you -"

204

"*Okay?* I was," said Tyler, displaying mock concern. "That is … until you asked me. I ought to be used to it by now. What is it?"

"I'm not sure. You look different, that's all?"

"Perhaps it's how I brushed my hair this morning."

"If I didn't know better," said Mills.

"Yes?"

"Nothing."

"No, go on. You've planted a seed so let's hear what's on your mind."

"Well, sir, if I didn't know better, and if I wasn't afraid of speaking out of turn ..." Tyler eyed his watch sarcastically. " ... I'd have to say that you'd either solved a difficult case ... or found romance."

"I see," said Tyler.

"Sir?"

"And they pay you to be a detective!" He let the moment grow. "Solved a difficult case? I should be so lucky. Come on, let's go and see Mr Fairbrother."

The home was one of the few to have survived the relentless changes that the council had implemented over the years, and Fairbrother was one of the few to have weathered those changes. A large, stout man approaching sixty, he was now the manager of the Family Resource Centre, and he was a year from retirement and counting. He was also clearly intrigued by the arrival of two detectives on his doorstep, despite Tyler insisting that these were routine and general enquiries.

In Dan Fairbrother's small office the detectives joined him, tea and biscuits in attendance and Mills determined to stay on his best behaviour.

Fairbrother wasn't fooled for a second by the DCI's downplaying of the visit, thought Mills, trying to keep his eyes off the chocolate digestives that Fairbrother seemed to be making short work of. Licking the chocolate off his thumb and taking a good slurp of tea, the keyworker-turned-manager looked thoughtful when Tyler asked him about Smee.

"This is off the record, naturally?"

"Naturally," said Tyler.

"Toby Smee was one on his own."

Having said this much Fairbrother reached for another digestive, causing Mills to panic as there were now only four left on the plate. The custard creams had likewise taken a hammering, which meant that if he didn't make a move soon it would be down to the dross - or, the way Fairbrother was going at it, only the crumbs.

Having demolished his latest conquest, he appeared to look at the detectives as though to say: is there anything else I can tell you? But the look from DCI Tyler seemed to galvanise him, causing him to sit up slightly in his chair and paint an unexpectedly vivid picture of his old charge.

The detectives listened to the description of Toby Smee as a young man who gave the impression that butter wouldn't melt, no matter what he was getting up to. "I actually found him fascinating. You could catch him with a fiver out of your wallet, still warm in his hand, and he would give the impression that you were the one with the problem for even suspecting him."

The man paused, his eyes fixed on the surviving biscuits. "The funny thing was, it was never Toby with the fiver in his hand, though. He would always get somebody else to do it and then he'd take his cut."

"Sounds like a born business man," said Mills, finally grabbing at the plate and coming back with a prized digestive, despite the look from the other two men.

"I did a lot of work with that young man," said Fairbrother, "preparing him for moving on, you know the drill: ready for the outside world and all that. They tried to place him a few times, but all the foster parents gave in eventually. It was always the same old story: Toby was disruptive and manipulative. He would play the victim, accuse all and sundry of treating him unfairly. The pattern was the same, virtually identical, in fact, and Toby was the common denominator."

"You didn't like him?" asked Tyler.

"On the contrary. I did like him. That was just it. That was what was so frustrating. He was sharp; he could be very witty; quite charming in many ways. But he had this part of his personality that let him down. It was like he had to be the victim; had to play the wounded part."

"I don't suppose that any of us are perfect," said Mills, reaching for the penultimate digestive.

"I didn't expect him to be perfect," said Fairbrother, taking no chances with the last surviving chocolate biscuit, "but it was ... he was so calculating. So - what's the word ... well, manipulative, I suppose. He liked to make the bullets for others to fire, and he seemed to delight in getting other youngsters into trouble. It was as though he couldn't help himself."

He thought for a moment, savouring a last mouthful of biscuit. "I'm no psychiatrist, and perhaps I'm talking out of turn here, but it was like it was a compulsion with him. He tried to get me into trouble a couple of times, accusing me of various things. Nothing very serious, thank goodness. It was as though he was testing the waters. Seeing how far he could go. What he could get away with. You take all of that away from Toby Smee and you were left with a smashing young man. I've often wondered how things turned out and whether that part of him ever changed." He eyed the two detectives. "Or if it kept getting him into trouble?"

The implied question failed to draw Tyler, who merely batted it off with a cursory, "You never know. People do change, sometimes."

Fairbrother looked disappointed; his candid divulgences not reciprocated.

"Was Toby ever caught doing anything serious?" asked Tyler.

A sly look came over Fairbrother. "That depends on what you mean by *serious*."

"Anything involving the police?"

He shook his head. "He was way too smart, like I've said. What kind of things did you have in mind?"

Tyler tried hard not to smile at the man's desperation for clues as to what his old charge had been up to.

"Like I said, Mr Fairbrother -"

"Dan, please."

"These are routine enquiries at this stage."

Dan Fairbrother appeared to survey the remains of the biscuits with regret, as though he had wasted abundant hospitality for little reward. Only the fig rolls had survived.

"Toby Smee hasn't kept in touch?" Tyler asked him.

208

"They never do. You bump into the odd one around town sometimes, and maybe get the chance to catch up a bit on how life's turning out for them."

"And how does it usually turn out?"

"There are winners and losers, like with the rest of society, I suppose. Most of the girls tend to be pregnant for the umpteenth time and living in squalor on benefits, the boys in and out of the nick or in dead end jobs."

"Doesn't sound like many winners to me," said Tyler.

"I had Toby down as a winner. I'd love to know how he's doing these days."

"A winner whether he changed or not?" asked Tyler.

"Now there's a question! I'd have to think about that one."

"Answers on a postcard," said Tyler standing up and stretching out a hand. "You've been very helpful. Thank you."

Walking out across the car park Mills appeared deep in thought.

Tyler said, "Mourning the might-have-beens? He's quick off the mark when it comes to a plate of biscuits, there's no doubt about that."

Mills unlocked the car. "*Makes bullets for others to fire.* I take it you're thinking what I'm thinking, sir?"

"And what am I thinking, Danny?"

"Smee using Summers?"

"His own hit man?"

"Just a thought," said Mills.

Tyler climbed into the passenger seat. "Then the question you would have to ask," he said, "is *why*?"

209

CHAPTER THIRTY ONE

In the high security wing at Cheddleton Hospital, Tyler sat in the sterile room with Luke Summers and Arlene Mitchell. Summers still had no recollection of being in the derelict house or of being in Penkhull. He was communicative when the detective asked how he was doing, and seemed to be in good spirits.

After a few minutes Tyler decided to move the conversation from a pleasant social call to the present murder enquiry. "Luke, I'd like to ask you about an old friend of yours."

Summers nodded, and smiled across at Arlene.

"Toby Smee," said Tyler, watching Summers carefully. The name failed to provoke a reaction. "Do you know Toby Smee? Do you remember him?"

Summers nodded.

"Have you seen him recently, Luke?"

"I bump into him from time to time."

"When's the last time you saw him?"

Summers appeared suddenly concerned. "Is he okay? He's not in any trouble?"

"Does he get himself into trouble?"

"No, not particularly; no more than the rest of us I suppose. He's alright is Toby."

"I understand that you met him fairly recently - at a group meeting that you both attended, in the Moorlands."

Summers looked directly at Tyler but didn't answer.

"You do know the group I'm talking about, don't you, Luke?"

Summers nodded. "*Chapter Six,*" he said. "Charles and Rose Blackwood."

"That's right."

"What a farce," said Summers. "It's supposed to be a secret cult." He laughed. "Not very secret, is it?"

"Did Toby invite you to the meetings?"

"We're not allowed to discuss any part of it. Those are the conditions for joining. It's a bit like the Freemasons but without the perks. I don't attend any more, but you're still not supposed to discuss it even after you've left."

"You have an interest in the occult?" asked Tyler.

"I thought I did. It looked interesting but in the end it wasn't. They liked dressing up and having sex with each other."

"You witnessed that?" asked Tyler, but Summers laughed.

"Just the vibe I was getting," he said. "They seemed the sort, you know."

"We know that Toby Smee attended the group, Luke, so you aren't breaking any confidences with regard to him. Did he invite you?"

"I don't want to answer your question," said Summers. "I'm sorry about that."

"Perhaps he got in touch about something else?" said Tyler.

"Like I said, we bump into each other here and there. I've not seen him since I left the group."

"And you've had no contact of any kind with him since then?"

"No."

"What about the other members of the group? Have you had any contact with any of them since leaving -?"

"No!" A hint of agitation, but quickly suppressed.

"Do you recall redecorating your flat?" asked Tyler. "I hear that your landlord wasn't too impressed."

"I don't remember doing any of that. I remember you though. I remember you coming to that cold house. I don't know how I got there. I don't know what I was doing there."

Tyler leaped at Summers' recollection of being in the derelict property. "Did anyone else visit you at that house, Luke?"

"I don't think so."

"Someone brought you food. Who was that?"

"Did they? I don't remember anybody."

Tyler was struggling to weigh the man up. It wasn't clear that Summers was lying, though it was hard to tell.

He was getting nowhere.

Outside the room he spoke with Arlene Mitchell. "I'll keep trying," she said. "Some of it might come back to him in dribs and drabs. I've known cases of temporary amnesia before, and sometimes patients regain full memory of events they had apparently forgotten."

"You don't think he remembers but is conveniently choosing to give a different impression?"

"Covering for this Mr Smee?"

"I don't know," said Tyler.

"It must be frustrating."

"It is."

She glanced at her watch. "I'd better get moving," she said. "No rest for the wicked."

"I know the feeling."

"Like I said, if anything comes up, I'll be in touch."

Tyler thanked her and they exchanged smiles. Her smile told him that she was a woman who kept her promises, and it hinted at something more than that. But whatever it hinted at, Tyler tried to put such thoughts from his mind as he strode out to his car.

Heading back to the station, the DCI took a sudden detour, arriving back at the care home and asking to speak again to Dan Fairbrother.

"Is it urgent?" asked the woman on the desk. "Mr Fairbrother has left for the day. He's in tomorrow morning, if that's any help to you."

Tyler said that it wasn't particularly urgent. Then he asked for the man's contact number.

"Are you the policeman who called to see Dan earlier?"

The woman, he thought, appeared to be sniffing scandal in the air.

Wishing to quash it before it took flame, he said it wasn't important, just something he had forgotten to ask.

The woman seemed unconvinced, but passed on the contact details anyway, with a distinct twinkle in her eye as she did so.

Fairbrother would likely be getting the third degree in the morning, thought Tyler, as he rang the number from the phone in the big man's office.

"Sorry to disturb you at home, sir. I meant to ask if you recall a child by the name of Luke Summers?"

"The name doesn't ring any bells," said Fairbrother, sounding like he was tearing through another packet of biscuits. "Was he with us at the home?"

"He was never admitted, as far as I know," said Tyler. "But he may have visited Toby Smee. I think they had been friends earlier."

"I never forget a face," said Fairbrother, the sound of a rustling packet giving way to a resounding, unmistakable munching, "but I'm not the best with names. So many kids have passed through our doors over the years, let alone the occasional visitors. You just can't keep track."

"I understand," said Tyler, a further rustle issuing followed by another loud crunch. "If I could get a photograph to you, would you take a look at it for me?"

"You sound keen on following up this young man. A person of interest, is he?"

"Just-"

"I know," said Fairbrother. "*Routine enquiries at this stage!*" He laughed. "With all of this confidentiality it's a wonder any of us ever get anything done! I'm in tomorrow from nine. If you want to call by I'll take a look."

Tyler returned to the home where Summers had last attended and asked for a photograph from the file. The staff on duty were more than happy to oblige a senior police officer in the course of his investigation and wasted no time in providing a choice of photographs of the young Luke Summers. They'd heard about their old charge being whisked off to Cheddleton High Security Hospital, and were keen to know more. Had he killed the vicar? Had he been involved with a group of Satanists, killing them off one by one?

Driving away from the home, on an impulse Tyler called at the Records Office and asked to see a press photograph of Father Berrington, the priest killed along with his wife in the fire at the rectory. The priest who had become Luke Summers' adoptive father, giving him a home after the boy's natural parents had tragically died.

The curate, Marion Ecclestone, was busy preparing for a funeral, when Tyler turned up at the church. He assured her that he would only require five minutes of her time. One of the church wardens, Phyllis Wagstaff, was also in the building, and looking thoroughly flattered when the DCI invited her to join them in the office. He showed them photographs of Toby Smee and Luke Summers as children, along with the more recent photo of Summers.

The women both shook their heads. "Should they look familiar?" asked Ecclestone. She looked again, but there was still no sign of recognition. Phyllis Wagstaff likewise couldn't say that she recognised them, though she was eager to quiz the DCI. "Are these the ones responsible?" she said. "I have to say, there's some shifty eyes on those photos."

"Oh, Phyllis!" said the curate.

"It's alright you saying 'Oh, Phyllis,' but I know shifty eyes when I see them." She was about to ask another question when Tyler thanked them both for their time, and made a hasty exit.

That evening, at his home in Penkhull, Tyler looked again at the photograph of Father Berrington, and placed it alongside the photo of Father Peterson.

215

Was there a resemblance, or was he seeing merely what he hoped to see? *A motive?* It was far too tenuous.

The following morning he showed the photo of the young Luke Summers to Dan Fairbrother, and a spark of recognition lit the man's eyes. "Yes," he said, tapping at the photo with a large index finger. "As a matter of fact I do seem to recall him. Are you certain he was never here, at this home?"

"You tell me," said Tyler.

He told the detective to wait a second, before disappearing from the room, and returning a few minutes later. "It would seem that he was never here under that name, certainly. Is it possible that his name was changed for some reason?"

"Luke Berrington?" suggested Tyler.

Fairbrother scratched his head. "That name sounds more familiar, for some reason."

Tyler knew that Summers had never been admitted to the home, as the records of his placements had been continuous, and always under the same name. But the fact that Fairbrother recognised him, that was interesting enough.

"Do you associate him with Smee?" asked Tyler.

"Well, they're a similar age, by the look of them. Have you asked Smee?"

No, I hadn't thought of that! The man was digging again.

"Berrington, *Berrington* ..." muttered Fairbrother, before suddenly clicking his fingers, loudly. "The priest who was killed along with his wife! A fire, wasn't it? I remember hearing about it at the time. It was all over the papers and on the news. And there was a rumour about a child going into one of the other homes. So that was him?"

The facts were piling up inside the head of Dan Fairbrother, and he looked hungry for more.

Tyler thanked him for his time.

From his car he rang Mills. "Danny, I'm coming in. There's something I'd like you to take a look at."

In the CID office the detectives compared notes, and Tyler took out the photographs once again.

Mills thought that both Summers and Smee looked like "a right couple of urchins, full of mischief. They remind me of some of the kids I used to hang around with at school. I've nicked a few of them over the years, and probably not for the last time, either."

He picked up the photograph of Summers' adoptive father, in dog collar and black robe. "Another one of Father William Peterson?" he said.

Tyler looked at him.

"What?" said Mills.

"Look again, Danny."

Mills studied the photo and handed it back.

"You spotted the resemblance, I take it?" said Tyler, his tongue circling the inside of his cheek.

"Perhaps it was the dog collar," said Mills.

"The late Father Berrington; consumed in the flames along with his wife."

"So, Luke Summers has a motive. He killed his parents and anyone who reminds him of his dad?"

"Just a remote theory at this stage," said Tyler. "Sounds a bit unlikely when you put it like that."

But Mills recognised the look on Jim Tyler's face only too well.

CHAPTER THIRTY TWO

As Mills parked up outside the hospital's high security wing, Tyler said, "It's often worth getting a second opinion. Is Luke Summers our man? Has he fooled everyone, intimidating and recruiting Smee as his accomplice to kill Peterson because he reminded him of his adopted father?"

"Are you intending to ask him?" said Mills.

"Not in so many words. Not at this stage."

"But what was Smee's motive?"

"Fear, perhaps."

Mills didn't look convinced.

Arlene Mitchell was out on visits and expected back in an hour. But Tyler wanted to speak to Summers right away.

The two detectives sat with him in a room on the ward. Tyler told staff stationed outside the room that it was an informal chat and to please let Arlene know they were there.

The DCI struck a casual tone, introducing DS Mills and suggesting that, as they were passing, they thought they'd pop in to see how he was doing, and maybe clarify a couple of points. "Is that alright, Luke?"

Summers offered a somewhat relaxed persona, and Mills couldn't help but wonder how long that might last once the DCI got going.

"Yes, that's alright," said Summers.

Tyler allowed Mills to excel with a few minutes of small talk, before moving in, asking Summers how he had first got involved with the cult run by Charles and Rose Blackwood.

Mills saw the way Summers had stiffened; he was suddenly anything but relaxed. He told the detectives that he wasn't sure how he had first heard about the cult. Tyler asked if Smee had told him about the group. Still Summers seemed to be having difficulties recalling the details, shaking his head repeatedly and sighing heavily.

Mills sensed Tyler's growing impatience. The DCI was in the process of coming back around to the same subject by a different route, when Arlene Mitchell appeared in the room.

Tyler stood up and welcomed her to join them. "I didn't realise you were visiting Luke today?" she said.

"Just a couple of routine questions," said Tyler. But it seemed to Mills that the CPN was far from convinced.

"I was asking Luke how he first came across the *Chapter Six* cult," said Tyler.

"I see." Arlene Mitchell looked at Summers, and he returned a frail smile. "Are you okay, Luke?" she asked him.

"A bit tired, but not bad, thanks," he said.

Tyler picked up the thread again. "Did someone invite you to a meeting at the home of the Blackwoods?"

When Summers failed to respond, Tyler said, "Did you say that Toby Smee invited you along?"

Summers looked nervous, and Arlene Mitchell moved to sit close to him.

"You knew Toby Smee from one of the care homes, isn't that right, Luke?" said Tyler.

"He was there for a bit, yes. You get moved around. I did, anyway."

"You kept in touch, though?"

Summers didn't answer.

"Did you go to visit him, or hang around with him? Maybe he visited you?"

"Not really. I might have bumped into him here and there, but we didn't really hang around. I didn't hang around with anyone."

"It must have been a difficult time for you, Luke. With what happened to your parents."

Summers nodded. "These things happen," he said. "My dad got ill and my mum couldn't cope. He had cancer and then my mum killed herself. I was on my own then."

"You were adopted, I understand?"

He looked at Tyler, and then at Arlene.

"Are you feeling comfortable talking about this today, Luke?" she asked him.

"I'm alright," he said.

"I can't imagine, Luke, how it must have been for you, after the tragedy of your mum and dad. I mean, your adoptive parents dying in that terrible fire." Tyler watched Summers carefully. "You're lucky to be alive, Luke."

"It was so long ago," he said. "I don't really know how I was feeling."

"Did you get on well with your adoptive parents?"

Arlene was eyeballing Tyler, but the DCI went on. "It couldn't have been easy for you, Luke."

"They were alright," he said. Then: "I didn't kill them, if that's what you're getting at."

"That's an interesting comment," said Tyler. "Has anyone accused you of starting that fire?"

"Not until now."

His agitation was quickening. He looked again at Arlene Mitchell. Before she had chance to respond, Tyler asked, "Did you know that Toby Smee was a member of the cult before you attended? Was it Toby who first invited you?"

Summers was coiled up now, as tense as an overwound spring.

"Perhaps you would prefer to leave it at that for today, Luke," said Arlene Mitchell, looking at Tyler.

But Tyler hadn't finished. "If there's something about Toby Smee that you aren't telling me -"

"There's nothing!" said Summers, his tone rising. "I don't know how I knew about the group, but it was nothing to do with Smee - he was just there and I don't know any more than that - so stop asking me!"

"He's not the reason that you stopped attending?"

Summers was beginning to rock forwards and backwards, looking at Arlene, and appearing tearful.

"I think," said Arlene, "that we should leave it there for today."

"Are you afraid of Toby Smee?" asked Tyler.

Summers had his hands over his ears, clutching at the sides of his head. "I don't know I don't know I don't know I ..."

Arlene Mitchell stood up. "That's enough for today," she said, and this time it wasn't a question.

*

The detectives retired to the empty visitors' lounge, while the CPN remained with Luke Summers for a little while. At last she emerged and joined them. Her look was stern.

"Are you intending to charge Luke?" she asked.

"Not at this stage," said Tyler. "I'll put my cards on the table, such as they are. Luke Summers' father dies of cancer and his mother, fanatically religious, is unable to cope and kills herself. Luke is adopted by a priest. Not long after the adoption there's a fire at the rectory killing the priest and his wife. And moving forward we now have the murder of a priest who, it's fair to say, shares a striking resemblance to Luke's late adoptive father. Now, all of this may be pure conjecture, circumstantial hogwash - but I trust you can see where I'm coming from."

"I've already said that I will do my best to talk to Luke," said Arlene Mitchell. "But to get him to open up fully may take time, particularly if his memory of events is fragmented and partial. Put too much pressure on him and, well, you see what happens."

"I appreciate that," said Tyler. "But I can't wait forever. If Luke's fooling everyone -"

"We don't know that."

Tyler eased back. "You're right," he said. "I'm sorry."

The detectives walked in silence out towards the car. As they were getting in, Tyler asked Mills for his thoughts.

"Impossible to say," said Mills.

"Don't be like that."

"Like you said, sir - it's all circumstantial. It adds up that Summers might be responsible, but there's no evidence."

A call was coming in.

The detectives listened.

Another woman had been found nailed to a church door.

Faye Winkelman.

CHAPTER THIRTY THREE

Mills took in the gruesome scene.

Faye Winkelman had been nailed, hands and feet, to the door of St Chad's church, close to Cheadle town centre, and a matter of a hundred yards from her mother's home. The scene, observed the DS, was almost identical to the one involving Jane Hopkins. Both women suffering the same hideous fate and presumably at the hands of the same killer. A priest, and now three female members of the same cult, all killed. Four murders, three with hammer and nails and one by fire.

Tyler finished a conversation with a scene of crime officer and came over to where Mills was standing.

"Copycat or the same killer?" asked Mills.

"Which murders are we talking about?"

Mills blinked. "Well - Jane Hopkins and this one, sir. The two nailed to church doors."

"Early indications suggest it's the same person. It's merely a matter of deciding *who*."

"Looks like Summers is off the hook, for two at least," said Mills.

"It would appear so," said Tyler. "Exactly the same manner of execution, in every detail apart from the location. What does that tell us, Danny?"

Mills was about to speak when Tyler said, "The men in white are now certain that Jane Hopkins was dead before she was crucified. The asphyxiation didn't occur as a result of that act of barbarism, but by being smothered. Early signs are that Faye Winkelman was dispatched in the same fashion. Your thoughts?"

"The killer didn't want to risk either of the women being found alive, and so took no chances?" suggested Mills.

"Go on," said Tyler.

"If the women knew their attacker – or attackers – and could identify them. But then why take the risk of being seen nailing two corpses to the doors? If the killer merely wanted them dead … the crucifixion part must have been symbolic. Or a warning, perhaps, to others to keep their mouths shut?"

Tyler nodded.

"Sir?"

"Let's go and find Smee."

Toby Smee was at home; his day off. He had spent it on his own, catching up with jobs around the house. He hadn't been through the door and he hadn't spoken to anyone.

Without an alibi, or even an attempt at one, it wasn't long before DCI was reading him his rights and taking him back to Cedar Lane Police Station where, in the presence of a solicitor, he would be interviewed under caution.

Awaiting the arrival of Smee's solicitor, the detectives sat together, looking over case notes and statements.

"I have modified my theory," said Tyler.

"Which theory was that, sir?" asked Mills.

"The one about Summers recruiting Smee under duress to help assassinate, or execute, a priest who dared to look like his adoptive father."

225

"And what have you come up with, sir?"

"We got it the wrong way around."

"A schoolboy error," said Mills. "So ... it was Smee recruiting Summers all the time?"

"Danny," said Tyler with a sigh, "whilst I find your master class in insubordination as fascinating and refreshing as ever, bear with me. Right, try this for size, and let's see if it fits. The likeness between the priests gives Summers a motive for killing Father Peterson. A chance encounter, perhaps, who knows, but let's run with that for a moment. It causes a reaction in Luke Summers that he can't control; but rather than acting spontaneously, he confides his feelings to Toby Smee. Knowing Summers' past, Smee exploits that ..."

Tyler appeared to be running out of steam. He battled on with the imagined scenario.

" ... So, when Smee's little harem catches wind of what has happened, and threatens to expose him, he quietens them down by killing Jane Hopkins - her death also serving as a warning to the others."

Mills looked unimpressed, and finally Tyler gave it up.

"I know," said Tyler, "you don't have to tell me. That's the part that doesn't make sense."

"One of the parts, sir. What's Smee's motive for killing the priest - for killing that particular priest? Unless of course Smee is just a nasty piece of work with a hump on his shoulder who decided to use Luke Summers to make some mischief."

Tyler shook his head. "It's not beyond the realms, but there are not many court room scenarios I know of where a motive like that can stand much scrutiny. Not without a shit-load of rock-solid evidence. Which takes us back to Summers wanting the priest dead, which does make sense ... possibly. Yet why would Smee act as his accomplice? We're back to fear. Was Toby Smee afraid of Luke Summers? I still think the other murders were cover ups. Unless …"

Tyler's phone was ringing.

Arlene Mitchell.

The DCI listened carefully before placing the phone down.

"She's been talking to our old friend again, Danny. She is nothing if not tenacious. Luke Summers, in her professional judgement, is scared shitless."

"She said that?" asked Mills.

"A technical term, no doubt. She's spent quite a bit of time with Summers since our visit and any mention of the cult seems to generate something of an acute reaction."

"That would tie in with our theory about Smee putting the frighteners on Summers, sir. But possibly not with our theory about Summers putting the frighteners on Smee. But I don't suppose that we can have it both ways."

Tyler eyed the DS in a parody of disdain.

"There's an old management technique long employed on the Force for dealing with those kinds of questions from lower ranking officers. It involves a polished boot and a proffered backside."

"Good to see that things have moved on from those good old days, sir. Couldn't Summers be more specific? I mean in regard to what exactly he's so scared of?"

"Either Summers is playing Arlene and the rest of us for chumps, or else something has seriously frightened that young man. He is giving every indication of not

227

wanting to ever leave the security of that hospital again."

Tyler stood up.

"You were about to say something, sir."

"Was I?"

"I mean, before the CPN rang. About cover-ups?"

"Ah, yes," said Tyler. "This latest killing. Faye Winkelman."

"Sir?"

"Something isn't ringing true."

Mills waited, until at last Tyler shook his head. "No, Danny, there's something but I just can't see it. Not yet. Come on, let's move."

"Time to visit Mr Smee downstairs, sir?"

"Smee can wait," said Tyler, "solicitor or no solicitor."

Audrey Winkelman was distraught, barely holding it together. Her friends had rallied and two of them were staying with her.

" ... My daughter was terrified," she told the detectives. "Her last days were full of nothing but torment. I've never seen her like that. It's all down to that damned cult she was messing with. I knew no good would come of it. But she wouldn't tell me what was bothering her. All her life, if she was worried about something, Faye would tell me about it. We were so close; we were more like sisters in some ways than mother and daughter.

"... I kept on asking her to tell me what was bothering her. I asked her if it was Smee but I knew there was more to it. She had his card marked, and she told me all about him. How he was having his affair

228

with Jane Hopkins and God alone knows who else, and how he was always trying to use the membership to get close to the other women. Yes, Faye told me all about that piece of dirt ..."

" ... Every time I asked her about that wretched group of weirdos she would just say that she was sworn to a code of secrecy. But there was something that she knew but wouldn't tell me. It was tormenting her."

"Do you have any idea what that might have been?" asked Tyler.

"If I knew don't you think I would tell you!"

Tyler looked at Mills and was about to signal that it was time to leave, when Audrey Winkelman said, "I was gone less than an hour. She had no reason to go through the door. Someone came for her. Someone turned up here and enticed my daughter to her death. They waited for me to leave. It must have been someone she knew."

"Do you have any suspicions about who may have been responsible for the death of your daughter?" said Tyler.

The grief was gathering and Audrey Winkelman looked ready to fall apart.

"That bastard Toby Smee," she said, "he wants hanging by the balls, there's no question of that. But I can't put my hand on my heart and say that I think he killed my daughter. She wasn't frightened of him; let down, yes, but her fear was somewhere else, *someone else*."

As the woman broke down, her friends moved to offer what support they could, and the detectives headed back to Cedar Lane to interview Toby Smee.

CHAPTER THIRTY FOUR

Tyler and Mills entered the interview room. Smee was looking notably nervous. Sitting next to him was his solicitor, who made a point of checking an expensive wrist-watch as the detectives sat down opposite.

"Sorry to keep you waiting," said Tyler.

"We've been waiting over an hour," said the solicitor.

"I'm afraid that murder investigations have a habit of keeping us busy. Talking of which ..."

Tyler allowed his gaze to settle over Toby Smee, moving the tension in the room up a further notch. "So, Mr Smee. Have you had the opportunity to rethink whether you have anything that might constitute an alibi for Faye Winkelman's death?"

Smee was sticking to his original claim of having been in his house alone.

"I understand that you had a close relationship with Miss Winkelman."

"That's right."

"You also had a relationship with Jane Hopkins."

Smee confirmed that this was also true.

"Were you having a relationship with Evie Ryles?"

"No."

"You said that Summers threatened you, saying that you would be next if you spoke to the police. Do you believe he was responsible for killing Jane Hopkins and Evie Ryles?"

"It's possible."

"For what reason?"

"I don't know."

"Because you were having a relationship -"

"My client has already answered your question," said the solicitor.

Tyler glanced at the solicitor and then asked Smee the question again.

"Might Summers have killed Jane Hopkins because she had been in a relationship with you?"

"I really don't know. I suppose anything's possible."

"But then why would he kill Evie Ryles?"

"I've no idea."

"Do you think Luke Summers killed Father William Peterson?"

"How would I know? I don't know that much about him. I hadn't seen him since childhood, apart from him turning up to a few meetings - and then on the carpark in Hanley."

"But you felt intimidated by him?"

"Yes. He threatened me. Of course I felt intimidated."

"Were you close to Summers as a child?"

"I wouldn't say that we were close. I knew him for a short time, that's all."

"You knew about his history?"

"Only what he told me. I think he used to make up stuff. I think he said a lot of things to get attention."

"How did you feel when he turned up 'out of the blue' at one of your meetings?"

"I was surprised to see him, naturally."

"You recognised him?"

"I did when he introduced himself, yes. I thought he looked familiar, his mannerisms, and when he said his name I remembered him."

"Mannerisms?"

"I mean - he was always nervy, full of energy. That's how I remembered him being."

"How long have you been a member of the cult?"

"I don't know exactly."

"Years?"

Smee glanced across at the solicitor. "I should think so."

"How many years - five, ten?"

"I'm not sure. Not as long as that."

"Are you the longest serving member?"

"I doubt it."

"Who's been there longer than you?"

Silence.

"Mr Smee?"

"No-one."

"You are the longest serving member?"

Mills noted Smee's increasing nervousness, and sensed that something was coming up to the boil.

"Did Charles and Rose Blackwood set it up?" asked Tyler.

The ambiguity of the question appeared to throw Smee, who glanced again at his solicitor.

"Is all of this really necessary?" asked the brief. "My client -"

"It might be relevant," snapped Tyler.

The DCI repeated the question, and when Smee still failed to answer, Tyler said, "Is something troubling you, Mr Smee?"

"It's just that ..." he said, again looking at the solicitor.

"Yes?" prompted Tyler.

"There is a strict code of confidentiality ..."

"And I'm trying to conduct a murder investigation!"

The solicitor interjected, again asking if this was relevant.

"It becomes more relevant with every passing minute," replied Tyler. "Your silence around the subject of this cult intrigues me, Mr Smee. So, I will ask you again: did Charles and Rose Blackwood originally set up the group?"

"I think so. I can't recall anyone else running it."

"And how did you hear about it?"

"I don't remember exactly. Through the grapevine, I suppose. I knew a few people who were interested in the occult, and one of them must have mentioned the group. I gave it a go and I stayed with it."

Tyler was pondering something, and Mills noted the deep thought lines creasing the DCI's forehead.

At last Tyler spoke again. "Are you afraid of Luke Summers?"

"Why wouldn't I be? He's threatened me. He ambushed me on a car park and threatened me!"

"Did he force you into helping him kill the priest?"

"I haven't killed anybody."

"Were you so afraid of Luke Summers that you would do anything he told you to do? Is that why you couldn't talk to us - because of what you had done?"

"I haven't killed anyone!" he repeated, and Mills could see that his hands were shaking. The solicitor was watching his client carefully, but still holding back.

"You had a nice little harem going, didn't you?" said Tyler. "Jane Hopkins, Evie Ryles, Faye Winkelman - have I missed anyone?"

"I didn't have a relationship with Evie, I've told you."

"Are you certain about that?"

"Of course I'm certain!"

"Why did Luke Summers kill the priest?"

"I've no idea."

"But you knew about it."

"I didn't know anything about it until I saw it on the news."

"When Faye found out about your affair with Jane Hopkins, she threatened to expose you, didn't she?"

"No."

"You shut Jane up, then Evie and Faye. They knew that you and Luke Summers had killed Father Peterson, and so you silenced them, each in turn. That's what happened, isn't it, Mr Smee?"

"No - none of it's true," said Smee. "Anyway, you were at my house the night Evie was killed."

"That's true," said Tyler. "How convenient."

The solicitor, still to break sweat, announced cheerfully that as DCI Tyler clearly had no evidence against his client, and could offer only mere conjecture, Mr Smee would presumably now be free to leave.

"How far would the cult go to honour the code of confidentiality?" asked Tyler.

Mills noted that with each mention of the cult, the tension on Smee's face deepened. The man was frightened of something, or someone, there was no question of that.

When Smee didn't answer, Tyler said, "If one of the members committed a crime, regardless of the seriousness of the crime, would the others be expected to maintain this *code of confidentiality*?"

"That's never happened."

"Let's suppose, just for a moment, that it did happen."

The solicitor made himself heard again. "More conjecture, DCI Tyler?"

"Mr Smee?" said Tyler.

Smee didn't answer.

"If one of the cult was responsible for something as serious as, let's say, *murder* ... would you break the code of silence?"

"Of course I would, yes."

"Are you sure about that?"

"DCI Tyler, my client has already answered your question."

The detective eyed the solicitor before returning his glare to Toby Smee.

"What is the penalty for breaking confidentiality, Mr Smee?"

Smee was close to tears, thought Mills, but he didn't have the look of a man about to blurt anything out.

Tyler suspended the interview.

"My client is free to go, I take it?"

"Your client is staying where he is," said Tyler.

Out in the corridor Tyler leaned against the wall.

"What did you make of Smee's solicitor?"

"Funny thing, sir, but I actually thought Smee seemed afraid of him."

"That's not how it's supposed to work, is it?"

"Hardly, sir."

"How many guesses do you need, Danny, to work out where we're going now?"

"To visit Charles and Rose Blackwood?" suggested Mills.

"Any idea why?"

"To find out what the penalty is for breaking the code of silence?"

"Get your coat."

CHAPTER THIRTY FIVE

They travelled the now familiar road out to where Charles and Rose Blackwood's farmhouse nestled in the Staffordshire Moorlands. The remoteness struck Mills and brought with it a renewed sense of foreboding. And yet, turning the case over, all the people they had interviewed, the DS kept returning to Jordan Wilson. He had not witnessed anger like that for a long time. Wilson's anger ran deep.

Grief can do strange things to people.

His instincts had screamed out that Jordan Wilson knew something; that he was in some way responsible for the death of Father Peterson.

He was suddenly aware that Tyler was looking at him.

"Cracked it, Danny?"

"I was thinking about the Wilson family."

"You're not holding a grudge, are you?"

"Not at all, sir."

"You'd be entitled to. They might have damaged your career, destroyed it, even."

"I was out of order, sir. I didn't handle it very well at all. I don't hold it against them for making that complaint."

"That's very noble and forgiving."

"I don't know about that."

"For my sins, Danny, my thoughts have been back in Stroud. I thought we were onto something with the

Pickerings. It seems we were both barking up the wrong tree."

"Certainly seems like it, sir."

They were approaching the farmhouse.

"Of course, we might be barking up the wrong tree now."

Mills didn't respond, turning off the main road and driving through an opened gate before pulling the car up and switching off the lights.

The darkness and the silence seemed to surround the detectives as they stepped out of the car. Together they walked up the path to the front door of the farmhouse.

Tyler rang the bell, and a few moments later Rose Blackwood appeared, looking surprised though not particularly concerned at being visited again by two police officers. Opening the door wide she ushered them inside and told them that Charles was in the back reading.

They were taken through to a large study filled with books, where they found Charles Blackwood sitting in an armchair, an old tome placed down on his lap as the detectives entered the room.

"Sorry to disturb you, Mr Blackwood," said Tyler.

"Don't be. I'm only catching up on an old favourite." He held up the battered hardback: *The Divine Religion* by A.F. Machen. "I can heartily recommend this one. I can lend you a copy, if you like. I have a couple of spares for potential converts," he said, grinning. "We might even get you along to one of our meetings once you've acquainted yourself with the truth."

"The truth?" asked Tyler.

"About how this world *actually* works."

Laughter issued from behind the detectives.

"He's always recruiting," said Rose Blackwood.

"It's our duty to spread the word, my dear. The real word," he added.

"I wouldn't have thought the forces of law and order would be welcome at one of your meetings," said Tyler.

"That's because you don't understand what we're about," said Blackwood, placing the book carefully on a side table before standing up. "We're not a band of anarchists and nutters out to destroy civilisation. That is a common misconception, no doubt; but one that a thorough reading of that book can easily dispel. Still, perhaps that's for another day. Enough of the hard sell. So, how can I help?"

The detectives took their seats while Rose Blackwood made drinks. They waited until she had returned, and then Tyler said, "Are you not concerned that three of your members have been killed over the last few days?"

"Naturally we are concerned," said Charles Blackwood. "But are you any closer to finding the killer?"

Tyler ignored the question and asked one of his own. "Do you have any theories as to why someone is killing members of your organisation, or who?"

Rose poured the tea.

Charles appeared to consider the question.

It felt, thought Mills, like a game of poker was underway; everyone waiting for the others to reveal what cards they were holding.

"I really have no idea," said Charles Blackwood at last. "Some crackpot Christian group, possibly, I really don't know."

239

"You haven't received any threats?" asked Tyler.

"No," said Charles. "Of course, we take our secrecy very seriously. Unless one of our members has inadvertently attracted the wrong kind of attention ..."

"Clayton Shaw was doing his best to," suggested Tyler.

"Mr Shaw is I suspect nothing more than a harmless buffoon. And, I might add, no longer a part of our group."

"There are a lot of strange people out there," said Rose. "Far more sinister than the likes of Mr Shaw."

Tyler frowned, appearing baffled for a moment by the seemingly unintended irony. "I wouldn't have expected strange, sinister types to be attracted to occult groups with an interest in - *amongst other things* - Satanism," he said. "Call me old-fashioned. But suppose the danger came from within?"

"One of our members?" said Charles. "Did you have anyone in mind?"

Mills looked from Charles to Rose, and tried to decide whether the cool innocence was genuine or contrived. It was a difficult call.

At last Tyler mentioned Luke Summers, and again Mills watched Charles and Rose Blackwood carefully. There was little or no reaction from either of them. Then Rose looked at her husband and said, "I'm afraid to say that he wasn't a man I particularly cared for."

"Dear!" said Charles, in reprimand. "We shouldn't act as judge and jury when we don't know the facts of the matter."

"I know that," said Rose. "But still, there it is."

"As I believe we indicated to you before," said Charles, "I didn't think Mr Summers was right for our

240

group. I did not ask him to leave, you understand, though I was not disappointed when he ceased to attend. His rather impetuous and unpredictable nature had, I would have to say, an unsettling effect on our membership. I think, had he stayed, others may not have done."

"Though they might still be alive," said Tyler.

"Inspector, I detect a subtext," said Charles.

"Would you care to elaborate?" said Tyler.

Charles was enjoying the game, thought Mills. But Rose appeared less comfortable.

"Correct me if I'm wrong," said Charles, "but I wonder if you think that Luke Summers may have had reason to go around murdering our members."

"And what do *you* think?" asked Tyler.

"I wonder what his motive would be. A deep-seated hatred of *Satanists*? Wishing to infiltrate our little group so that he could pick us off as a warning to others, possibly?"

"You hardly seem frightened by the prospect," said Tyler.

"We heard that he had been found and arrested," said Charles.

"And you felt relieved by that?" asked Tyler.

"Yes, as a matter of fact I did feel a certain relief. I will not bad mouth the man when I don't know the facts, but possibly your actions in searching and apprehending him confirmed something that had been in the back of my mind."

He looked to his wife.

"I would agree with Charles," she said. "Actually, I would go further. There was something about that man that I didn't trust, though I couldn't quite put my finger

241

on what it was. Aside from his disruptive qualities, alienating others in the group, there was a profoundly *disturbing* quality about him, I would have to say. I was relieved when he stopped attending and equally relieved when I heard that he was helping you with your enquiries."

"What about Toby Smee?" asked Tyler.

"What about him?" said Charles.

"Mr Smee is also currently *helping us with our enquiries*. How do you find him?"

"In what sense?"

"You can assume that I'm still talking about our enquiries," said Tyler, and Mills tried hard not to smile at the turn of phrase.

"Surely you don't think that Toby Smee had anything to do with any of this?" said Charles.

"Did you know that he was having an affair with at least two of the dead women?"

"I didn't. Even so, that's hardly an arrestable offence, as far as I understand. Or am I mistaken? The law can change so quickly these days I find."

"Were you aware of any particular tensions in the group recently?" said Tyler, ignoring the sarcasm.

Charles Blackwood shook his head.

"Mrs Blackwood?" asked Mills.

"Not at all," she said. "With the exception of Mr Summers - and I suppose Clayton Shaw, in his own way - we are a very cohesive group. Mutually supportive, despite our diverse range of occult interests, which is all credit to our membership, of course."

A look of sudden realisation seemed to overwhelm her. "Are you by any chance suggesting that three women have died because of an alleged affair?" She asked the question with an evident lack of belief that such a thing could be possible, but Mills sensed a whisper of insincerity.

Tyler's expression darkened, and his eyes narrowed. He was coming to the nub of the matter, and Mills braced himself.

"I understand," said Tyler, looking from Rose to Charles and back again, "that you operate a strict code of confidentiality. That what happens in this group remains in the group. I wonder how far your code extends."

Charles Blackwood smiled and shook his head. "You are asking me if I, or Rose, or any of us would conceal a murderer. Do I really need to answer that?"

Tyler looked at Rose Blackwood.

"Absolutely not," she said. "If for a moment we suspected anyone of committing such a crime, any crime, for that matter, we would be on the phone to the likes of you immediately. We have no interest in breaking the law, or protecting those who choose to do so."

"You don't seriously suspect Toby Smee of murder, Inspector?" said Charles, appearing somewhat flabbergasted at having to even frame such an outrageous question.

"We are following up a number of leads," said Tyler.

Rose looked almost hurt. "If we thought that Toby Smee or Luke Summers or Clayton Shaw or anybody else had anything to do with these dreadful killings ... rest assured that we would not hesitate to come forward with our suspicions."

"And yet you've already said that you were relieved when Summers was apprehended," said Tyler.

243

"We had no reason to suspect Luke Summers of anything. But when we heard that you were out looking for him, well, you begin putting two and two together, don't you."

Mills noticed something interesting. It was the look in the eye; a flicker of something that lasted no more than a moment; the subtle change in the expression on Rose Blackwood's face.

Gone was the innocence, the willingness to help, replaced by a glint of ice that assured the DS that here was a woman you wouldn't wish to be on the wrong side of.

"I'm not sure that we can be of much more help to you," said Charles Blackwood, glancing towards his wife, as though checking that she was alright. But already the glint of ice had vanished, replaced by congeniality, and a weary sadness for the troubles of the world.

"I have one last question," said Tyler, and again Mills noticed a tightening of Rose Blackwood's features, while her husband retained his poker look.

"What happens to members of your cult who break your code of silence?"

Charles Blackwood laughed. "Why, that's easy," he said. "We light a circle of black candles and conjure up the Devil! And then we offer up the offender as a living sacrifice."

"Charles, really!" said Rose.

Outside the farmhouse, the detectives got back into the car; neither spoke, yet both, in equal measure, appeared to feel the chill wind that was blowing across the moors, gathering its forces in the darkness of the bleak November night.

CHAPTER THIRTY SIX

The following morning Tyler received an early phone call from Arlene Mitchell. Luke Summers was asking to speak to him.

She was at the hospital when the detectives arrived. "He's practically on the ceiling," she told them. "He won't tell me what it is." Her focus was now squarely on DCI Tyler. "He was adamant that he would only speak to you. You should be highly honoured."

Summers was sitting on his bed, his eyes darting towards the detectives as they entered the room. Mills thought how like a frightened child he looked. His face appeared swollen, his eye sockets blood red.

They sat on the chairs provided, a few feet from the bed. Arlene asked Summers if he wanted her to remain in the room, and he said that he did. Tyler was about to speak when Summers said, "Smee made me do it. He made me kill the priest. He came to see me at my flat."

"When was this?" asked Tyler.

"I don't know. He saw me going into my flat. He made out that he happened to be passing, like it was a coincidence. But he'd been waiting for me to return. I think he'd been following me. I'm sure of it."

Tyler opened his mouth, but then held fire. He gestured to Luke Summers to continue.

"He came into my flat and he told me all about the cult he was part of. He said it was something I would be interested in. I told him I wasn't sure but then he turned up again and I could tell he wasn't going to let it go. I

246

went along - twice in as many weeks. I didn't like it and I stopped going. He turned up again and he said there was something I had to help him with."

Summers was gulping at the air, as though the rush of words had left him short of breath.

"Take your time, Luke," said Tyler.

"He said he knew about me, knew what I'd done in the past. I used to make things up - I didn't kill anybody, I've never killed - but Smee said nobody would believe me once he went to the police about it. He told me they'd lock me up and throw away the key for what I'd done."

He was gasping for breath again, and Arlene sat next to him. She took his hand and comforted him, assuring him that everything was alright and that nobody was going to hurt him. After a few minutes he indicated that he was ready to continue.

"He picked me up. He had a truck waiting outside. He drove to the entrance - Trentham Park. It was cold and raining and there was nobody around. In the back of his truck he had two planks of wood. He made me put gloves on and carry the planks into the woods. Then we waited there until the priest came. I'd never seen the priest before, so why would I kill him? Smee said that if I didn't do it he would say it was me anyway and they would believe it because I was a priest killer. Because I had killed my adoptive parents and that I hated priests."

He was sobbing. "I'd never killed anyone. I never started the fire."

Tyler waited until Summers had calmed down again. "Why did Toby Smee want to kill the priest, Luke?"

"I don't know. He wouldn't say. But I think he was scared like I was. I think that someone was threatening him, making him do it."

"Do you know who was threatening him?"

"I wondered if it was to do with the cult. I don't know."

"Why did you think it might be to do with the cult, Luke?"

Summers thought for a moment. "It was the way he was. At those meetings, I could tell that he was under pressure. The people who were running it."

"Charles and Rose Blackwood?" said Tyler.

"It was like he was under their power. I stopped going. They spooked me. I didn't want anything to do with them."

"And the two of you killed the priest in the woods?"

"We watched him coming towards us. Then Smee jumped him, took him down and taped up his mouth. He made me hammer nails into the cross to join the two sections and then I had to help lift the priest into position. He made me hammer in the nails, into his hands and his feet."

Summers buried his face into his hands, weeping.

They all waited. At last Arlene Mitchell said, "Are you okay to continue, Luke? Do you need to take a break?"

Summers looked up and shook his head. "I have to tell it," he said.

"Take your time," said Tyler.

Summers went on: "We waited until we were sure that he was dead. It didn't take long. He was an old man. The shock most likely killed him. It was a mercy if it did. Then we left, and Smee said that if the police

248

came around asking questions ... that if I said anything
the truth would come out about my past or worse I
would end up being nailed to a cross myself ... and then
he turned up one night again and said that the police
were after me and that I had to be moved ... he took me
to that house ... he brought me some food and water ... I
had to stay there."

He looked at Tyler. "Then you came for me and
that's the God's honest truth, I swear it. But they'll kill
me. They'll kill me!"

"It's alright, Luke," said Arlene. "You're safe,
nobody can hurt you here. You've been brave today,
and I'm proud of you."

Tyler asked about the other killings, the three
women.

"I don't know anything about that. I killed the priest
but I didn't hurt anyone else. I'm going to hell for what
I've done."

Again his head was buried into his hands, and he
was weeping, intermittent screams piercing the room.

The CPN quietly suggested that the detectives allow
Luke Summers some space.

Tyler stood up to leave, nodding at Mills as he did
so. Then the DCI hesitated. "Luke," he said. "Did Smee
show you a photograph of the priest?" Summers didn't
answer, his face still in his hands, sobbing. The CPN
was gesturing towards Tyler, but the DCI didn't move.
"Luke," he said, "did he show you a photograph? Did
he ask you if the priest reminded you of somebody?"

Summers stopped weeping, and a silence descended
over the room. Then he took his hands away from his
face and shouted, "I killed them!"

Tyler sat back down.

"That bastard who adopted me ... I fucking killed him and his wife. I burnt their fucking house down while they were asleep in bed and I did it because I wanted them both dead. The things he was doing to me ... every fucking night when I went to bed. I couldn't stand any more ... and when I tried to tell her, she said she didn't believe me and that little boys who made up nasty stories about people like that were going to hell ... and she told him what I'd said and she watched while he beat the daylights out of me every night for a week ... and he said that if I ever told tales like that again that was only the beginning ... and I couldn't take any more of it and so I waited until they were asleep one night and I burnt their fucking house down and I hope they're still burning in hell ..."

Tyler listened, his own eyes filling, catching the silent gaze of Arlene Mitchell.

Summers was heaving great sobs while Arlene held him close to her, his face buried into her chest as he wailed.

Tyler stood up, and Arlene mouthed to him, "*Are you alright?*"

The detectives left the room and waited outside until the CPN joined them. Emerging at last from the room, she looked quizzically at Tyler, and he asked for her thoughts on whether Luke Summers was telling the truth.

"I can't see inside a person's head," she said, "but it sounded like the truth to me. It had that unmistakable ring, wouldn't you say?"

Tyler nodded, for a moment unable to look her in the face. "Particularly the part about his adoptive parents," he said.

As the detectives turned to go, Arlene Mitchell said, "DCI Tyler?"

He turned around; her expression was beckoning him, and he walked back towards her. "What is it?" he asked.

"In there," she said. "I couldn't help ... listen: if you ever need - if you ever want to talk ... I'm here for you."

"It sounded like the truth to me, too," said Mills, as the detectives made their way across the car park. "Smee recruiting Luke Summers as the perfect fall guy - it makes sense. He knew Summers wasn't making it up about killing his adoptive parents."

At the car Tyler stopped, looking back towards the hospital; to the high-security wing housing Luke Summers.

"But why did Smee want the priest dead, and in such a brutal fashion?" he said. "On the other hand, if he was afraid of Summers ... but that only begs the question, and then we're back to why Summers would want Father Peterson dead. We have a problem with motive - unless it really was because Peterson reminded him of the man who was abusing him as a child. Or else ..."

"What are you thinking?"

"Suppose someone hurt Toby Smee just as badly."

"I'm inclined to trust Summers more than I do Smee," said Mills. "He's just confessed to murdering his adoptive parents, and his part in killing Peterson. He's not going anywhere soon and you could argue that while he was on a roll he might as well have confessed to anything else that was on his mind. And he has an alibi for the murder of Faye Winkelman, after all."

251

"Not for the others, though." Tyler shook his head. "There's more to it. We're not seeing the full picture. We're seeing ... as if through a glass darkly. Let's see if Smee can pour light into our darkness."

CHAPTER THIRTY SEVEN

Toby Smee and his solicitor were not impressed at the length of time they had been kept waiting. The solicitor made the usual noises about a complaint and Tyler didn't look the least bit concerned. He pulled out a chair and sat opposite Smee, while Mills felt the walls of the interview room begin to close in.

"I've been to see your old friend Luke Summers, Mr Smee. It looks like you've done a good job of scaring the daylights out of him."

"I don't know what you're talking about."

"I'm talking about murder and intimidation. You forced Summers to act as your accomplice."

Smee laughed.

"The two of you waited in the woods beyond St Barnabas church, and there you killed Father William Peterson. You threatened Summers with the consequences of not keeping his mouth shut."

"That's what he told you?" Smee laughed again. "He's off his head." He looked at Tyler, at Mills. "You don't believe him?"

"Why should I have reason to doubt him?" said Tyler. "He's confessed to murder already."

Mills was looking at Smee's solicitor, who appeared alert and composed. Somehow his demeanour was different to that of most of the briefs Mills had come across in his time. He couldn't quite put his finger on the difference; it was there in the relationship between him and his client.

253

Then Smee glanced at his solicitor and Mills thought: *Your brief's not just here to look out for your rights, is he, Mr Smee? He's here to make sure you don't speak out of turn.*

Mills tried to recall something. Summers had said that Smee was afraid of the Blackwoods. Mills would have put his season ticket at Stoke City on the man sitting next to Toby Smee turning out to be in the employment of Charles and Rose Blackwood.

"So," said Tyler, "why would Luke Summers try to implicate you, given that he has already made a confession of his own part in three murders?"

"How should I know what goes on inside a warped mind like his? I've already told you, he's off his head. He spent his childhood boasting about murdering his *priest-father*, for Christ's sake!"

Tyler maintained a fixed gaze on Smee.

"Isn't it obvious? He's got a thing about priests. I never even met the one he killed, so why would I have anything to do with it? Luke Summers is sick, I tell you. He's sick and he's dangerous."

"But why implicate you specifically?"

"I've told you, I don't know."

"Does he have reason to hurt you, to bear a grudge against you?"

"Not that I'm aware of. I've no idea. Who can tell with a nut like that?"

Mills leaned forward. His eyes were pointing straight at Toby Smee, but his peripheral vision was trained on the solicitor. "Could this have anything to do with the cult that you have both been members of?" he asked. "The one run by Charles and Rose Blackwood?"

Mills felt Tyler's glance, but the DS didn't flinch. He had seen the tightening in the expression of the brief at the mention of Charles and Rose Blackwood. And it had confirmed his suspicions that the Blackwoods were more than a name to this man.

He was there to make sure that they were kept out of it.

Mills eased back in his chair.

"Let's go back to the murders of Jane Hopkins, Evie Ryles, and Faye Winkelman, shall we, Mr Smee?" said Tyler.

"I take it Summers has blamed me for those too?"

"You were having a relationship with at least two of those women before they died."

"That hardly means I killed them. Did Summers reckon he was my accomplice in killing them as well?"

"On the contrary," said Tyler. "He maintains that he had nothing to do with any of those deaths."

Smee laughed again, sardonically. "And you take his word?"

"Is there any reason I shouldn't?"

"It seems obvious to me," said Smee, "that Summers is crazy enough to have killed them all."

"Why would he kill them?"

"Who knows what goes on in the mind of a psychopath? But I can have a bloody good guess."

"Be my guest," said Tyler.

"Well, he's already admitted to killing the priest, so I reckon the other killings were about keeping people's mouths shut."

"But how would the women know that Summers had killed the priest?"

"That's your job to find out, isn't it?"

"It doesn't seem to add up, does it, Mr Smee? On the other hand, you were close to the women; you had known them all for some time, and had been having an intimate relationship -"

"It doesn't mean I killed anybody!"

"Why did you invite Luke Summers to the meetings?"

"I didn't. He just turned up. And everyone could tell that he was unstable. Maybe he targeted the women because he thought they'd upset him in some way. He was paranoid, ask anyone who's ever met him. He's a scary guy."

"You were scared of Luke Summers?"

"Yes, I was scared of him. It doesn't surprise me that he's a killer."

"Do you believe that he was envious of you, Mr Smee?"

"Why would he be envious of me? He hardly knew me."

"Perhaps he thought your life was working out better than his," said Tyler. "Perhaps he was envious that you had a girlfriend - and maybe more than one."

Smee looked about ready to react, when his solicitor gave up his apparent vow of silence. "You wouldn't be attempting to lay a trap for my client, would you, DCI Tyler?"

Tyler ignored the question, keeping his eyes trained on Smee.

Whether Smee needed the cautionary reminder from his brief, he heeded it anyway. "Summers wouldn't have known that I had a girlfriend," he said at last. "I had very little to do with him." He seemed to be thinking over the conundrum, before appearing to experience a light-bulb moment. "Unless - unless he's been spying on me."

Mills noted the glib way that the sudden 'revelation' was expressed, the DS suspecting that it had been prepared well in advance. Suddenly Luke Summers did have a motive after all for killing three women: to hurt Toby Smee and implicate him in killing the priest.

Except that Summers couldn't have killed Faye Winkelman ... but neither could Smee have killed Evie Ryles.

Mills noted the smug look on the solicitor's face. It was a look suggesting that his client had played everything according to plan.

There was little left to be said, and the solicitor didn't delay playing the last card of the session, asking if his client would now be free to leave the police station as there was clearly no evidence on which to charge him for any of the murders.

All four men in the interview room knew it: Toby Smee was free to go.

CHAPTER THIRTY EIGHT

"I want him followed," said Tyler, watching Smee leaving with his brief.

Mills organised the tail on Smee while Tyler made phone calls. As the DCI was ending a call, he looked up to see the DS standing in front of him, clearly bursting with news. "Go on, then," he said. "You look like the cat that's got the mouse by the balls."

"He's turned up at the Blackwoods' farm, sir."

Tyler's expression slowly unfolded into a broad, consuming grin. "The mists begin to clear at last," he said, standing up and reaching for his jacket.

According to staff at the hospital, Luke Summers had been much calmer since talking to the detectives. On the journey over Tyler had suggested to Mills that perhaps confession really was good for the soul. And yet, as they again entered the man's room, he appeared anything but calm.

"What do you want?" he shouted. "I've already spoken to you. Leave me alone!"

Mills tried to assure him that he was safe from harm, that no-one was going to hurt him, but that it would be helpful if he could answer a couple more questions.

"I'm tired, why can't you leave me alone, I've told you everything I know and I'm not saying anything until Arlene's here!"

Arlene Mitchell was out on a visit. She would, according to the office diary, be back in a few minutes.

Tyler told Luke Summers that he was prepared to wait, if that's what he wanted. But Summers changed his mind and said that he would rather get it over with.

Tyler came straight to the point. "I want you to be very honest with me, Luke. I want you to cast your mind back to your recent dealings with Toby Smee."

Mills watched as Summers' agitation began to accelerate once again.

"Did Smee ever talk about, or mention, the priest - Father Peterson, I mean - abusing children?" Tyler asked him.

Summers looked frightened, and on the edge of tears.

"This is very important, Luke," said Tyler.

"I'm not sure. I can't remember."

"Take your time," said Tyler. But Summers was becoming increasingly distressed, tears running down his face.

"Toby Smee can't hurt you, Luke. You're safe here."

But still Summers wouldn't say anything; and he was swinging his head from side to side, sobbing loudly.

Tyler waited for a lull in the storm, and then he tried again.

"Is there someone else you're afraid of, Luke? Someone else who's frightened you? You mentioned the cult. Charles and Rose Blackwood -"

Without warning, he exploded.

"Why can't you leave me alone I've told you everything I know you're killing me you're fucking killing me." Summers was on his feet, looking around the room as though trying to establish an escape route,

259

and then looking at the detectives, gulping at the air and screaming for help.

Two members of staff came running into the room.

"It's alright," said Mills, "we're not here to hurt you, Luke. Arlene will be back in a moment. We'll wait until she gets here, shall we?"

Summers nodded, crying.

The two staff members held back.

"Then we'll wait," said Mills, catching Tyler's eye.

He recognised again the impatience in the DCI, and thought: *Two damaged souls in this room.* He smiled, from one to the other. "I wonder if they do nice cakes here?" he said. "I bet they do, in a place as good as this. I don't know about you two, but I'm famished." Then he stroked the dome of his belly for good measure. "Let's see what they can come up with, shall we?" he said. "By the time we've had a nice cuppa and a few biscuits and cakes I reckon Arlene will be back."

Mills nodded at the two staff, and winked. "I reckon a bit of chocolate on those biscuits and some cream in those cakes is just what the good doctor ordered."

The three men sat drinking the teas provided, and Luke Summers and Danny Mills shared an evident love of custard creams and chocolate éclairs, while Tyler sat looking on, intermittently checking the time.

When Arlene Mitchell finally joined them, only crumbs remained, and the tea had been drunk.

"I'm sorry to have kept you," she said. "I hadn't realised you were -"

"We wanted to ask Luke a couple more questions," said Tyler. "He prefers you to be here."

She sat down with Luke and asked him how he was feeling. His eyes filled. "I told Toby Smee what I did," he said. "When I met him in care I told him."

The words began to pick up pace. "I told him about my dad dying, and my mum couldn't handle it, and she killed herself." He took a few breaths, and then he launched into a retelling of his tale. "... She was obsessed with religion and then she hated God ... and they made me live with a priest and his wife ... and he used to torture me, if I didn't get it right ... and I tried to run away, but they wouldn't believe me and they kept saying that he was a man of God and wouldn't do those things ... and they made me go back and then things got worse and then things got a lot worse and in the end I couldn't stand any more of it and I started that fire ... I killed him, I killed his wife, and Toby Smee was the only person I ever told and then I pretended that I'd made it up ... but I knew he didn't believe me."

Summers was telling it as though for the first time, and reliving the fear, the pain and the anger. Arlene was comforting him.

The detectives waited until he had regained some composure.

"Smee told me that there was a priest who had been just like that one who tortured me and called himself my father. But he was never my father or anything like my father. My dad was a good man, he was the best ever, and he was always good to me and kind to me and he would never hurt me. Smee said I would feel better if I helped him to teach this other 'monster' - that's what he called him: *a monster* - he said I'd feel a lot better once we taught him a lesson. He said it was my duty to do it, and that I had been given a special opportunity. He convinced me. He said that the *monster* even looked like that bastard who tortured me ... and he did, too. He was older, and when I saw him ... I still wasn't sure I could go through with it - but when I saw him approaching us through the woods, I thought: it could be him, a few years older, *it could be him.* I knew it wasn't, but a part of me ... a part of me almost believed that it was ..."

As the words began to peter out, Tyler said, "Had this priest - the one in the woods – had he hurt Toby Smee?"

Summers shook his head.

"Had he hurt someone Smee knew?"

Summers nodded.

"Did Smee tell you the name of the person he hurt, Luke?"

"I don't know. I don't remember."

"How did Smee know what your adoptive father looked like?"

"He said that he'd seen the story in the papers and on the news."

"Was it recent, when the priest - when Father Peterson - hurt this other person?"

"It was a long time ago. It wasn't around here. He said that the priest had moved to this area because of what he'd done ..."

Tyler looked at Mills and nodded in confirmation. "Does the name Pickering mean anything to you?" Summers again shook his head. "Was it something that happened when the priest lived in *Stroud*?"

"Somewhere like that, I don't know. He reckoned that I would be doing everyone a favour. That I owed it to those other victims."

"Did he offer you money for helping kill Father Peterson?"

"He said there would be money for me. He said it was my compensation for what had happened to me - in the past. But it was never about money, not as far as I was concerned. He tricked me. He *used* me."

Summers cried, softly.

"It was Smee," he said. "... He told me that *he* was abused at one of the homes. That there was a syndicate and Peterson had been part of it. He said that he had abused youngsters all over the country. He said he had lived down south and had to move up here because of accusations against him. He said Peterson had lived here before, when Smee was in care. He told me the things Peterson had done to *him*. It was all bullshit."

"Did Smee say anything to you about Faye Winkelman, Evie Ryles, or Jane Hopkins?"

"I knew he was seeing one of the women from the group. I didn't know any names."

Tyler frowned. "But you do know those names, and you met those women?"

"I don't know what I know ... I didn't hurt any of those women."

"What about Charles and Rose Blackwood?"

"What about them? They ran the group. I've told you, I found them scary."

"What else do you know about them, Luke?" asked Tyler.

"I don't know anything else about them."

"Were they involved in the killings?"

Summers was sweating, his agitation building once again. "I don't know anything about them. I've told you everything I know."

"You said that Smee was afraid of them. Why was he afraid of them, Luke?"

Summers was on his feet. "Leave me alone; I don't know any more than I've told you already, why do you keep on hounding me?"

"Are you afraid of them, Luke?"

He started screaming, and Arlene Mitchell tried to calm him down as the detectives left the room.

Berkins was on the phone when DCI Tyler entered his office. When the CS had finished his call, Tyler brought him up to speed on the latest developments.

"So, Luke Summers has confessed to killing his adoptive parents, as well as assisting with the crucifixion of Father Peterson. Is he prone to making confessions?"

"Apparently not, and his CPN is inclined to believe that he's telling the truth. I want to make a request," said Tyler.

"A request?" said Berkins, nervously. "What kind of request?"

"I want to check out recent financial transactions of the Pickerings and the Blackwoods."

"Is that all!"

"For the moment."

"You're suggesting some sort of a contract taken out on Father Peterson because of the alleged assault on Tony Pickering?"

"I know," said Tyler, "when you put it like that."

"I'm not sure how else I can put it, Jim. Those I have to answer to are likely to ask me what kind of films my staff are watching these days."

"The Pickerings know something, and they were determined to see justice done. That is, if you can ever call doing something like that to another person 'justice'. But then again, a part of me does understand it."

"Jim?"

"Forgive me. I was thinking aloud."

"*So I noticed!* I've never asked you about your past, and I'm not going to start now. But suffice to say, I need to know that you're not ..."

"Leaping to conclusions that are convenient to settling old scores?" Tyler shook his head. "If that was the case, then I might be inclined to say that Peterson *did* get what he deserved. But then I would be the last person to be going after the Pickerings, wouldn't I? In fact, I might rather be inclined to say good luck to them."

Berkins weighed up the man sitting in front of him. "I trust your integrity absolutely, Jim. I will do everything I can to grant your request. Leave it with me."

Tyler was at looking at the phone when Mills entered the office.

"Expecting a call?" asked the DS.

"I'm hoping for third time lucky," he said, lifting up the handset and punching redial. After a few moments his eyes brightened and he lifted a thumb towards Mills.

"Mr Pickering?"

Ending the call Tyler thought for a moment. "That was interesting," he said. "Gerald Pickering received a phone call a couple of weeks ago. At first he thought it might have been a crank call. The caller said he

265

understood that Pickering had a problem with a priest who had moved to Staffordshire."

"Interesting," said Mills. "Was the priest named?"

"No, he wasn't. The caller said that he sympathised with anyone who had been abused, and that sometimes justice could not be gained through traditional methods. That sometimes, what he called 'alternative routes to justice' had to be explored. The caller told Pickering that one simple transaction would ensure that justice was achieved."

"A hit job?"

"That was the strong implication. Pickering said that he was given twenty four hours to think about it, and that the caller would ring again after that time. Pickering said that he was scared, and that he intended going to the police. He thought the whole thing was a scam to get money, and he hadn't a clue how the person had got hold of his number."

"He hardly made a secret of his son's accusations against Father Peterson," said Mills. "Gerald Pickering is fairly high profile, and easy enough to trace."

"Anyway," said Tyler, "the caller rang back and Pickering said he wasn't interested."

"And that was the end of it?"

"It seems so. But when he heard about the death of Peterson he panicked. He said that he was afraid that if he went to the police, either it would make him look guilty for the murder of the priest, or else whoever had done this would go after him."

"Do you believe him?" asked Mills.

"Sometimes," said Tyler, "I surprise myself. As a matter of fact I do believe him. I knew he was hiding something, and this fits. You heard me tell him that I was requesting access to his recent finances?"

"I did, sir."

"And you thought no doubt that it was good of me to give him advance warning?"

"Now you mention it, sir."

"Well, he told me he had nothing to hide and that I was welcome. I'm not that big a fool, Danny. I know that rich men like Gerald Pickering can keep a great deal of their funds hidden from the prying eyes of any authority, be it the tax man or the detective. Looking over Pickering's finances will I'm sure tell us nothing at all."

"But his manner on the phone told you a great deal?"

"I also want to see the Blackwoods' dealings."

"If they're involved, won't the same thing apply?"

"It might."

The internal phone was ringing. Tyler picked up. "Thanks, Chief," he said. "Much appreciated."

"Berkins has authorised it already?" asked Mills.

"He's sending out officers to secure the finances of both parties."

CHAPTER THIRTY NINE

Charles and Rose Blackwood hadn't put up much of a fight, by all accounts.

"The officers tasked had the impression that they had anticipated something like this happening and hadn't seemed surprised to have a detail of officers descending unannounced to scrutinise their business dealings."

"That alone makes me suspicious," said Tyler, sitting across from the CS.

"It had a similar effect on the officers, Jim."

"What have they found?"

"It's hard to say. The financial dealings are vast and complex. There's a particular transaction that may be of interest. It's substantial, and incoming; a one-off; an indirect feed into one of their concerns. It would have been easy to overlook, given the way it was set up."

"Nothing on the Pickerings?" said Tyler.

"Nothing at all."

"I'm not surprised."

CS Berkins picked up an incoming call, and Tyler watched as the Chief's expression fell into a deep frown. "I see. Okay. Yes, I understand. Thank you." Berkins placed the phone down and sighed. "Apparently it's all 'above board and accounted for'."

"And that's it?"

"It looks that way. There's nothing else giving cause for suspicion, and nowhere else to go. It was a good try, Jim."

Later that evening Tyler put on his running clothes and set out into the dismal November darkness. The case had seemed to be coming into focus, but either they had been barking up the wrong tree, or else the Blackwoods had been too well prepared and too clever.

The miles stacked up, and Tyler at last returned to his home in Penkhull feeling tired and frustrated. The run had done nothing to ease the tension that was building inside him.

Loneliness began to descend on Jim Tyler. He hoped that Danny Mills was having a better evening.

Mills had spent the remains of the evening in front of the television with his wife, watching a crime drama that he hadn't been following. His mind had taken flight elsewhere, busily going back over the investigation and failing to come up with anything new. At last, when the programme had ended, he followed his wife up to bed. She was reading a magazine when he entered the bedroom.

"So, what now?" she said, without looking up.

"Good question."

As he climbed into bed, his wife looked over. "You're tired," she said. "Maybe things will look a bit clearer after a good night's sleep."

"I wouldn't bank on it. You know, I would have put my pension on this having something to do with that family."

"You mean the Wilson family? You're not still a little bit sneeped because they made a complaint against you?"

"Thanks!"

269

"I'm sorry, I didn't mean ..."

"That I'm a small-minded little man who takes offence too easily?"

"Danny -"

"I know," he said. "Perhaps you're right."

"It was a bit of an over-reaction on their part," she said.

"It was. And that's what I keep coming back to."

"But like I said before: grief can do funny things to people."

Mills watched his wife reading for a few minutes; mulling things over without making any progress.

She was still the beautiful woman he had once fallen in love with, and even if she had dragged him and his kids out from the city and into the God-forsaken country, he doubted that he would ever stop loving her. A swell of desire took hold of him, and he was about to make his request for a nightcap when she yawned, heavily. She was a woman who knew when she wanted to sleep, and nothing as humdrum as mere physical desire could ever get in the way of her insatiable need to close her eyes and find rest once a yawn of that magnitude had been issued.

On cue, she turned to him and kissed him once on the cheek, before bidding him a sleepy goodnight and turning out her light.

Turning out his own light, he lay in the darkness, listening to the familiar sounds of his wife settling down and the soft snores that soon followed. His mind once again moved over the investigation, as something seemed to edge closer, almost within reach, almost in focus in the last moments before he too gave up the fight and succumbed to the overpowering call of sleep.

DCI Tyler was awake early, and he climbed out of bed wondering whether to take to the streets again. If one more run would bring clarity.

He thought of Arlene Mitchell, and wondered if he would ever take up her offer; and if it was something more than the offer of someone who would listen, that was calling him to her. He'd had his fill of living in the past and reliving it, wasn't it time to move on? He thought of Luke Summers, confessing to parenticide, and to killing Father Peterson and accusing Toby Smee of coercing him into murder.

But Smee had no evident reason to kill the priest. Unless his 'confession' to Summers of having been a victim of Peterson's had any truth to it, which seemed unlikely. Or unless Smee was motivated purely by money. *A hitman*? Was Smee the anonymous caller who had contacted the Pickerings? But if that was the case, who had taken out the contract on Peterson if not the Pickerings?

Whose money was at the bottom of this?

Mills was dreaming. He was munching on a nice warm burger down at the Britannia Stadium and watching his beloved Stoke City putting five goals past the European Champions. And then he was out in the country, feeling lost and disorientated. Someone was holding up a card and he couldn't quite read what was written on the card, and so he walked closer ...

Danny Mills woke up in the darkness of the room.

"The date?" he said.

His wife murmured next to him.

Mills sat up and tried to collect his thoughts.

271

Something and nothing? He checked his watch; it was still early. He wondered if Jim Tyler was out running again, pounding the streets to clear his mind.

Without thinking any further he allowed instinct to win the day, leaping out of bed and rushing downstairs.

Tyler was about to set off into the darkness when his phone started ringing. He picked up.

"That transaction," said Mills. "The Blackwoods - what was the date?"

Tyler thought for a moment, and told him. After a few moments of silence from the other end of the line, Tyler said, "Why do you ask?"

"I'd have to check," said Mills. "But I think that was around the day of the funeral."

"Whose funeral?"

"Marjorie Wilson," said Mills.

"You're not going to leave that one alone, are you?"

"Can we get access to the Wilsons' finances?"

"We can try."

CS Berkins was shaking his head. "We have absolutely no evidence, Jim. We've already had one complaint from that family."

"*Exactly.*"

"Meaning?"

"The more I think about it, the more I see it as a strategy."

"What are you talking about?"

"Scaring us away from closer scrutiny."

"I'm not convinced," said Berkins. "I'm not convinced at all." Then he placed his hands over his face. "I shouldn't," he said. "Jordan Wilson will hang us out to dry. He has the wealth and the influence ..."

Berkins slammed a fist down on the desk. "Okay, Jim - granted! I will get the authorisation and begin planning my retirement this evening."

"I believe golf is very popular with retired Chief Superintendents," said Tyler.

Jordan Wilson and his solicitor had erected every block available to them, yet the transfer from his account still stood out like a sore thumb. His legal team, however, didn't bat an eyelid. The attempts by the police to harass a family grieving from their tragic loss did not make the business dealings the least bit suspect. The money could be accounted for by legitimate means.

"The Blackwoods and Jordan Wilson have complex businesses, covering a multitude of sins, I don't doubt." Tyler appeared to be thinking aloud, and Mills listened attentively. "The difference, however, is that the Blackwoods have almost certainly done this kind of thing before," he continued. "Their dealings were strictly business, but not so for Jordan Wilson. He acted impulsively, out of anger and pain, and he's tried to cover his tracks."

Tyler smiled as he looked at Mills.

"That's all conjecture and speculation on my part, you understand? Still, he's left enough of a question mark for us to go back to the Blackwoods and dig deeper. Maybe they should have spaced the payment out. An instalment plan. Was someone greedy for their money, and somebody else too eager to see the job done? Perhaps the Blackwoods were wise enough to hold off payment to Toby Smee, or to disguise payment, but failed to demonstrate the same wisdom and restraint when it came to getting their hands on Wilson's blood money. The link was disguised on the recipient's side, but Jordan Wilson has been less canny."

He put on the brakes. "Sorry, Danny: more conjecture and speculation. I find that once you start it's hard to stop. Let my example be a lesson to you."

"Shall we bring them in, sir?"

"I think it's time to throw a party."

"It's close to the season for it, sir."

"So let's invite Charles and Rose Blackwood - and not forgetting Jordan Wilson." A broad grin crossed his face. "Actually, I have an idea."

Mills steeled himself.

"I want to add two more names to the guest list. I want Gerald and Tony Pickering."

"I'll send out the invites right away, sir."

CHAPTER FORTY

The interview rooms were all in use. Charles and Rose Blackwood; Jordan Wilson; Gerald and Tony Pickering. They had all arrived protesting innocence and threatening complaints.

Charles Blackwood's solicitor was the same one who had represented Toby Smee, and Tyler pulled no punches in telling the man that it was an unexpected treat seeing him again so soon. The solicitor scowled but said nothing. He clearly preferred to let his client do the talking.

And Charles Blackwood talked; he was openness personified. He had nothing to hide. Rose Blackwood, the more tight-lipped partner, took a different approach. She allowed the solicitor to play his part, and an hour later the detectives were no further forward. The Blackwoods had done nothing wrong; and whilst they were happy to aid the police in their enquiries, arresting them on the flimsiest so-called evidence that they had received money in payment for an execution - well, it was plainly ridiculous.

"It's polished and it's rehearsed," said Tyler in hushed tones, out in the corridor. Mills concurred. "We can't prove a thing and they know it. Which leaves us with one last hope."

"Smee?" said Mills.

"They'll be subtle about it," said Tyler. "If they're too obvious it will come back on them when we arrest Smee. But then it won't look good that they kept their suspicions about him to themselves. Come on; let's see how they play it."

The detectives took their seats once more opposite Charles Blackwood.

"I want to ask you about one of the members of your cult," said Tyler.

"Fire away," said Blackwood. "I'll assist you as far as I'm able."

"Toby Smee," said Tyler.

"What about him?"

"We have reason to be believe that he is involved in at least one murder, and quite possibly more."

"Have you spoken to him?"

"You don't seem particularly surprised by my accusation," said Tyler.

"Nothing much surprises me anymore."

"Have you had your suspicions about him already?"

"No," said Blackwood. "Not at all. But I don't know him that well, you understand."

"I *understand*," said Tyler, "that Mr Smee has been a member of your cult for some considerable time. Many years, in fact."

"That's true. We meet perhaps a couple of dozen times a year and exclusively because we share an interest in the occult. We don't meet socially. We don't *really* know each other beyond our shared interests. In the same way a rogue employee in any organisation does not prove that his or her manager is also corrupt."

"Are you suggesting that he's the rogue member in your organisation?"

"No, I'm not. I'm merely using an analogy to illustrate a point."

276

"You are aware that he was having affairs with female members of the group?"

Charles Blackwood shrugged. "That's his business. Why would I wish to interfere in his private life?"

"Do you like Mr Smee?"

"*Like* hardly comes into it. As I say, we shared a common interest. He had many interesting views on the subject. We were hardly friends, but that's true of all our members. We shared an interest and we met regularly to indulge our passion."

"Okay," said Tyler. "I'll put it another way. Did you trust Mr Smee?"

"I never had reason not to trust him."

Tyler paused for a moment. He looked first at the solicitor, who was sitting quietly by his client's side, and then he turned his focus back on Blackwood. "You didn't like Luke Summers, Mr Blackwood, and yet Smee introduced Summers to your group."

Blackwood frowned. "I'm not aware that he introduced him."

"But it was clear that the two men knew each other, that they had a history. Didn't Smee answer your inevitable questions about Luke Summers?"

Blackwood appeared to consider the question carefully, and DS Mills noticed a tightening in the demeanour of both Blackwood and his brief. For a moment it looked as though the solicitor was about to step in with a response, but then Blackwood said, "I did ask Toby about Luke Summers. It was clear that their paths had crossed. I got the distinct impression that Toby was not especially keen to renew the acquaintance of Luke Summers."

"So, if Smee hadn't invited him along, how did Summers come to attend?"

"I really have no idea."

"Do you not look into the backgrounds of your members?"

"We are not the police," said Blackwood. "We don't have to vet our membership. Having an interest in the occult is generally our sole requirement."

"And Summers had that?"

"He appeared to, yes."

"But?"

"He had something of a disruptive personality. He made other members feel uncomfortable."

"Did he make Smee uncomfortable?"

"I think it's fair to say that he had more of an effect on our female membership."

"Smee didn't ask him to be removed from the group?"

"No," said Blackwood.

The interview was paused, and the solicitor asked if Rose would now be re-interviewed. When Tyler confirmed that was the case, the brief left the room to walk the short distance to find his other client.

On the way along the corridor to re-interview Rose Blackwood, Mills said, "He's hardly hanging Toby Smee out to dry, sir."

"Perhaps he believes that to be the duty of a wife," said Tyler.

The solicitor was sitting with Rose Blackwood when the detectives entered the room.

Tyler asked the same questions, and received a more muted response than the ones her husband had given.

But there was nothing contradictory, and nothing damning of Toby Smee.

DCI Tyler prepared to play his card.

"Were you at all intimidated by Luke Summers?" he asked her.

"As a matter of fact, I was."

"In what way?"

"There was something unsettling about the man. I was glad when he stopped attending."

Tyler offered a conspiratorial smile. "And you thought the same about Toby Smee, didn't you? You never liked him, or to put it another way, you never entirely trusted him."

The detectives watched her hesitation, her glance towards the solicitor. *A fine thread to hang Smee with,* thought Mills.

"Can you tell me exactly why you didn't like or trust Mr Smee?" said Tyler.

"I didn't say that I didn't like or trust him," she said. "Those were your words."

"You knew he was having relationships with female members of the group?"

"That was his business, and nothing to do with me."

"Do you think that he was the reason Summers began attending?"

"He may have been. I wondered if that was the case, though Toby suggested that he wasn't responsible and that neither was he keen on the man."

"But still?"

"I must say," said Rose Blackwood, "that despite Toby Smee telling us that he wasn't keen on Mr Summers, they seemed to get on rather well."

"Do you think it possible that Smee and Summers conspired to murder the priest?"

"I have no reason to think they did. Summers struck me as somewhat unstable. As for Toby Smee ... now that you mention it, they did seem to, how can I put this? They seemed to gravitate towards each other."

"Did any of the female members ever express concerns to you about Toby Smee?"

Rose Blackwood shook her head.

"None of them came to you regarding anything that they had witnessed, or that they wanted to discuss regarding Toby Smee?"

"No," she said. "That never happened."

"Have you ever recruited the services of Toby Smee for any part of your business dealings?"

"No."

"You have never paid him for anything?"

"Not that I'm aware of. Have you checked with Charles? He generally deals with the financial side of things."

Rose Blackwood looked about to say something, and then hesitated.

"What is it?" asked Tyler.

The woman held up her hands. "I'm sorry," she said. "I should have said something."

"About what?"

"Jane Hopkins. She had concerns."

"Regarding?"

"Regarding Toby Smee. Nothing concrete, you understand. She felt that he was acting what she called *strangely*, but wouldn't elaborate. Evie and Faye also mentioned him. I put it down to jealousy. I'm not stupid. I knew Toby was having an affair with Jane and

Faye at the same time, and probably with Evie too. I know how women can be about these things. I wondered if they were out to cause trouble."

"And when the three of them were murdered you didn't think it worth mentioning?"

"I've been stupid, haven't I? I never imagined that Toby Smee could have been capable of killing anyone. He just ... didn't seem to be the type."

She looked at the detectives with a sudden expression of horror. "You think he really did kill them? And you think ... you think he may also have killed the priest?"

Out in the corridor, Tyler said, "Subtle enough, would you say?"

Mills grinned. "I'd say that she played that about perfectly. I don't have any doubts."

"It's going to be hell proving it."

The detectives walked into the third interview room, where they found Jordan Wilson and his brief.

"Glad you could join us!" said the solicitor.

"Sorry to have kept you waiting," said Tyler. "These murder enquiries never seem to go to plan."

"A complaint has already been made against ..." the solicitor looked at Mills ... "one of your officers."

"On the day after your mother's funeral, Mr Wilson," said Tyler, ignoring the solicitor, "a large amount of money was moved from one of your business accounts. I would like you to explain the nature of that transaction."

"Isn't that confidential?" asked Wilson.

"Not in the context of a murder investigation it isn't. What dealings have you had with Charles and Rose Blackwood?"

Wilson looked rattled.

"A large sum of money appears to have been paid *indirectly* into Charles Blackwood's account by you on the day following your mother's funeral. I want to know what services you were paying for, Mr Wilson."

Wilson appeared less angry now, his natural belligerence giving way to fear and uncertainty.

Tyler, tiring of a barrage of "No Comment" paused the interview.

He walked back across to the interview room where Rose Blackwood was sitting alone.

"Jordan Wilson," he said, "is sitting a few yards from here, answering questions, some of which concern you and your husband."

"I want my solicitor present if you're going to interview me again," she said.

"The Pickerings didn't take the bait, did they? You thought they would have paid to find justice, your kind of justice. You've had dealings with Jordan Wilson before, though, haven't you?"

Rose Blackwood looked confused. "Yes," she said. "I believe so. Some time ago. We have done business with him, and it was all above board - I'm sure you will have checked. My husband will -"

"You heard about his mother?"

The coolness slipped from Rose Blackwood's expression.

"It must be difficult, coming to terms with a loved one dying a horrible, lingering death like that," said Tyler. "She was a Christian. Her husband was a

Christian. They put their faith in God, and in a priest named William Peterson. God, or the priest, whichever way you choose to look at it, let poor Mrs Wilson down. Jordan Wilson doesn't like people letting him or his family down, does he?"

"I don't know what you mean. I want my solicitor -"

"Has a temper, doesn't he, Jordan Wilson, and he wanted to even the score, as he saw it, didn't he? But he was never going to get his own hands dirty, not a man of wealth and status like him. You told him you could find justice for his mother, didn't you? That for a price you could ensure that the priest died a death just as brutal as his mother had died."

"I have never heard anything quite so preposterous."

There was fear and trembling in her eyes, though, thought Mills.

Tyler went on: "Like Wilson, the Blackwoods don't get their hands dirty either ... *do you?* That's what the likes of Toby Smee and Luke Summers are for. Smee recruited his old friend, a useful accomplice and the perfect fall guy. But then a few of your members - who Smee was cavorting with - started to have suspicions about him, and they weren't best pleased with the way he was carrying on. Jane Hopkins made the fatal mistake of coming to you for help, didn't she? And signing her own death warrant into the bargain when you tipped off Smee, isn't that right, Mrs Blackwood?"

Rose Blackwood was shaking her head, demanding to see her solicitor.

Tyler looked deep into the eyes of Jordan Wilson. "You and Charles Blackwood go back quite a way, Mr Wilson. There's nothing wrong with that, intrinsically.

The only thing I'm not sure about is whether you knew what services - under the counter, as it were - the Blackwoods were offering. Or if they came to you, making an offer that you couldn't resist; dealing with the priest who had let your mother down so badly. Either way, Mr Wilson, it amounts to the same thing: you paid a substantial amount of money to the Blackwoods to have Peterson killed."

Tyler continued to eyeball Wilson. "How do imagine your father will feel when he finds out? Do you think he will feel grateful to you?"

He could see the venom rising in Wilson's eyes.

"Not only has he lost the woman he loved to a hideous disease, but that tragedy turned his son into a killer. Or are you telling me that your father already knows?"

Mills watched it unfold, as though in slow motion, the solicitor moving to intervene a fraction too late. Wilson was on his feet. "Leave my father out of this!"

The solicitor urged calm, but Wilson was beyond taking advice.

"You think that scumbag priest deserved to go on living? There was other treatment that could have been tried. I had the money, but my mother wouldn't listen. She had every faith in that bastard. And he promised her ... he promised she could be healed!" Tears were exploding down his face. "You don't know what it was like seeing my mum going down like that, and my father sinking down with her. We could have done something, I tell you, but that priest and his empty promises ..."

Wilson stopped, looking around the room.

"I don't regret ..."

284

"Yes, Mr Wilson?" said Tyler.

"He got what he deserved. He had it coming and I hope he's roasting in hell."

Wilson collapsed back into the chair.

The detectives watched as grief consumed him.

At last Tyler said, "The Blackwoods came to you, didn't they? And their services didn't come cheap. Did they assure you that you would get your money's worth?"

Jordan Wilson didn't answer.

"*Did you get your money's worth, Mr Wilson?*"

Wilson leaned forward, his face pressed hard into his knees.

"Please, Mr Wilson," said Tyler. "For the tape, if you don't mind."

Wilson looked up at Tyler. "I haven't a clue what you're talking about," he said.

The detectives returned to the interview room where Rose Blackwood was waiting. Her solicitor was present, and he didn't look happy. "I believe," he said, "that you've been trying to intimidate my client."

Tyler offered him a look of disdain, and turned to Rose Blackwood. "I think the next part of this interview will work best if we invite your husband to join us. DS Mills, would you do the honours."

As soon as Charles Blackwood was present in the room, Tyler began.

"... Jordan Wilson didn't come to you, Mr Blackwood. You offered your services to him, the same as you did for the Pickerings. Except that Gerald Pickering didn't take you up on the offer."

Charles Blackwood looked at his wife, as though ascertaining what she might already have said. Satisfied with her coded response, he turned back to look at DCI Tyler, offering him an expression of quiet defiance.

"I wonder when Toby Smee was going to get his cut," said Tyler. "After all, he's the one who got his hands dirty. He's the one who took the risks." Tyler's eyes narrowed. "But what kind of cut was he getting? Did he already owe you? Was his part in this the repayment of a debt? I wonder what other jobs Smee's done for you - and why."

"I don't know what you're talking about," said Charles Blackwood. "And whatever Wilson's said ... he's either mistaken or else he's still grieving for his mother and doesn't know what he's saying."

Outside in the corridor Tyler looked frustrated and angry. Mills said, "We've got nothing and they know it."

Tyler reached into his jacket and took out a small tape recorder. "Desperate times call for desperate measures, Danny."

Mills looked baffled as he followed the DCI into the room.

Gerald and Tony Pickering sat together. As soon as the detectives entered the interview room, Gerald Pickering was on his feet. "What's this about?" he said. "We've told you everything we know. This whole thing has got out of hand. Dragging us all the way up here! We are not murderers, and we wouldn't want what happened to Peterson, despite what he's done."

"I don't intend keeping you very long," said Tyler. "I'm not accusing either of you of anything. I'm not interviewing you under caution, and that's why I suggested that you do not require legal representation. I hope that as far as you are both concerned, today marks the end of your involvement in this enquiry."

Gerald Pickering sat down, appearing somewhat dazed. His son, Tony, continued to look terrified.

"You received an anonymous phone call, Mr Pickering," said Tyler, looking at Gerald Pickering." Before the man could say anything, Tyler said, "I want to play you recordings of four voices, and I want you to tell me if any of the voices sound familiar. Okay?"

Pickering frowned, and then nodded. "Okay," he said.

Tyler produced the small cassette recorder that he had shown to Mills. "You said it was a man who rang you?" said Tyler.

"That's right," said Pickering.

Tyler took out four cassette tapes, each labelled with initials. He inserted the first cassette into the machine.

Gerald and Tony Pickering waited, and DS Mills was perched on the edge of his seat.

Tyler pressed play, and the sound of Luke Summers' voice filled the room. A few words spoken, Tyler and Summers.

Tyler stopped the tape. "Did the voice that was not mine sound familiar to you, Mr Pickering?"

Pickering shook his head. "Definitely not," he said.

Tyler inserted a second tape into the machine and again he pressed play. This time it was the turn of Jordan Wilson, and again the extract had been carefully edited so that the voice was both calm and not betraying any sensitive material that Pickering ought not to be privy to.

Tyler stopped the tape. "Familiar, Mr Pickering?"

Again Gerald Pickering shook his head. "No," he said.

Tyler inserted a third tape. Charles Blackwood. The DCI watched Gerald Pickering intently, but again he betrayed no hint of recognition. Tyler stopped the tape. "Do you recognise the voice on the tape, Mr Pickering?" Again Pickering said that he didn't.

Tyler inserted the fourth and final tape into the slot and pressed play.

After a few seconds of DCI Tyler's introductions, the voice gave way to another, again speaking calmly; no names, nothing to give any clue pertaining to his identity or any details about the present enquiry.

Tyler watched Pickering's expression begin to reflect something: *recognition*? He let the tape roll on, the look on Gerald Pickering's face becoming unmistakable. Tyler stopped the tape.

"That's him," said Gerald Pickering. "No question about it. That's the man who rang me."

"The man who rang you, asking if you were willing to pay to see justice done ... justice for what had been done to your son by Father William Peterson?"

Gerald Pickering was nodding. "Yes," he said, swallowing hard.

"Mr Pickering?" said Tyler.

His eyes were swollen, his cheeks wet with tears. He looked across at his son. "You'd better say something, Tony."

Tony Pickering started to speak, his words coming out in an indecipherable stammer.

"Tony!" said his father. "For God's sake, take a breath!"

"He didn't do anything," said Tony Pickering. "The priest ... he never touched me."

The detectives emerged from the room and headed up towards the CID office.

"As we thought," said Tyler. "Saving face until it was too late to tell the truth."

"A weight off both their shoulders by the look of it, sir. I thought we'd have to swim out of that room."

"There was no question when Gerald Pickering heard that tape," said Tyler. "No question at all. He recognised Smee's voice straight off."

"Mind you," said Mills, "I'm not sure how Berkins will take it when he finds out."

"Berkins is not going to find out, though, is he?"

"Not from me, sir."

"And I can't imagine Gerald and Tony Pickering wanting to make a song and dance about my methods. So, what are we waiting for?"

CHAPTER FORTY ONE

Mills checked with the surveillance team. "He's just left his property, sir. They believe he's heading for the Blackwood farm."

"That'll do," said Tyler. "Let's go."

Mills drove out towards the Leek Moorlands, Tyler silent at his side watching the city recede and the rain-sodden countryside taking over. It was close now to the darkest part of the year, he reflected, as they by-passed the town of Leek and headed into the wilds. The spirits of winter held sway more evidently in this bleak, God-forsaken land, he reflected, at the same time secretly acknowledging Danny Mills' feelings of exile from the city he loved.

A deep well of compassion opened up in the heart of the DCI: compassion for the victims of everyday brutality, the tragic deaths of people like Marjorie Wilson, and the consequential ripples of anger and despair that such deaths sent out to all who had loved them in this fragile life. He thought of those waiting in the wings to exploit the anger and desolation - the vultures' content to feed off the hopelessness of ordinary people suffering unimaginable loss.

He thought of Luke Summers, broken in childhood, and living in the shadows of such brutality and betrayal; and of the dark secrets that the youngster had once tried to share with the world, and that had come back to haunt him. Becoming a tool of the unscrupulous, of those not acting from misguided notions of restoring justice where none exists but acting solely from the motives of greed and self-interest. The Toby Smees, the Charles and Rose Blackwoods of this world.

But what did they have on Toby Smee?

They were a mile away from the Blackwoods' farm. Surveillance had reported that Smee had taken a detour, calling for petrol. He was approaching the farm from the opposite direction.

Tyler instructed surveillance to hold back but to remain close to the property, offering backup as required.

Mills drove the last few hundred yards with a growing sense of foreboding, his deep breaths alerting Tyler.

"Are you alright, Danny?"

"I will be, sir."

"Rest assured, I'm not planning on playing the hero. Any signs of resistance and we use the backup available, okay?"

"Okay, sir."

"Now, there's only one way off the property, at least by car, so we close the gate behind us."

Surveillance had parked discreetly whilst maintaining visual contact with Smee from their roadside station, using the cover afforded by the trees surrounding that side of the farm buildings. Smee had parked outside the front entrance, and was already out of his car. According to surveillance, he appeared to be banging on the front door of the farmhouse.

Mills drove in through the gate, not visible from the main door, and pulled the car to a halt. He secured the gate, as Tyler had instructed, the unmarked car acting as a further barrier to prevent any attempt by Smee to drive away from the property.

Tyler got out of the car, the rain falling heavily now. He started towards the farmhouse, Mills catching up as they turned the corner of the building.

Smee was waiting beneath the front porch awning, his jaw dropping when he saw the two detectives approaching.

"I didn't realise there was a meeting planned for today," said Tyler. "I need to update my diary. Are you sure you have the right week?"

Smee tried to smile, but the effect was close to grotesque.

"They were expecting you, Charles and Rose?" said Tyler. "How remiss of them."

Smee hesitated.

"So, a social call? Just popping by?"

"What do you want?" asked Smee.

Tyler read the man his rights.

"I haven't killed anybody. Luke Summers is the one you should be arresting."

"Wouldn't that be convenient, Mr Smee?"

"I want to speak to my solicitor."

"You're in luck. He's waiting for you down at the station. He doubles up for the Blackwoods - but then I suppose you know that."

"I don't know what you mean."

"They've set you up."

"I haven't a clue what you're talking about."

"I'm sure he will explain it all to you, down at the station. If you're ready. I believe it's time to go."

"What do you mean *they've set me up?*"

292

"They had Faye Winkelman killed after your fall guy Luke Summers was already in custody. Things were getting messy and so they've pointed the finger at you. I'm surprised it's taken you this long to work that out. Or to not work it out."

Smee looked confused. But Tyler could see that the truth was slowly dawning on him.

"Did you ever meet Jordan Wilson?" asked Tyler.

Smee tried to look blank at the mention of the name, though unconvincingly.

"I see. Just the hit man, were you? Recruiting Summers and getting paid off. It's less complicated if you're not given the name at the other end of the contract, isn't that right? Father Peterson was nothing to you, was he? He was merely a handsome payout. But when Faye Winkelman and the others started to suspect something was going on, they went to Charles and Rose; and then Charles and Rose tipped you off. You already had Summers in the frame for an 'occult killing', and so you dispatched three women in a fashion that linked back to the man in the frame."

"I don't know what you're talking about."

"Then you're the only one who doesn't," said Tyler. "Come on, let's go."

Smee started to move forward, and then side-stepped, moving towards his vehicle. Opening the door he climbed inside and started the engine, tyres squealing in the thickening mud as he revved the engine and sped around towards the gate.

When he saw the unmarked police car blocking the closed gate, he reversed, cranking the engine and ramming at the vehicle from behind, shunting it a few feet forward, then reversing again and doing the same thing a second time, the car almost clear of the gate now. Tyler opened the car door and pulled at Smee's arm, trying to yank him from the cabin while Mills radioed for assistance from the waiting surveillance crew parked a hundred yards up the main road.

Smee pushed Tyler back, the DCI losing his balance, falling backward into the mud. He reversed again before barrelling headlong into the car, this time shunting it clear of the gate.

Tyler was back on his feet, pulling again at the driver's door, and clutching at Smee, who was kicking out at him. Mills was scrambling around to the passenger door now as Smee let out a savage kick that caught Tyler square in the mid riff, folding him over. The DCI had caught hold of Smee's foot and he was tugging him out of the car as Mills clambered in, an arm across the man's throat, Smee lurching back, his crown contacting with Mills' face and issuing a splintering crack, causing the DS to fall backwards. But Tyler still had hold of Smee's foot, and was pulling him out of the car.

Smee landed on the sodden ground, and sprang up, shoving at Tyler as he ran past him. Tyler set off in pursuit as Smee headed up towards the woods at the far side of the farmhouse. He was closing in on the woods when Tyler dived forward, catching hold of one of his legs, and bringing him down into the mud. Smee turned over, fists primed, but Tyler was on him, pinning his arms down with his knees and holding him to the ground.

"I hope they were paying you well enough," said Tyler.

"I don't know what you're talking about," said Smee, struggling to get his breath.

"You're going down for multiple murder while the Blackwoods walk away with the money. Are you that afraid of them?"

Smee was still breathing hard, and wincing under the pressure of Tyler's weight bearing down on him.

"What's the price for such loyalty these days?"

"This was never about money," said Smee.

Tyler laughed.

"For them maybe - but not for me."

"What, then?" asked Tyler. "Blackmail, intimidation?"

"I killed a woman, years ago. Karen Wildig. I was off my head, and *they* took me in. I had no-one else to turn to. I was already working for them. They helped me conceal what I'd done. They provided an alibi when the police interviewed me. The police interviewed a lot of people but they never charged anyone for Karen's murder. I loved her; we could have been married with kids. But like I said, I was out of my head in those days. They kept me out of prison and I cleaned up my act."

"That's one way of putting it. Killing to stay clean? I've heard it all now. And you've been paying them back ever since? Tell me, what other jobs have you, their keenest, loyalist operator performed for them over the years?"

Smee held the DCI's glare for a few moments, and then looked away, the side of his face resting on the cold, wet ground.

"Too many to mention?" said Tyler. "You rang the Pickerings and Father Peterson and you approached Jordan Wilson, isn't that right?"

"I had nothing to do with Wilson. I knew there was a contract. I knew the situation and that's all I needed to know. More than I needed to know."

"And you used Luke Summers as accomplice and fall guy?"

"I owed him one."

"For what?"

"Giving me the idea in the first place."

"Are you saying it was all *your* idea?"

"No, not really. The Blackwoods exploited Wilson's *situation.* They're good at that sort of thing. And when they gave me the job - when they showed me the target - *the priest* - I spotted the likeness and I knew Summers was perfect. That part was all mine. So I invited him along to a meeting so they could all see he was crazy and unhinged. Charles and Rose agreed I could use him."

"And all the time they were using you," said Tyler.

"This was my big chance. If I pulled this one off, my debt was paid. I was a free man."

"And you believe they would have honoured that; that they wouldn't have been back for more?"

Smee began to laugh.

"Have I said something funny?"

"It hardly matters now, does it? If I tell the truth I'm a dead man. So keep it to yourself, Inspector. You'll get a promotion and I stay alive. Everyone's happy. I killed the priest and Jane - I make that three including Karen. Summers killed Evie. He's good at starting fires, don't you know? I can't prove that anybody *made me do it.* So what do I gain by putting my head in the Blackwood noose?"

He looked up to see the circle of officers now surrounding him. "It was me!" he shouted. "Me and Luke Summers! I'm admitting everything, case closed!"

Tyler stood up, looking down at the pitiful figure on the ground.

"And what about Faye Winkelman?"

Smee looked uncertain. "What about her?"

"They set you up, didn't they?"

Smee beckoned Tyler to lean closer. But the DCI didn't budge.

As the officers took hold of Toby Smee, lifting him up from the ground, he lurched towards Tyler, pressing his mouth against his ear. "Okay, that was me too, if you like," he whispered. "Keeps it all simpler, doesn't it?"

Tyler nodded to the officers. "Take him away."

As the officers led Smee back towards the crumpled vehicles, and the waiting squad cars beyond the gate, Mills, still holding his face and groaning, came over to the DCI. "I thought you said no heroics today, sir?"

Tyler smacked his own forehead in an attitude of forgetfulness. "You're right," he said. "I did, didn't I? You should have reminded me."

CHAPTER FORTY TWO

In the CID office the mood was far from celebratory. It felt like half a job done at best. Mills was trying hard to be upbeat but Tyler was having none of it. Then the phone rang and Mills picked up. At the end of the call he placed the handset down as Tyler prepared to return to his mountain of unwritten reports.

"That was Marion Ecclestone," said Mills.

"The curate? What does she want?"

"Graham Wilson has been at the church most of the day, and he's still there now."

Tyler looked up.

"He was in early. He didn't look well," said Mills. "He's been on his knees praying for hours."

"Is there a point to this?" asked Tyler.

"He's been hinting at wanting to get something off his chest. She thinks it may not be the kind of confession that requires a priest."

Tyler grabbed his jacket.

Marion Ecclestone met the detectives at the back of the church. "When he came in this morning he was crying and saying that he was sorry," she told them. "Then he took his place in one of the pews and he's been there since. I spoke to him a couple of times, offered him a hot drink. He didn't want to talk and he wouldn't accept a drink. But an hour ago he said that he wanted to talk. He said that he wanted to confess something that ... he asked me to contact you."

298

The detectives moved down the aisle. In one of the front-row pews, a frail, stooped figure was muttering, his face upturned towards the crucifixion scene at the main altar.

Tyler waited for a few moments, and then he said, "Mr Wilson?"

The man didn't look around. He nodded, and stood up. Graham Wilson hadn't looked good the last time, thought Tyler, and appeared to have aged another decade in the interim. His eyes looked empty, fixed in a dull flotation above dark bags.

He walked with the detective towards the office. Marion Ecclestone asked if he would prefer that she was there and he indicated that he would.

He sat, in an aspect of prayer, in the presence of the two detectives and the curate, and at last he said, "My family has meant everything to me. Marjorie, Jordan, my grandchildren. Everything has fallen apart."

After the echo of his words had trailed off, a deep silence fell over the small gathering.

"I wanted God to do as Graham Wilson instructed. In our hour of need - *in my beloved Marjorie's hour of need* - I wanted God to simply obey *my* orders. Marjorie ... I can see it now ... she was reconciled. But I wasn't. It was all about me, what I wanted."

Marion Ecclestone started to speak, but Wilson shook his head.

"No, it's taken me a long time to recognise the truth, so let me say it while I have the will to. I blamed Father Peterson - as God's proxy I blamed him. But my wife had found peace and Father Peterson was wise enough to know what I couldn't see. If she saw what happened, how I turned my back on God ..." A wave of pain appeared to consume him. "If Marjorie could see how I allowed my anger to inflame our son's anger, infecting him with it ... I want God to forgive me. I want Marjorie to forgive me."

Graham Wilson looked at the detectives. "I fear for what my son has done. He is not an evil man. He could not have been in his right mind. He loved his mother. If I could have maintained a fragment of the faith that she kept to the very end ... Jordan could have let go. He could have let go of all that hurt and pain and *desolation*."

The silence deepened once more, and Graham Wilson stood up. "I want God to forgive my son. And he will. I came here today to make my peace with my saviour and redeemer ... and then I was going to tell a pack of lies to save my son. I was going to tell you that I arranged the murder, because in a way it's true. In my heart I did. But I know my son. I know what he has done, even though he has never spoken a word about it. Now he has to make his own confession and find the forgiveness waiting for him, and the peace that only God can grant him."

Jordan Wilson sat in the interview room with his solicitor. A further complaint of police harassment had been issued already and Tyler let the brief have his say. Then he nodded at Mills.

A few moments later the DS returned to the interview room with Graham Wilson.

Jordan Wilson was on his feet. "Dad! What the hell are you -"

Graham Wilson embraced his son. The solicitor started to speak but Jordan Wilson waved him down.

Mills watched as the son's rage turned, transforming into a deluge of tears as the two men held each other and gave in to the onslaught of grief.

Nobody in the room spoke; and yet, Mills was later to reflect, everything was said.

When at last the two men pulled apart, they looked at each other, and Graham Wilson said, "It's time, Jordan. For *Mum's* sake and mine. But most of all for yours."

After a moment Jordan Wilson nodded, and sat down.

"I want to make a statement," he said.

CHAPTER FORTY THREE

Mills cracked.

Rifling through his desk drawers in the CID office he found his emergency snacks. Tearing the packet open, he was holding up the first biscuit when DCI Tyler came through the door.

"Caught red handed!"

Catching Mills' slightly sheepish expression, Tyler added, "I suppose you feel you've earned a treat because of those few cuts and bruises. No doubt you've been milking it at home, too."

Mills grinned. "My wife does get motherly when it comes to the marks of war, sir. I put my old vest on and she thinks I'm Bruce Willis in *Die Hard*."

"Lose five stone and it's a mistake any fool could make."

"Bit harsh, sir."

"Go on," said Tyler. "For your fine instincts and tenacity regarding Jordan Wilson, I'm going to allow it this one time. But, please, not the whole packet in one sitting."

Mills devoured the first biscuit without tasting it, and was lining up its successor when he paused to say, "That only leaves one loose end that I can see, sir."

Tyler frowned. "What loose end?"

"The CPN," said Mills, sinking his teeth into the biscuit.

"I didn't realise that she was under suspicion."

"I suspect," said Mills, "that she might be interested in helping you further with your enquiries."

"And what evidence do you have for this outrageous accusation, Detective Sergeant Mills?"

"I've seen the way she looks at you. And the way you look at her, for that matter."

"Then you are clearly mistaken," said Tyler. "You should be concentrating on catching criminals."

Mills had thrown all caution to the wind, and was demolishing the pack with abandon. But all the while his grin was fixed on the DCI.

"You can grin at me all you like. It doesn't alter the facts of the matter."

"Facts, sir?"

"That pleasure and business rarely mix, at least not in my experience."

The outside line was flashing.

"Perhaps it's Charles or Rose Blackwood, deciding to confess all and save us a load of time and trouble," said Tyler.

"You reckon, sir?"

"We'll get them, Danny, even without help from Smee. When things got messy, they set up him up, having his girlfriend killed in the same fashion that he killed Jane Hopkins - and with Summers out of the frame. It'll take hundreds of hours of police time, but even if we never nail them directly for any of this, we'll still ruin the bastards, one way or another."

The phone stopped ringing.

Mills said, "But we've got Jordan Wilson's testimony, sir."

"The money he paid to the Blackwoods can't be proven to have links to any murders. But my hunch, for what it's worth, is that when Smee's had time to fully reflect on how royally he's been shafted, he'll provide us with the final nails in the Blackwood coffin, so to speak. They're part of a far bigger network. *Chapter Six*? There's an entire compendium of books out there! We'll never touch the sides of the wider organisation, and they might have imported an operative from virtually anywhere to take care of Faye Winkelman. But they screwed up using Smee and it's going to cost them. We'll close down the Staffordshire cell and hang Charles and Rose out to dry, *God bless them.*"

The phone began ringing again, and this time Mills picked up. A few seconds later, he handed the phone across the desk to his colleague.

"It's for you, sir."

Tyler gave him a questioning look.

"Arlene Mitchell," said Mills, sitting back to observe, and at the same time reaching for another handful of biscuits.

The call was brief, and at the end of it Tyler looked thoughtful.

Mills rustled the packet, somewhat surprised when he realised that he was extracting the last survivor from the onslaught.

When Tyler finally looked up, poker faced, Mills said, "Anything to report?"

"Only," said Tyler, "that it seems I have been proven wrong once again."

"You don't want to make a habit of that, sir."

"Quite."

"So," said Mills, "when are you planning to ..."

But DCI Tyler had answered enough questions for one day, and he was pointing at the unfinished reports

304

stacked high on Mills' desk. "I've kept you from your work too long already. They're not going to write themselves."

"Very true, sir. By the way, some more good news: the diet starts tomorrow."

"It always does."

Tyler checked his watch, stood up and grabbed his jacket.

"Going anywhere nice, sir?"

"I'm afraid," he said, "that's classified ... and strictly confidential."

THE END

NOTE FROM THE AUTHOR

Many thanks for reading **The Devil Wore Black**, I hope you enjoyed it. You may be interested to know that other books featuring Tyler and Mills include **Red Is The Colour**, and **Blue Murder**.

Also by the same author: **Silver, Sextet, The Man Upstairs,** and **Coffin Maker.**

Printed in Poland
by Amazon Fulfillment
Poland Sp. z o.o., Wrocław